# Saving Olympus

## The Spellcaster

### Book Two

Written By:

## R.D. Wolfe

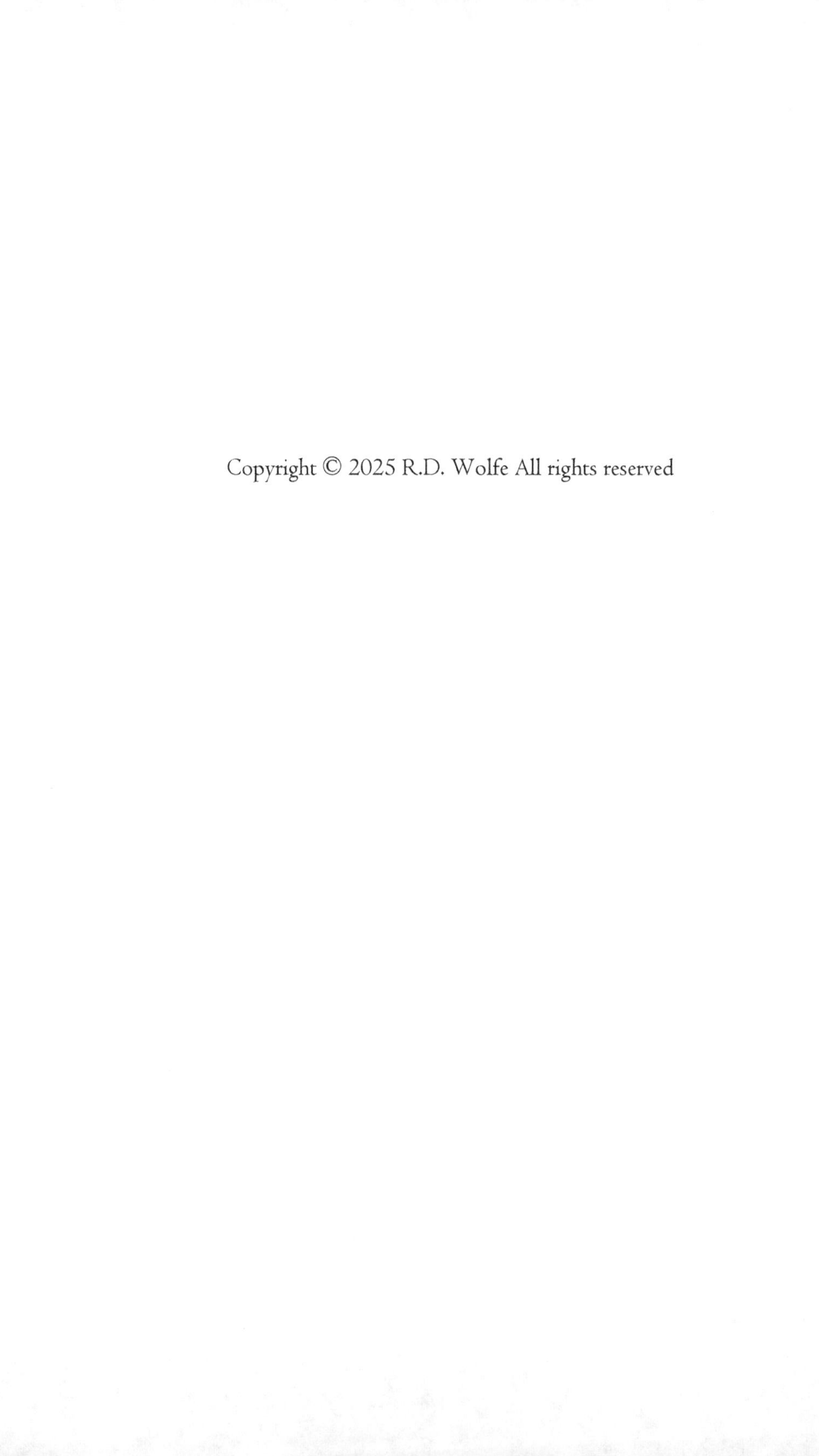

# Contents


Chapter 1: The Pyrrhic Victory ..................................... 1

Chapter 2: The Transition Orb ....................................21

Chapter 3: The Stolen Champion ..................................42

Chapter 4: The Unlikely Scholar ..................................56

Chapter 5: The Master's Valley ....................................71

Chapter 6: The World Revealed ...................................88

Chapter 7: The Lessons Begin ....................................107

Chapter 8: The Journey Continues................................126

Chapter 9: The Desperate Plea....................................139

Chapter 10: The Unraveled Balance ............................154

Chapter 11: The Wounded Mentor ..............................164

Chapter 12: The Marauders Resolve ............................180

Chapter 13: The Burdened Past...................................195

Chapter 14: The Serpent Court ...................................209

Chapter 15: The Hidden Trap ....................................230

Chapter 16: The Ravine Edge .....................................245

Chapter 17: The Master Revealed................................263

Chapter 18: The Imprisoned Hope ..............................287

Chapter 19: The Answered Questions ..........................305

Chapter 20: The Hero Returns....................................318

Chapter 21: The Friends Reunited ...............................331

Chapter 22: The Journey Retold ..................................348

Chapter 23: The Agents Fall ......................................359

Chapter 24: The Students Return .................................375

Pronunciation Guide .................................................398

For those who've felt the weight of the world lately—
may you find in these pages a breath, a spark, a way
forward.

# Chapter I: The Pyrrhic Victory

Darien stood at the edge of the turret, hands braced against the cold stone, staring down at Silver Lake. The water was still, smooth as glass, waiting for the funeral pyres that would soon set it alight. He tried to picture it—the glow of flames licking at the surface, their reflections stretching long and thin in the ripples. Would it bring closure? Or just another reminder of how many they had lost?

Farkland Reach still stood, but it no longer felt like the same city. The battle had changed it, carved grief into its foundations. Below, merchants arranged their stalls, farmers hauled goods into the market square, but the usual energy had dimmed. Too many faces were missing. Too many voices would never be heard again.

"Darien! Darien, come down here!"

The call jolted him from his thoughts. He turned, looking down into the castle gardens where Rist stood, draped in his ever-present robes, an unmoving shadow against the sunlit stone. The fabric stirred slightly in the breeze, but it revealed nothing. Darien had never seen what lay beneath those robes. Some part of him wasn't sure he wanted to.

"I'm coming!" he called back, stepping away from the ledge. He climbed down the ladder, then made his way through the winding corridors, his footsteps echoing in the unnaturally quiet halls. The castle had always been alive with movement, with the constant shuffle of soldiers and messengers. Now, only the hushed sounds of cleaning and quiet conversation remained. The war had ended, but its weight still hung in the air.

When he stepped into the gardens, Rist was watching him, unreadable as ever. "You spend a lot of time up there."

Darien exhaled through his nose. "It helps me think."

"And what are you thinking about?"

Darien hesitated, glancing back at the castle walls, at the distant horizon beyond. "That it doesn't feel like we won."

Rist nodded slightly, as if he had been expecting that answer. "It never does."

They stood there for a long moment, the silence stretching between them, neither willing to break it. Then Rist turned, gesturing for Darien to follow as he led them along the stone path that wound through the garden, toward the castle's inner halls.

"The city is already rebuilding," Rist said, his voice even. "But it will take time. And time is the one thing we may not have."

Darien frowned. "You think Cyprin will attack again?"

"I think we don't know what he'll do next. And that's exactly why we can't sit idle."

They passed through archways where servants worked quietly, scrubbing soot from the castle walls, repairing banners that had been scorched in the fighting. No one spoke unless necessary. Everyone had a task, a purpose—something to keep them from stopping, from thinking too much about the past few days.

Darien finally asked, "What do you think we're supposed to do next?"

Rist stopped walking. Turned his hooded head toward him. "Are you asking what we should do, or what we will do?"

Darien hesitated, then admitted, "I don't know."

Rist let the silence stretch before he answered. "Then maybe you should figure that out before asking the question."

There was no mockery in his tone, no judgment— just a simple truth.

Darien sighed, rubbing a hand across his face as he glanced back toward the city, toward the people slowly rebuilding the world around them. The battle had ended, but the weight of it had only just begun settling into their bones.

Darien moved through the halls of Fenway Castle, his steps slow but steady as his eyes traced the towering walls. The castle, standing at the heart of Farkland Reach, was beginning to feel familiar. The corridors gleamed under the mid-afternoon light, its walls adorned with artifacts of Olympian history—mostly Troll relics, collected over thousands of years. Busts of past rulers lined various alcoves, their stone gazes fixed on a future they would never see.

One statue made him pause. King Aghemnon. The craggy features had been carved with remarkable care, the Troll craftsmen capturing the warmth in the late king's eyes despite the roughness of the stone. Darien swallowed. He remembered the last time he had seen Aghemnon alive—just before he had rushed after Tahmer, the troll who had stolen the ancient sword. The same sword that Darien and the others needed to challenge Cyprin on Mount Olympus.

He had fought for that sword. Lost. Tahmer had been faster, stronger—likely enhanced by Cyprin's magic. That thought unsettled him. How many others, like Tahmer, were already in place, waiting? How many unseen enemies moved in the shadows?

He lingered a few more seconds before exhaling sharply and stepping away. The courtyard awaited.

Sunlight struck his face the moment he stepped outside, forcing him to lift a hand to block the glare. The heat of the afternoon weighed on his skin, the scent of earth and stone rising from the ground. Three figures stood near the center—Rist, Breyman, and Airlyn, all members of The Eldric. His companions in this war.

Darien studied them briefly. Breyman, the towering Lystran warrior, was a mountain of muscle and patience, his presence steady and unmoving. Fur covered his entire body. If not for the fact that he walked upright and had clearly defined facial features, Darien would have likened him to a tiger. Especially given the stripes that lined his coat.

Airlyn, in contrast, was sharp edges and intensity. Her green eyes narrowed as she crossed her arms tightly over her chest. Something about her always felt like a viper, coiled and waiting to strike.

"There you are," Airlyn said, her voice clipped. "We have much to discuss."

Darien took a measured breath. "Sorry. I was thinking."

"You and your thinking." Airlyn scoffed. "You'll have plenty of time to do that on the road. I wouldn't have to explain that to someone from Evindor. Don't you take this seriously?"

Darien clenched his jaw but forced himself to stay level. "Of course I do."

"It doesn't show," Airlyn said, flicking her dark hair back over her shoulder. The movement was dismissive, her expression unchanging.

His irritation flared, but he swallowed it. He had learned by now that arguing with Airlyn was like fighting the wind—useless and exhausting. She was built from a different world, with expectations and traditions he didn't understand. The sharp angles of her face, the pointed ears, the piercing green eyes— she was unlike any race he had encountered, yet still, she stood beside them, bound by the same fate.

"That is enough," Breyman's deep voice rumbled, cutting through the tension. The power in his tone made even Airlyn pause.

Rist, ever composed, turned his attention to the table behind him. A map lay stretched across its surface, marked with locations Darien didn't recognize. "Let's focus," Rist said, his voice like ice and certainty. "We need to decide our next move. We have the sword, but the final weapon remains in Zanarchin, to the east. The other two lie to the west—one in Atlantis, the land of the Mers, and the other in Minotatha, home of the Peronia."

Darien glanced at the map, but the geography meant little to him. The symbols and markings blurred together, as foreign as the world itself.

"The Mers seem the easiest to reach," Airlyn said flatly.

"Yes," Breyman agreed, his voice measured.

"Easier, perhaps," Rist said. "But it would require crossing the mountains, and I don't know of any safe passage. If we had wings, I might consider it. Instead, I suggest we move west to Minotatha, then take the Laynor River south to Atlantis."

All three turned to Darien.

He hesitated. He had no real strategy to offer. His experience in Olympus had been defined by survival, by reacting, not planning. He wasn't like the others. They had chosen this fight. He had been thrown into it.

"Oh. Well, I agree with Rist," Darien said, forcing a nod.

Airlyn rolled her eyes. "Of course you do."

"Fine. We go to Minotatha. And we leave as soon as possible."

Breyman gave a slow, approving nod before stepping away, settling onto the grass beneath the sun. He lowered himself cross-legged, resting his massive hands on his knees, closing his eyes in quiet meditation. Darien watched him for a moment, then exchanged a glance with Rist. The two of them shrugged in unison.

Airlyn let out a quiet noise of irritation and turned sharply, vanishing into the castle without another word.

Darien smirked. "You know, I can't help but enjoy irritating her."

Rist tilted his head slightly. "She makes it easy. But I would tread carefully. Her emotions are... troubled. She may not have come to Olympus as willingly as the rest of us."

"Yeah, you're probably right," Darien muttered, filing the thought away for another time and working to keep his own ignorance of Olympus before arriving to himself. "Hey, do we have anything else to do right now?"

Rist shook his head. "Not at the moment."

"Good," Darien said, already turning back toward the castle halls. "Then I'll see you tonight."

The truth was, there was somewhere else Darien wanted to be. He enjoyed Rist's company, and Breyman was someone he hoped to get to know better. Airlyn, on the other hand, made him nervous. He never knew when she might lose her temper and go off on another tirade.

Darien stepped into the bright sunlight as he exited the entrance hall of Fenway Castle. The heat pressed down on him; the light glinting off the pale stone. He moved through the sparse city streets, angling southeast toward his destination. As he neared the outskirts, the air changed. The quiet hum of the city gave way to the open countryside, where rolling grasslands stretched toward thin forests of needle-covered trees. It was a sight he had grown used to, yet every so often, he would catch himself staring, as if seeing it for the first time.

A voice pulled him from his thoughts.

"Darien! Hey, Darien!"

He turned toward the sound. A squat, green-skinned goblin was making his way toward him, moving quickly despite his short legs. He carried a sheathed sword, gripping it tightly in one hand. Darien recognized him but couldn't place his name. After meeting so many new faces, they had all begun to blur together into one tangled mass.

"Hello," Darien said, keeping his tone friendly.

The goblin reached him, lightly panting. "I've seen you come to the camp a few times now, but I didn't have my sword around. You said you'd teach me a few tricks. Thought I'd collect."

Darien hesitated. "Uhh—"

"You know, when you and Evatra came to see Atreya before you got the wraith out of her? I asked if you'd teach me, and you said you would."

"Oh!" Darien exclaimed, realization clicking into place. "Wret, right? Listen, I'm here to see Evatra right now. Can I catch you another time?"

Wret's expression faltered, his grip tightening on the sword's hilt. "Sure."

Darien felt a pang of guilt. "Thanks, Wret. Look, why don't we meet tomorrow morning, after the funerals? There's just a lot going on right now."

That seemed to ease Wret's disappointment. He nodded, managing a small smile. Darien clapped him on the shoulder before continuing on toward the camp.

The marauders had been a thorn in his side when he first arrived in Olympus. He had been their prisoner, dragged through the dirt and barely given a second glance. But things had changed. He had survived a raid that wiped out a number of them, earned Totra-Dal's favor, and, somehow, carved a place among them. Now, walking through their ranks felt less like stepping through enemy territory and more like wading into unpredictable waters.

It still felt surreal—this life he had stumbled into. If things had gone differently, he would have been teaching at The Academy, maybe even with Kara.

A pang of guilt struck him at the thought of her.

Seven months. That was how long they had been together before everything had changed. Back then, they had spoken of the future like it was something certain, something solid. Even after he had decided to stay at The Academy, some part of him had still hoped they could make it work. And then Olympus had stolen him away. Now, he had left that life behind.

Left her behind.

And in her place, there was—

"Darien!"

Evatra's voice broke through his thoughts.

He barely had time to react before she reached him, closing the distance with effortless grace. Without hesitation, she kissed him, her lips warm against his. The contact shattered any lingering thoughts of Kara. When he was with Evatra, everything else faded. His doubts, his exhaustion, even the weight of what lay ahead.

"Hey," he murmured, smiling as he tried to shake off the unease still clinging to him. "How's it going?"

She exhaled, brushing a strand of black hair from her face. "As well as can be expected. The marauders are getting restless. They want to leave and go back to what they know best."

Darien frowned. "And Totra-Dal? Any word?"

Evatra's face darkened. "He still hasn't woken up. The knife damaged his heart. The healers have done all they can, but it's up to him now."

Darien nodded, not trusting himself to speak. He had seen Totra-Dal take that wound. Had watched him fall at the hand of Kort, one of his own men. The idea of the marauders without their leader was a dangerous one. Without him, they would splinter. Scatter. And Evatra—

He sat down in one of the chairs near the fire pit, watching the embers smolder. "So, are the marauders going to leave soon?"

Evatra regarded him for a long moment before answering. "I don't know. That depends on what happens with Totra-Dal. You know they aren't ones to stay in one place for too long. "

Darien hesitated. "What about you?"

The question felt heavier than he intended. It had hung between them for days, unspoken but ever-present.

Evatra's shoulders tensed. "I don't know," she admitted. "These people are my family, and right now they still look at me as their leader. But being here at the city… it's been nice. Quiet. Plus, you're here." She paused. "But that's going to change too. I don't know. Can we just spend today together and worry about tomorrow, tomorrow?"

Darien held her gaze for a moment before nodding. "Sure."

He didn't want to wait for tomorrow. He wanted to talk about it now. But that was what he and Kara had done, wasn't it? They had put it off. And before they had a chance to figure it out, he had been ripped away from everything he knew.

Evatra turned back to her work, and Darien sat back, waiting for her to finish. He watched as she moved through the camp, answering questions, issuing commands, keeping the marauders from losing what little order they had left. When she finally returned, her smile was small but real.

"Sorry about that," she said, pulling him to his feet. "The Queen keeps sending messengers with complaints. Noise, smell, the camp being an eyesore. It never stops."

Darien smirked. "Can't imagine why she wouldn't want a bunch of thieves and cutthroats camped outside her gates."

Evatra rolled her eyes but didn't argue as she led him toward her horse. She climbed up first before offering a hand, pulling him up behind her. Darien wrapped his arms around her waist as they rode out toward Silver Lake. The scent of her hair filled his senses—woodsmoke and something faintly floral.

For a while, they just rode. No words, no planning. Just the rhythm of hoofbeats against the earth and the quiet pull of the horizon. Darien shifted uncomfortably, his grip tightening around Evatra's waist as the horse moved beneath him. Riding bareback still unsettled him—the constant sway, the uneven motion, the lack of a saddle to brace against. He felt every shift of muscle, every jolt as the horse adjusted its gait, and no matter how hard he tried, he couldn't relax. It was an uneasy reminder of just how much of this world still felt foreign to him.

Eventually, they reached a grassy hollow beyond the hills. Evatra dismounted, letting her horse wander freely. Darien followed, their fingers intertwining as they walked along the lake's edge. They spoke about nothing—about training, about the absurdity of some of the city's customs. It was easy, and Darien found himself holding onto the simplicity of it.

But as the sun dipped lower, reality crept back in.

"We should head back before it starts," Darien said reluctantly.

Evatra only nodded.

They rode back in silence, but it wasn't uncomfortable. Just… temporary. Like everything else.

Darien walked quickly back to the castle, pushing against the dull ache forming behind his eyes. The faster he moved, the stronger it grew, settling like a weight between his temples. He rolled his shoulders and exhaled slowly, willing it away. There was no time for it now.

Inside, the halls of Fenway Castle were dim, the light from the setting sun filtering through the tall arched windows, casting long shadows along the stone. He navigated the familiar corridors, passing tapestries of battle scenes and statues of rulers long dead. In his chambers, a fresh set of clothes awaited him—silk-like fabric woven by troll hands, meant to mark the occasion.

Tonight, the city would honor its dead.

The thought wrapped around his ribs, tightening until he could hardly breathe. The men, women, and children who had stood against Cyprin's army had paid the ultimate price. Families shattered, lives cut short. The city still stood, but it would never be the same.

Darien dressed in silence, pushing down the memories that clawed at the edges of his mind. The battlefield was still fresh in his head—bodies strewn across the ground, the air thick with smoke and blood. He had never seen anything like it before Olympus. He had trained for war, but war had never felt real until now.

His hands clenched involuntarily, nausea rising at the memory. He forced himself to move, to focus on the task ahead.

By the time he reached the castle entrance, Rist, Airlyn, and Breyman were already there, standing in somber silence. No words were exchanged. None were needed.

Moments later, Queen Marenya emerged from the grand hall, her silver hair braided tightly behind her crown. She gave a small nod, then turned toward the waiting carriages.

Darien climbed into the rearmost one, following Rist inside. He was grateful for the lack of company. With anyone else, he might have been expected to speak. With Rist, silence was natural.

The carriage rocked forward, wheels creaking against the stone path. Outside, the streets were quiet. The usual murmur of city life had dulled, replaced by an eerie stillness. People gathered in hushed clusters along the roadside, their faces lit by the glow of lanterns.

Rist broke the silence first. "Are you well, friend?"

The back of Darien's neck prickled. Rist rarely called him 'friend.'

"Yeah," Darien said, shaking his head as if to clear it. "I'm fine. Just ready for this to be done."

Rist tilted his head slightly. "Are you unfamiliar with death?"

The bluntness of the question caught Darien off guard. He hesitated before answering. "No, I mean—not really. I don't have experience with anything so… real." He exhaled, glancing toward the window. "Most of what I studied was how to fight in small, controlled engagements. Sparring, drills. No one ever died. I guess it's just not something I was prepared for."

"I see," Rist murmured.

Darien shifted uncomfortably. Had he said too much? Chorrun had warned him against revealing his lack of knowledge to the others. The Eldric were warriors. They were expected to lead, to know Olympus as if they had always been part of it. He was still catching up, still trying to piece together a world that had existed long before him.

Rist didn't press further, and Darien let the silence settle again as the carriage bumped along the uneven roads. He turned his gaze to the city beyond the window. The streets blurred past, candlelight flickering in the dark.

"How is Evatra handling the marauders?" Rist asked suddenly.

Darien let out a breath. "Well enough, I guess." He ran a hand over his face. "It'll be easier if Totra-Dal recovers. I think part of her enjoys leading them, but another part just wants to leave. Go back to moving from place to place."

Rist's hood inclined slightly. "And you?"

Darien hesitated.

He and Evatra had never discussed what came next. They had avoided it, dancing around the truth instead of facing it. He knew why. He just didn't want to admit it.

"There's your relationship," Rist said, breaking the silence.

Darien huffed a quiet laugh. "I guess it's not so secret after all, is it?"

"If it was, your efforts at hiding it were half-hearted at best," Rist said, something like amusement flickering in his voice.

Darien gave a small, guilty smile but said nothing. The carriage rattled on, the road growing rougher as they neared the lake.

When they arrived, the air was different. Still. Heavy.

Darien stepped out onto the packed dirt, the scent of water thick in the air. The lake stretched before them, its surface dark and waiting. A raised platform had been built at its edge, its structure illuminated by the glow of thousands of tiny lights.

Candles.

They flickered in the hands of the gathered crowd, stretching across the shore like a sea of golden fireflies. Each flame represented a life—a warrior, a healer, a child too young to understand why their world had been torn apart. A mother, a father, a son, a daughter. People who had fought not for power or conquest, but because they had no choice.

Darien swallowed hard, his throat tight as he struggled to steady his breathing. Then, a single note broke the silence. Soft. Fragile.

Marenya's voice carried over the water, low and mournful, weaving through the air like the first gust of an oncoming storm. Alone, she sang—her voice the only sound in a world that had stopped to grieve. The ancient words, foreign and aching, pressed against Darien's chest, reverberating through him like something old and forgotten had been awakened.

The trolls stood motionless, their eyes fixed ahead, their hands tightening around the candles they held. The song deepened, rising with slow, deliberate sorrow as Marenya stepped forward, her torch flickering against the black of the night.

Darien turned his gaze just in time to see movement in the crowd—a child, no older than five, break free from his mother's grasp. The boy staggered forward, his small hands reaching desperately for the wooden vessel floating just beyond the shore. His breath hitched in a quiet sob as he grabbed at the pyre, fingers slipping against the wet wood. He tried again, straining against the water, refusing to let go, as though holding it back would bring the one inside it back to him.

His mother caught up to him, her trembling hands clutching at his cloak, pulling him away. But he fought, his cries breaking through the solemn quiet, raw and full of heartbreak. "Please," he whimpered, his voice cracking. "Please, don't go."

Her strength gave out. She sank to her knees, arms tightening around her son, holding him as sobs racked her body. The pyre drifted further, slipping into the waiting embrace of the lake. The child watched, his breath shuddering as his fingers clenched into tiny fists, powerless to stop it.

Marenya's voice never wavered. As the flames caught the edge of the king's pyre, her song swelled, rising to meet the cries of the boy, to carry his grief in its melody. And then, as if answering, the voices of the trolls joined hers, one by one, their mourning hymn rippling across the water, filling the night with sorrow and reverence.

The lake had swallowed their dead, their names drifting skyward in embers and smoke. A hush lingered, vast and endless, as if Olympus itself had paused to mourn.

# Chapter 2: The Transition Orb

The days passed in a blur of preparations. The streets of Farkland Reach were busy but subdued, its people forcing themselves forward in the wake of battle. Supply wagons creaked under the weight of provisions. Smiths hammered out last-minute repairs to armor and weapons. Soldiers drilled, their movements precise but mechanical, as if going through the motions could force some sense of normalcy back into their lives.

Darien moved through it all, his mind elsewhere.

He had walked these streets every morning since the funeral, nodding at familiar faces, but not stopping to talk. The air carried a heaviness that hadn't been there before. Conversations were hushed, glances lingered just a little too long. The city had won its battle, but it had not yet recovered.

Their journey north to Minotatha loomed ahead, and Darien had tried to gather what information he could about the Peronia. But asking questions about them yielded little more than quiet deflections and vague answers. The people of Farkland Reach spoke of them carefully, as if saying too much would invite unwanted attention.

It wasn't that they didn't know anything. It was that they didn't want to say it.

He had already encountered the Peronia once before, during his time with the Marauders. A tense moment—an accidental brush of shoulders in a crowded space that had almost turned violent. The Peronia were patient, calculating, and untrusting. They spoke in low, deliberate tones, watching everything but saying little. Garik had stepped in before the situation escalated, but his warning had stuck with Darien.

"They deal in information and favors," Garik had told him. "That makes them powerful, but it also makes them paranoid. They listen. They watch. And they don't forget."

Darien had held onto that warning. Now, hearing the way people avoided his questions, he realized how true it was.

He made his way through the market square, sidestepping merchants setting up their stalls. The scent of fresh bread mixed with the lingering smell of scorched stone. The damage from the battle had been patched up, but the wounds it left behind hadn't healed.

He was nearly at the Marauder camp when he saw her.

Evatra was moving toward him with purpose, her ebony hair catching the light, her sharp features set in focus. Before he could call out, she was already in front of him.

"Darien," she said, her voice urgent but low. "I just got a message from the Queen. Totra-Dal is awake."

Darien felt his breath hitch. Relief surged through him, sharp and unexpected. He had feared this moment wouldn't come—that Evatra would be forced to choose between staying behind with her niece or leaving with the Eldric. Now there was a chance she could go with him in a way Kara would never have been able to.

"Where is he?" he asked.

"They have him in a room in the castle," she said. "I was going there now. Come with me."

She turned sharply, already making her way back toward the city. Darien hesitated only for a second before falling into step beside her. Neither of them spoke as they moved through the streets. There was too much to say, and no time to say it.

The guards at the castle entrance barely spared them a glance before waving them through. Inside, the corridors were brighter than they had been the last time Darien walked them, sunlight pouring in from high-arched windows. The walls of Fenway Castle had held steady through the battle, but for the first time, they felt fragile. As if the war had not yet left them.

They rounded a corner and nearly collided with Queen Marenya as she stepped out of a chamber, the heavy door clicking shut behind her. She turned at the sound, her gaze landing first on Evatra, then on Darien.

"Ah, there you both are," she said, her voice calm but edged with exhaustion.

Evatra bowed slightly. "Your Majesty. I came as soon as I received your message. I ran into Darien in the city and brought him with me." Her eyes flicked toward the closed door. "Is he…?"

Marenya's lips curved in a small, knowing smile. "He is most certainly awake, and exactly as I expected him to be. You should go in and speak with him. I think he might welcome familiar faces."

Evatra didn't wait for further permission. She stepped past the Queen and pushed the door open, Darien following closely behind.

The room was plain, almost stark, compared to the chambers Darien had been given. No ornate furnishings, no symbols of wealth or status. Just a sturdy chair, a table, and a man who had been on the edge of death days ago.

Totra-Dal sat at the far end of the room, his massive frame dwarfed slightly by the chair. He looked tired, but his eyes were sharp, assessing, as they landed first on Evatra, then on Darien.

"Ah, Evatra!" he boomed, slapping a hand against his thigh. "I wondered if you'd come to see me. Tell me, how is Atreya? Did you bring her with you?"

Evatra didn't answer.

Instead, she took two steps forward, then sank to her knees before him, pressing her face into her hands as a sob broke free.

Darien stood motionless, struggling to process Evatra's reaction. She had always been composed, unreadable even in the worst moments. She had rejected Totra-Dal's claim to Atreya, treated him with cool indifference, and yet—here she was, breaking apart in front of him. He had no words for it. No reference point for this kind of vulnerability.

He took a hesitant step forward, instinct urging him to comfort her, but Totra-Dal shook his head, the movement barely perceptible. Darien's eyes flicked up, meeting the older man's gaze. There was no arrogance in it, no amusement—just an understanding he hadn't expected. A quiet acknowledgment of pain shared, of wounds that time alone couldn't heal.

"Come now, Evatra," Totra-Dal said, his voice softer than Darien had ever heard it. "You didn't think Kort could do away with me that easily, did you?"

Evatra remained where she was, her fingers digging into her arms as she fought to steady herself. Her breath hitched, her shoulders trembled, but she did not look away. Finally, after several long moments, she dragged the back of her hand across her eyes and pulled herself upright, though the effort left her visibly drained.

"I—" Her voice faltered. She swallowed hard, then tried again. "I'm glad to see you alive."

Totra-Dal exhaled, shaking his head with a small chuckle. "So am I."

She nodded stiffly, as if locking her emotions back into place. "Atreya isn't here. She's in the care of the Scillans. I wasn't sure what state you were in and didn't want her to worry more than she already has."

A deep, rumbling noise came from Totra-Dal's chest—not quite a sigh, not quite a grunt, but something in between. He nodded, rubbing a hand over his jaw. "I understand. That was wise."

Then, after a moment, his gaze sharpened. "Tell me, have the Marauders tried to unseat you yet?"

Evatra's expression flickered, her guard snapping back up. "How would you know I was leading them?"

Totra-Dal gave a knowing smirk. "Because if I'm alive, that means Kort is either dead or in chains. That leaves only a handful of people the Marauders would follow. I trust Darien isn't foolish enough to try and lead them, so that only leaves you. And when Marenya sent for someone, you were the one who appeared." He gestured toward Darien. "Didn't take much deduction."

Darien, despite himself, was impressed. He had seen Totra-Dal lead, had witnessed his strength and cunning firsthand, but even now, recovering from a near-fatal wound, the man was still five steps ahead of everyone else in the room.

"So, Marenya filled me in on what's happened since my injury," Totra-Dal continued, "but there is still a lot I don't know. Tell me everything."

Evatra inhaled slowly, then launched into a retelling of the battle. She spoke of the ride from the Marauder camp, the theft of the sword, Darien's failure against Tahmer, the discovery of Cyprin's army, the desperate plea to the Wraiths for help. She described the way the city had been nearly lost, the battle that followed, the moment Kort's blade had struck Totra-Dal down.

Darien listened in silence, offering details where he could, but he let Evatra lead the telling. Totra-Dal's eyes remained sharp throughout, nodding at key moments, filing every piece of information away in that ever-calculating mind of his. He gave no indication of pain or weakness, despite the bandages still wrapped around his midsection.

When Evatra finally fell silent, she remained kneeling, staring at the floor, as if lost in thought. The room settled into stillness, a shared weight pressing over them all. Totra-Dal leaned forward, rubbing a thumb over the edge of the chair's armrest.

"It appears," he said finally, his voice measured, "that things have turned differently in this cycle. I've never concerned myself with the Eldric in the past, but it seems I find myself in the middle of it now."

His gaze flicked to Darien, steady and assessing. "And you, my young friend—you seem to be the focal point of all of it. Wherever you go, events shift, as if fate itself sees you as her plaything." He leaned back, studying him. "Be wary, Darien. Fate is a cruel temptress. Do not let her sink her claws too deep."

Darien forced himself to hold Totra-Dal's gaze, though he wasn't sure he fully understood what was being implied. He was saved from answering when the older man turned back to Evatra.

"Stand up, Evatra. There's no need for you to be on the floor. Listen, both of you—I owe you a debt of gratitude."

Evatra rose, standing beside Darien. Totra-Dal's expression softened slightly. "You kept Atreya safe. You prevented the Marauders from turning on each other. And you defended Farkland Reach when it needed it most. That is more than most accomplish in a lifetime."

Darien hesitated, then blurted out the question that had been nagging at him. "You lived here?"

Totra-Dal's grin widened. "Oh yes. I lived here many years as a child and a young man. But that's a story for another time. For now, there is much to discuss—Evatra, your future, the Marauders, and mine. But not tonight. I need rest."

His grin faded slightly, and for the first time, Darien saw the exhaustion beneath his bravado. "The doctors say it's a miracle I'm alive. And I do not intend to waste that second chance. But for now, leave me to my rest. I'll send for you tomorrow."

Evatra nodded, her voice barely above a whisper. "I'm glad you're alive."

She turned sharply, walking toward the door without another word, not waiting for Darien to follow.

Totra-Dal's gaze lingered on her retreating figure before he turned back to Darien, an unreadable expression crossing his features. Then, after a moment, he nodded, dismissing him as well.

Darien stepped into the hall, spotting Evatra a few steps ahead. She gripped the railing, staring down at the levels below, unmoving.

Darien approached quietly, slipping his hand over hers. She didn't pull away, but she didn't acknowledge him either.

"I've spent weeks now," she whispered. "A turbulent sea of emotions. First the raid that killed my party. Then learning who you were. Saving Atreya. Finding out he was her father. Recruiting the Wraiths. Wondering if you had been killed by Tahmer. Saving the city. Leading the Marauders."

She exhaled shakily. "Seeing him alive means it wasn't all in vain. That Atreya won't suffer another loss."

Darien didn't speak. He only held her hand, letting her say what she needed to say.

Finally, after a long moment, she pulled away— only to turn and wrap her arms around him, holding on tight. Darien's arms instinctively encircled her, holding her as close as he could, offering whatever comfort he had to give.

Eventually, she pulled back, brushing her lips against his briefly before turning toward the castle halls.

"Darien! Darien, wait. Evatra!"

Oratrin's voice rang through the courtyard, sharp and urgent. Darien and Evatra exchanged a glance before turning toward him.

"What is it?" Evatra asked, lowering her voice as they neared to avoid drawing unnecessary attention.

"The Queen asked me to find you after your visit with Totra-Dal. She has something she wishes to show you. She's gathered the other members of the Eldric in the vaults below. I'm to take you both there now."

Darien straightened slightly, his muscles tensing. "Lead the way, then."

Oratrin turned sharply, guiding them toward a door at the rear of the grand entryway—one that, to Darien's knowledge, had always been locked. The heavy iron handle creaked as Oratrin pushed it open, revealing a dimly lit corridor that sloped downward, the air immediately growing colder. The scent of damp stone and aged dust filled Darien's nose, a stark contrast to the open halls of the castle above.

As they stepped inside, the door groaned shut behind them, sealing them into an uneasy silence. The darkness felt oppressive, pressing in from all sides as their footsteps echoed against the stone. The weight of centuries lay in these walls.

Darien counted the steps as they began their descent, only realizing halfway down how unpleasant the climb back up would be. Four landings later, the spiral staircase finally ended in a narrow passage, lined with unlit torches fixed to the walls. Oratrin grabbed a lantern from a nearby sconce, touching it to a smoldering ember on the opposite wall. The lantern flared to life, casting flickering shadows along the stone.

"Stay close," Oratrin warned, his voice quiet but firm. "The passages here are a labyrinth. Fall too far back, and you might never find your way out."

With that ominous caution, he led them deeper into the winding corridors, making sudden turns without hesitation, unlocking doors to narrow passageways. The air grew colder, and the silence stretched so thin that every footstep sounded deafening.

Something about the space made Darien uneasy. It reminded him of The Academy—the same long halls, the same countless doors leading to unknown rooms. It made him wonder—what lay beneath his home? What secrets had been buried beneath the Academy's ancient foundation? Whyn had hinted at something just before he left.

Finally, after what felt like an eternity, they emerged into a larger chamber bathed in torchlight. The sudden brightness forced Darien and Evatra to shield their eyes, adjusting to the shift. When he lowered his hand, his gaze fell upon the center of the room.

A pedestal stood before them, and atop it sat a small, pulsing blue sphere—roughly three inches across, swirling with an ethereal glow. The air around it hummed, vibrating in a way that felt familiar but eerily distant.

Darien frowned. Why did it seem so familiar? He struggled to place the memory, but it hovered just out of reach, like a forgotten dream slipping through his grasp.

To his left, Marenya stood with Rist, Breyman, Airlyn, Garil, and Chorrun—the centaur who had guided Darien to Farkland Reach before his capture by Totra-Dal's marauders. Chorrun gave him a warm nod, while Breyman and Marenya watched in measured silence. Airlyn, by contrast, looked bored and vaguely irritated. Garik, on the other hand, observed the scene with his usual sharp-eyed amusement, his lips quirking slightly, as if he had already determined how this would play out before anyone spoke.

"Thank you for joining us, Darien," Marenya said in her usual soft, composed voice.

Darien nodded, still eyeing the glowing sphere. "What is that?"

"That," Marenya said, stepping forward, "is why I asked you all here."

She moved toward the pedestal, gesturing toward the object. "We found this on the body of the thief Tahmer. When we retrieved it, it was completely black. But this morning, it began to glow."

The pulsing light intensified, as if responding to her words.

"We originally stored it in a vault on an upper level," Marenya continued. "Under standard security—nothing extreme. But earlier today, something happened. A servant, hearing the hum of the object, picked up the satchel containing it. According to those present, the orb slipped from the bag. The man reached down to grab it…"

She hesitated, her face darkening.

"And?" Evatra pressed.

Marenya's voice was grave. "He vanished. Without a trace."

A murmur of shock rippled through the gathered warriors.

"This thing," Airlyn spoke up, stepping closer, her previous irritation replaced with fascination, "looks exactly like the transitions that bring the Eldric to Olympus."

"Could it be magic?" Darien asked, hoping his question wouldn't betray just how little he still understood about this world.

Marenya inclined her head. "That is our best guess. Though, if history has taught us anything, Garik will likely suggest a far more elaborate and conspiratorial alternative."

Garik folded his arms, letting out a theatrical sigh. "Your Majesty wounds me. I am merely an observer of patterns, and the pattern here suggests something rather unsettling."

Darien's stomach twisted. He barely noticed Garik tilting his head, watching him closely. "You seem troubled, Darien. Well, more than usual," Garik mused. "

Darien didn't respond, lost in the tumult of his own thoughts.

*If it functioned like a transition… was it connected to the Eldric? To me?*

"There's more," Marenya continued. "After Tahmer's failure, we kept his body, hoping to determine if Cyprin had augmented him in any way. Our doctors and scholars attempted numerous tests."

She exhaled, tension lining her features. "Each one fell ill. Every attempt ended in sickness or failure. Realizing that something was preventing us from studying him, we decided to burn his body," She paused. "Or so we thought."

A cold unease settled over the room.

"Several hours after placing him on the pyre, we returned to find the timber reduced to ash." Marenya's gaze swept across the group. "But Tahmer's body remained—untouched."

Silence gripped them.

"How is that possible?" Evatra asked, her voice quieter now.

"Magic," Breyman rumbled, his deep voice rolling through the chamber like distant thunder.

Darien frowned. "I thought Cyprin controlled all magic. Isn't that why the war began in the first place?"

"He does," Chorrun answered, the usual historian's awe tinged with something darker. "Or at least he did at the end of the great war. No one in Olympus has been able to use magic since then, at least not to my knowledge. But it seems he may have given this magic to Tahmer. Or perhaps to the orb itself."

"That is our suspicion as well," Marenya confirmed, pacing slowly. "And there is more."

She turned back to face them, her expression severe. "At the same moment this orb came to life... Tahmer's body vanished."

A sharp, visceral panic gripped Darien's chest as the world around him seemed to constrict. The last time he had faced Tahmer, he had barely escaped with his life, and if not for Rist, he would have been just another name whispered among the dead. Now, Tahmer stood before them again, his presence carrying an unnatural weight that sent ice lancing through Darien's veins. His fingers twitched toward his waist, instinct commanding him to reach for his sword—only to grasp at nothing. His stomach dropped. The weapon he needed most was with the smith, far beyond his reach.

"—Do you have it secure?" Rist's voice cut through the suffocating tension, as sharp and steady as a blade being drawn from its sheath.

"The sword?" Marenya's nod was precise. "It has been moved to a more secure location. Handpicked guards, hidden corridors, alarm systems. No one is getting to it without facing dozens of warriors."

"So what now?" Airlyn asked, her voice edged with impatience, her body tense as if already preparing for the inevitable fight.

Before anyone could answer, a cold voice echoed from the passage behind them, carrying with it the weight of something inevitable.

"Now the cycles end."

Darien's stomach clenched as every muscle in his body went taut. He knew that voice.

The group turned in unison, the air in the chamber thick with the unspoken understanding that whatever came next, it would change everything.

Tahmer stood in the entryway, his masked face an unreadable void, but the eerie glow emanating from behind his darkened eyes betrayed something far worse than before. In his right hand, he gripped a blood-stained troll blade. In his left, wrapped in cloth, was something far more dangerous. A sword. Its hilt protruded from the wrappings, unmistakable even from a distance.

He had the sword again.

Darien's instincts screamed. He knew what was coming, but his body had already started moving before his mind could catch up.

"What do you want, traitor?" Marenya demanded, her voice measured, but carrying the force of command.

Tahmer's voice remained eerily calm. "What was given to me by my master."

He lifted his chin slightly, gesturing toward the pulsing blue orb at the center of the room.

Rist's voice cut through the tension like a knife. "Drop the sword. Leave the orb. If you do, we may let you leave."

Tahmer laughed, a hollow, empty sound that barely seemed to belong to him. "You'll let me?" His head tilted slightly, his expression unreadable behind the mask. "You can't stop me."

The moment Tahmer's gaze flicked toward the orb, something inside Darien snapped into motion, instinct overriding thought.

So did Tahmer.

Both warriors lunged, colliding in a brutal contest of speed and sheer will. The impact sent a shockwave through Darien's arms, his grip tightening around the cloth-wrapped hilt of the sword as Tahmer fought to wrench it free. The force of their struggle sent them careening into the pedestal, knocking the orb from its resting place. It hung suspended in the air for a fraction of a second before Tahmer's hand closed around it.

A low, reverberating hum filled the chamber. The air thickened, charged with unseen energy as a pulse of blue light rippled outward from the orb. Darien felt it wrap around him like an unseen tether, yanking him forward. His grip on the sword tightened as it began to slip, but his entire body locked up, his muscles freezing in place as the force dragged him into the swirling light alongside Tahmer.

Everything blurred. The world twisted, stretched, and folded in ways it wasn't meant to. Darien had experienced the transitions before, but this was different—wilder, untamed. The seconds stretched unnaturally, his sense of direction warping with each heartbeat.

Then, a violent jolt.

A secondary force pulled against him, like another current fighting to rip him away from the main stream of the transition. The turbulence sent his legs swinging sideways, yanking him off course. A silent scream clawed at his throat as he struggled to hold onto the sword, his grip slipping. He saw Tahmer's fingers tighten in response, but the same unseen force that had seized Darien wrenched at him as well. The connection snapped, and suddenly, they were no longer moving together.

Tahmer spiraled toward the point of light ahead, while Darien was flung violently in another direction.

And then—impact.

The ground hit him like stone, his body slamming into it with enough force to knock the breath from his lungs. Pain lanced through every muscle as nausea roiled through him, and before he could stop himself, he fell forward onto his hands and knees, retching into the damp earth. The acrid taste burned his throat, his entire body trembling from the aftershock of the transition.

Panic set in before he even looked up. His hands scrambled against the ground, searching—searching—

There. Just beyond his reach, half-buried in loose dirt, lay the sword. He dragged himself toward it, his fingers closing around the hilt. Clutching it against his chest, he collapsed onto his side, forcing himself to breathe, to fight the overwhelming darkness threatening to pull him under.

The world was eerily silent.

Then—footsteps.

Soft, methodical, approaching with unsettling precision.

Darien forced himself to look up, but his vision wavered, refusing to focus. The figure loomed above him, its features blurred in the haze of his fading consciousness. But something was wrong.

Pale skin. Human feet.

No.

Darien was the only human in Olympus.

His mind fought against what he was seeing, reality twisting at the edges of comprehension. His body screamed at him to stay awake, to move, to defend himself, but his limbs were too heavy, his thoughts sluggish.

The figure crouched beside him. Through the haze, through the blinding pain, through the sheer impossibility of it—Darien saw a face he knew. A face he had never expected to see until his journey was over.

Master Whyn.

The shock struck harder than the transition itself, knocking the breath from his body. His muscles locked up, the last threads of his awareness unraveling into the dark as he slipped into unconsciousness.

# Chapter 3: The Stolen Champion

Ristvahkbain stood still amid the roiling emotions that churned through the chamber, their intensity pressing against his senses like a storm threatening to consume him. Panic. Confusion. Despair. Fear. Anger. They crashed over him in waves, each distinct, each belonging to someone else, none of them his own. He had long since mastered the art of separating himself from the emotions of others, but in moments like this—when the room seethed with uncertainty—it took effort.

He pulled in a slow breath, siphoning the cacophony of feelings into the background, like distant murmurs in a crowded marketplace. It was a skill, one honed through years of necessity. He did not read thoughts. He could not pluck secrets from minds. He was no telepath. But emotions? They were impossible to conceal. They bled from people, raw and unchecked, and Rist read them as naturally as one might read the shifting clouds before a storm.

The silence in the room stretched unbearably. No one moved. No one spoke. Only moments ago, they had watched Darien—their human Eldric—be swallowed by the blue light of the orb, dragged away by Tahmer with one of their sacred weapons.

The orb that had stood upon the pedestal sat empty, lifeless. There was no following him now.

Evatra's voice broke the silence, a single cry filled with anguish.

"Darien!"

Rist flinched, but not at the sound itself. It was the weight behind it, the sheer depth of feeling that nearly drowned him in sorrow and fear. He focused on her for a moment, peeling back the layers of her emotion. Beneath the panic and despair, something steadier burned—determination, raw and unshaken. She would not let this be the end of it. That was good. That meant she could still be useful.

"Where have they gone?" Airlyn demanded.

Marenya shook her head, her usual composure slipping ever so slightly.

"WHERE?!" Airlyn's voice cracked like a whip, her rage palpable.

"I-I don't know." The Queen's voice faltered, a rare slip into uncertainty. Rist's focus sharpened. She was afraid, but not just for Darien. For all of them. If Tahmer had mastered something beyond their understanding, if he had somehow circumvented the cycle's constraints, then everything they thought they knew was flawed.

Airlyn's fury had not abated. "We have to go after them!"

"And where would you have us begin?" Rist asked, his voice a steady anchor in the rising tide of emotion. It was a calculated response, meant to force her into reason.

Airlyn hesitated, frustration flashing across her features before logic began to take hold.

"We can't just wait for him to come back!"

"What do you propose that we do?" Rist countered, his tone cool, deliberate. She was still angry, but her rage was shifting, becoming less wild, less dangerous. She was thinking now, not just reacting. He allowed himself a small moment of gratitude for his gift—it had given him an edge in controlling situations like these.

"So you think we just do nothing?" she pushed again.

"Calm yourself, elf." Breyman's voice was low and firm, rumbling like distant thunder. "Nothing has been decided."

Rist liked Breyman. He was steady, a pillar of reason amidst the chaos. Unlike the others, his emotions rarely flared beyond control. That made him easier to ignore when necessary.

"This will require some thought," Rist said, shifting his attention back to Evatra. She still stood frozen, her eyes locked on the space where the orb had sat, her sorrow radiating outward like ripples in water. He let her grief press against him for a moment longer before pushing it away. She turned toward him suddenly, meeting the void of his hood with burning intensity. A single tear slipped down her cheek, but she wiped it away before it had a chance to fall. The sorrow receded, replaced by something colder—resolve.

She would not break.

"Yes, yes, Master Rist, that is a good idea," Marenya murmured, shaking herself free from her hesitation. "Oratrin, please lead the way."

As they filed out of the chamber, Rist felt another presence slip into step beside him. Garik. He had been silent, watching, as he often did. His emotions were more difficult to untangle—layers upon layers of control, falsehoods woven seamlessly into truths. That was what made him dangerous, but also incredibly entertaining.

"I was wondering when you would say something," Rist murmured lowly.

Garik's lips quirked upward, the smirk audible in his voice. "I find it wise to let others exhaust their dramatics before offering my insights. And you, my friend, always know the right moment to stir the pot."

Rist didn't respond, but he could feel the weight of Garik's amusement. Beneath it, however, something sharper lurked. He was worried.

By the time they reached the council chambers, the tension had coiled itself into something heavy. The plans for the battle against the Dark Army lay rolled on the table, untouched since their victory. Marenya took her seat at the head, her presence commanding as always. The others followed suit, except for Darien's chair, which remained empty.

It did not go unnoticed.

"I have three points," Rist said, breaking the silence. He pitched his voice carefully, keeping it warm, steady, authoritative. "All of which should be obvious, should we pause to consider them." He counted them off with slow precision. "First, we have no way of knowing where Darien and Tahmer have gone. For all we know, Tahmer took him directly into the heart of Mount Olympus. That would be the most logical place for him to go."

Silence met his words, though he sensed several minds already spinning through counterarguments.

"Second, given their likely location, attempting to pursue either of them now is a foolish endeavor."

The tension in the room thickened. Some of them didn't like where this was going, but Rist pressed on.

"Third and finally, we must continue our journey regardless of what is done to find Darien or retrieve the sword."

The words hung there, heavy and unyielding. A beat passed before Evatra finally spoke, her voice laced with quiet defiance. "Are you saying we just do nothing?"

Rist turned his head toward her, letting the silence stretch before answering. "No. I am saying that we must build our next steps from a place of strategy, not desperation."

A ripple of discontent passed through the room, but no one argued. Not yet.

Marenya's voice cut through the tension, sharp with decision. "Then we will retrieve Darien and the sword. He saved our city. The least we can do is return the favor."

Rist didn't sigh, but he wanted to. This was about more than just Darien. More than just one lost warrior. But he knew better than to argue against loyalty.

As the discussion unfolded, Rist leaned back in his chair, letting the emotions of the room press against him. There was fear here, yes, but something else lingered beneath it.

Doubt.

He would have to watch carefully. There were always those who looked for opportunity in chaos, and he suspected they had not yet seen the last of them.

"No," Rist said, shaking his head. "I simply point out the foundation from which we can develop whatever plan seems best."

"Do you have any suggestions, then?" Oratrin asked.

Rist turned his hooded gaze toward the troll general, considering him carefully. Oratrin had been instrumental in defending Farkland Reach, but in the wake of battle, his rigid sense of duty had turned into something more grating. Rist liked him well enough, but found his approach trying.

"No," Rist answered simply.

Silence fell. The emotions around him became a tangled web of frustration, anxiety, and restrained arguments waiting to be voiced. Rather than try to parse them all, Rist let them settle into background noise, listening instead to the rhythm of the conversation.

"The priority," Chorrun finally said, breaking the silence, "seems as though it should be simultaneously the journey and the recovery of Darien and the sword. The path forward on the former seems obvious, the latter, however..." Chorrun trailed off, waiting for someone else to pick up his thought. Breyman did so.

"The Eldric will continue our journey. To Minotatha, then to the Mer's homeland in the seas."

"Well, thank you for pointing out the obvious," Airlyn sneered derisively, clearly annoyed at the lack of deeper insight. "But what about the rest? Can we take Olympus without the sword?"

All eyes turned to Chorrun, the room's expert on the cycle and its history.

"I—I'm not sure," Chorrun admitted, his voice unusually unsteady. "No one, other than the Eldric who have traveled up the mountain, knows the mechanism by which the gates to Cyprin's fortress are opened. I suppose it's possible, but we would be risking the very process of the cycle itself."

"Then we *must* recover the sword," Marenya said, her voice carrying a weight of finality. For the first time in the conversation, she sounded like a queen. "We will retrieve Darien and the sword for you. After all Darien did to save our city, the least we can do is to save him from the grip of that traitor." She nearly spat the last word before catching herself, resolve hardening once more. "The how will be decided later. But we will go in search of Darien and Tahmer as soon as a party can be assembled and sent."

"I'm going with them," Evatra stated flatly, leaving little room for discussion.

Marenya turned her hard, gray gaze toward her younger counterpart, her expression softer but still firm. "I knew you would volunteer for this. But we must consider a great many things before the final party is decided. I know you are not under my direct authority, but I urge patience from you as we begin to plan."

Evatra remained silent, but Rist could sense the tension radiating from her. She wanted to argue, but she held herself in check. Rist was impressed by the restraint.

"We must begin the journey as quickly as possible. We can't know what other chaos may have erupted in the other major cities since the battle. How are preparations coming?" Rist asked, keeping his voice warm, measured.

"Your horses are ready, though we had some trouble finding one large enough for you, Sir Breyman." Oratrin nodded toward the large Lystran before continuing, "Supplies are being gathered now, and everything should be ready by tomorrow morning."

"Good, then we can finally get on with this," Airlyn muttered, impatience dripping from her tone.

Rist examined the emotions flowing from her—fear, resentment, a cold undercurrent of rage. Something wasn't right with her, and he made a mental note to watch her carefully in the coming weeks.

"Then that concludes our council here," Marenya announced. "The rest of the Eldric will continue their journey the day after tomorrow once we are sure all is in order. The others and I will begin to make plans to pursue Darien and the sword."

Rist chuckled inwardly. The Queen spoke as though marching into Cyprin's domain was a simple matter, as if walking into the heart of darkness was merely another task to be completed. His own task would be difficult enough if what he suspected about the other cities proved true. He did not envy whoever was chosen to find Darien.

He turned his hood toward Evatra, finding her staring directly back at him with a deadly intensity. His head cocked slightly, curiosity piqued. The others had begun to stand, filing out around them, but she remained seated, unmoving. Finally, she rose, the last besides himself, and exited the room. Rist followed at a small distance, sensing the weight of something unspoken lingering between them.

She led him down the hall without a word, glancing back once before opening a door and stepping inside. She didn't ask him to follow, but she didn't need to. Rist could feel the expectation hanging in the air. Out of instinct, he rested a hand on the hilt of a small dagger hidden within the folds of his cloak and stepped inside.

She shut the door behind them and turned to face him.

"Is Darien alive?" she asked, her voice quiet but sharp with purpose.

"How would I know?" Rist asked, tilting his head slightly.

"I don't know," she admitted, her emotions swirling in a tangled storm. "You seem to... know things. You and Darien seemed to like each other well enough. I just need someone to tell me he's still alive."

Rist studied her for a long moment, sifting through the weight of her emotions. Her attachment to Darien was strong—stronger than it should have been given how recently they had met. He considered how best to answer her, choosing his words carefully.

"I cannot know," Rist said slowly. "But from what I know of our young friend, and what I can guess about Tahmer and the demon he serves, I would doubt Darien's immediate death is something that we should fear."

Evatra's gaze dropped for a moment. A tear slipped down her cheek again before she wiped it away as though it had never existed.

"You said immediate death," she said quietly. "So you think they'll kill him, eventually?"

"I'm not sure," Rist admitted. "Cyprin is twisted, his motivations all his own. That means he likely is somewhere between mad and cunning—possibly both."

Rist let a moment of silence pass between them before continuing. "I know you want to join the party in search of Darien. I urge you to reconsider."

"I won't." Evatra's response left no room for debate. Her posture was rigid, her hands curled into fists at her sides.

Rist continued as if he hadn't heard her. "You have proven yourself to be incredibly valuable, Evatra. You led the Marauders in their leader's absence, you fought in the battle of Farkland Reach, and your role in the planning has earned you prestige both among your people and within the city. You have brokered peace where few thought it possible." He stepped away from the wall, his movements smooth, deliberate. "The Queen could use you. If Darien is found, it is here they will bring him. Please consider that."

Evatra held his gaze, unreadable, her emotions suddenly distant. Rist had expected anger, frustration—something. Instead, she offered nothing. Without another word, she turned and strode out of the room, her steps quick but measured.

Rist watched her go, sensing her emotions shift the further she walked. She was seeking something—*someone*—to anchor herself to. He suspected she would find that in Totra-Dal. This was good. He had not met the man, but from what he had learned, Totra-Dal was wise beneath his bravado, his mind as sharp as his sword arm.

Giving her a moment of distance, Rist followed, though he took a different path, veering toward his own quarters.

Upon entering, the first thing he noticed was the light—bright, intrusive. The servants had drawn back the heavy curtains, letting the late afternoon sun spill across the chamber in golden bands. Rist exhaled through his nose, stepping forward and pulling the drapes shut with a sharp flick of his wrist. Darkness settled over the room like a familiar cloak. He much preferred it that way.

The opulence of the space was unnecessary, almost garish. The furniture was carved with intricate details; the tapestries embroidered with silver and gold thread. Displays of wealth that meant little to him. On Terrae, such things were seen as excess, distractions. Here, they were symbols of power.

He reminded himself, as he had many times since arriving in Olympus, that this was *not* his world.

Crossing the room, Rist adjusted the last folds of fabric, blocking out every sliver of light until the chamber was pitch-black. It made no difference to him. Sight was not dependent on light. He saw through *other* means, through the subtle ripples of energy in the world around him.

With a quiet sigh, he reached up and pushed back his hood. The air touched his face, cool and unrestricted. None had seen him without the shroud of his robes since he was a boy, since he had been named one of the Eld. He did not regret it, but the relief of shedding that weight, if only for a moment, was undeniable.

He let his thoughts drift. It was unusual for him to linger on people, yet he found his mind circling back to Darien. He had known the boy for only a short time, and yet, there was something about him—something that made Rist feel as though he were standing on the edge of a vast, unseen pattern. Wherever Darien went, events shifted. Fate twisted around him like threads pulled by an invisible hand.

Rist wasn't sure whether that was something to be admired—or feared.

With fluid movements, he loosened the clasp of his robe, letting the heavy fabric slip from his shoulders and pool onto the floor. He hovered a few inches above the ground, his body relaxing as he expanded outward, no longer confined by form. It was always in these moments, freed from restriction, that he felt most himself.

# Chapter 4: The Unlikely Scholar

The next twenty-four hours rushed by in a daze for Rist as final preparations were made for their company—now reduced by one due to Darien's brash yet daring action—to depart Farkland Reach and take the journey west.

On the final evening before their departure, Rist moved through the grey stone streets, the worn paths reflecting the faces of those who walked them. Though he kept his awareness open, allowing the hum of emotions to pass around him like the current of a river, he remained selective—muting the overwhelming waves of grief, exhaustion, and determination. He afforded those around him some privacy, but still kept a wary tether on his senses, always watching for the unseen dangers that lurked beneath the surface.

As he approached the door to the shop, he paused for a moment, considering what he might find on the other side. The emotions coming from within were chaotic—frustration laced with embarrassment. He stepped inside.

The shop was dimly lit, the cool air carrying the scent of hot iron and polished wood. A counter stood in front of him, unoccupied, though the faint glow of red light flickered from a doorway in the far-left corner. A bell chimed behind him as the door shut, and almost immediately, there was a clatter from the back room, followed by a sharp curse.

A squat purple face peeked past the doorway, eyes widening for a fraction of a second before ducking away again. A flurry of movement followed, the sound of something heavy scraping across the floor.

"Hello?" Rist called, his voice calm, measured.

"Uh—um—one moment, please! I'll be right there!" came the hurried response.

"Do you need help?" Rist asked into the void of the room beyond.

Rist heard another thud, followed by a strained grunt of exertion. "No—no, that's quite alright—I just need to—" The voice cut off again, replaced by a final scrape of metal against stone. "There," the voice said, satisfied.

A moment later, the same purple face reappeared, now hastily wiped clean—though streaks of dust remained, forming uneven patterns like war paint.

"Sorry about that," the figure said, brushing off his apron. "Had an… accident. I needed to clean up before Master Thron returned."

Now that Rist could see him fully, the small, winged man was unmistakably a fairy—his wings folded neatly against his back, his stature reaching just over half of Rist's height. Rist noted the sharp intelligence behind his eyes, despite the obvious nervous energy buzzing around him.

"Master Thron?" Rist asked.

"Yes, he's the smith in this shop. I just help out and hope to learn. Whatever he's willing to teach me, anyway—which isn't much."

"How long have you worked for this 'Thron'?"

"Not long by troll standards. Ages by mine." The fairy sighed. "But that's what I signed up for. Differences in life cycle don't grant special privileges among the trolls. Forgive me, I haven't even introduced myself. I'm Lark—Lark Whitebay, at your service."

Rist inclined his head slightly. "I am here to retrieve a sword."

Lark nodded absentmindedly. "We have hundreds of those. Who was the maker?"

"I am uncertain, but it was not of troll make. Foreign to you, likely."

Recognition flickered across the fairy's face. "Ah, the human sword." He clicked his tongue. "That proved tricky. Made using a method we couldn't quite place—the metals were… different. It took Master Thron hours to repair."

"That would be it," Rist said. "I am here to collect it."

Lark hesitated, his wings twitching slightly. "Oh, I'm sorry. I can't give it to you."

Rist let a pause stretch between them, then allowed the faintest note of icy irritation to enter his voice. "And why not?"

Lark, to his credit, barely faltered. "Because it's not your sword, sir."

Rist studied him, considering. It was rare for someone to hold their ground against him. "Do you know who I am?"

Lark tilted his head, a flicker of apprehension in his aura. "No, sir. Should I?"

"Probably. The one who left the sword here is Darien. He is a member of the Eldric, as I am. He is currently unable to retrieve the weapon, so I am here in his stead."

Lark visibly paled, shrinking down ever so slightly. "Oh—oh! Oh, I'm so sorry, sir. I didn't realize! How could I be so stupid? Master Thron is going to kill me—"

"Calm yourself," Rist interjected smoothly. "You caused no offense, and your master is not here. I simply wish to collect the sword and be on my way."

"Y-yes, sir! Right away!" Lark stammered, dashing back into the workshop.

Rist listened to the sound of metal shifting against metal, each clang and scrape giving way to hurried footsteps. A few long seconds later, Lark returned, carefully placing Darien's sheathed sword on the counter between them. His hands still trembled slightly as he let go of the black leather grip.

Rist stepped forward and drew the blade, letting the weight settle in his palm. It was a well-crafted weapon—balanced, sharp—but it held no inherent power of its own. Its worth lay entirely in the hands of the one who wielded it.

Lark watched him curiously. "He'll be pleased, I hope."

"He will be," Rist confirmed.

Lark exhaled, some of his tension easing. "Master Thron spent more time on that than anything I've ever seen him work on. Is it special?"

Rist met his gaze evenly. "There is nothing special about a blade—only the one who uses it."

Lark tilted his head. "True enough. But isn't one of the weapons you have to get a sword? Isn't *that* sword special?"

"The sword itself?" Rist turned the blade slightly, watching how the dim light played along the steel. "No. The sword we must collect is merely an instrument. If none remained to wield it, if no person or being were around to appreciate its value or its history, it would be nothing more than a piece of metal on the ground. It holds no power on its own—only in the hands of those who understand its value."

Rist returned the sword to its sheath and turned toward the door. Before stepping out, he glanced back over his shoulder. "Let no object become more important than the people who wield it. That is the lesson in this cycle."

Lark stared after him, his brow furrowed, as though still trying to decipher the meaning behind Rist's words.

Rist turned away, letting the door close behind him. His last glance at Lark showed the fairy still frozen in thought, his brow furrowed as though he were trying to untangle a puzzle he hadn't realized he was part of. Rist pushed the interaction from his mind and started back toward the castle, his pace unhurried, his senses attuned to the world around him.

The city had settled into an uneasy quiet. The weight of rebuilding still hung over Farkland Reach, its people moving forward because they had no other choice. Rist caught traces of emotion—determination, exhaustion, lingering grief—all layered atop one another like the cracked stonework beneath his feet.

Airlyn, Breyman, and he would be leaving in the morning. Marenya had suggested a small escort of trolls accompany them, but all three had refused. A larger party would only slow them down, complicating an already delicate mission. If Cyprin's agents had already begun infiltrating other cities, their best advantage would be speed and discretion. The Queen had eventually relented, though not without a few displeased glances.

Rist let out a slow breath as he entered the castle, his thoughts turning to a more immediate concern—Evatra.

She was an asset. A leader when her people had needed one, a skilled warrior in her own right. But she was also unpredictable. She would go in search of Darien, with or without approval. That much was certain. What troubled Rist was how far she was willing to go, what she was willing to risk.

Rist moved through the halls, his boots silent against the stone. His mind was still turning over the problem when another thought surfaced—Totra-Dal. The man could be invaluable, a force to stabilize the Marauders when so much else was uncertain. With a few quiet words to a passing guard, Rist redirected his steps toward the Marauders' quarters.

He reached the door and hesitated, stretching his awareness inside. A mind, sharp and alert, though softened at the edges by fatigue. Papers rustling. A slow breath, measured and steady. Rist knocked three times.

There was a pause, then a gruff, familiar voice. "Come."

Rist pushed open the door and stepped inside. The room was modest compared to his own quarters, stripped of excess decoration. A sturdy table sat in the center, scattered with maps and worn documents. Totra-Dal sat at its edge, his large hands resting atop an open scroll. He studied Rist with an expression that was equal parts curiosity and calculation.

"What brings you here?" Totra-Dal asked, wasting no time on pleasantries.

Rist inclined his head slightly. "I have heard much about you. I wished to meet you for myself."

Totra-Dal's gaze flicked to the sword still in Rist's grip. His emotions shifted, a flicker of wariness beneath his usual confidence. "What's that for?"

Rist followed his gaze, realizing he still carried Darien's blade. "Ah." He turned the weapon slightly, watching the light catch against the metal. "I have just retrieved this from the smith. I had intended to store it, but found my thoughts wandering here instead."

Totra-Dal grunted, reaching for the goblet at his side. "A man walking into another man's quarters with a sword in hand tends to raise questions." He took a slow drink before setting it down. "You're not from here, but even you must know that."

Rist said nothing, letting the statement settle between them. The silence stretched long before Totra-Dal leaned back in his chair, nodding toward the opposite seat. "Well? Sit. No need to loom in the doorway."

Rist crossed the room, lowering himself onto the offered chair. He took in the maps spread before him, noting the markings—Zanarchin, Minotatha, a network of tunnels traced with careful precision.

"So," Totra-Dal said, breaking the silence, "what does someone as important as yourself want with someone as insignificant as me Sir... what is it they call you? Roast?"

"They have taken to calling me Rist, and you may forgo the flattery," Rist replied smoothly. "I came to speak with you about several matters. First, these maps."

Totra-Dal chuckled, shaking his head. "A man immune to flattery—now that is rare. Fine, I'll answer your question, but answer one of mine first. I did ask before you."

Rist considered, then nodded. "Very well."

Totra-Dal's expression shifted, the humor in his voice dimming. "Evatra. What of her? She hasn't gone off on her own after that boy, has she?"

Rist's gaze didn't waver. "She intends to leave in search of Darien. I would prefer she reconsider."

Totra-Dal studied him for a long moment before letting out a low sigh. "Yes. That sounds like her." He leaned forward, folding his hands. "When Evatra decides on something, you have two choices—help her or get out of her way. And trust me, she won't be talked down. That kind of mentality suited her well in her life as a marauder but can create problems when there's bigger consequences involved. That's something she has never had to deal with. It allows her to complete raids with astounding precision, but she becomes so focused on her goal that she can sometimes lose sight of the larger picture."

Rist had suspected as much. "Why is she so determined?"

The older man's amusement faded entirely. A deep sorrow flickered beneath his otherwise steady presence, something even Rist hadn't expected.

"That," Totra-Dal said slowly, "is her story to tell."

Rist felt the truth of the words, the weight behind them. "But you know."

A long silence followed. Totra-Dal studied his clasped hands, his fingers tightening slightly against the worn wood of the table. "I believe I do. But I cannot say for certain." He exhaled through his nose. "She's lived a hard life. Always surrounded by outcasts, criminals. But she's not like them. Never was."

Rist absorbed the words, the emotion running beneath them. He had suspected there was more to Evatra's story.

"I think you have the beginnings of understanding," Totra-Dal said, his voice quieter now. "But you won't truly understand until she tells you herself."

Rist inclined his head in acknowledgment. He let the silence linger before shifting the conversation. "These maps," he said, tapping a finger against one of the parchments. "Tell me about them."

Totra-Dal's face lit with something new—excitement, curiosity. He straightened, tapping the scroll before him. "Ah, now this is interesting. These are the most recent maps we have of the lands north and east. They include Zanarchin and—most importantly—tunnels no one knew existed until now."

"If these tunnels weren't finished during the time of the civil war, what makes you think Cyprin's forces finished them? What evidence do you have the Cyprin even knew that they existed?"

"No, no, you don't understand." Totra-Dal said, shaking his head. "Let me try again."

"Please do." Rist said as he leaned back in his chair.

"These tunnels were discovered by Hephaesion, who was the engineer and master inventor who designed the last portions of the city of Zanarchin to be built before Cyprin's final rise to power. In fact, he is the man credited with inventing more contraptions than any before him, and his knowledge of building of all kinds was unparalleled. This," Totra-Dal held up a loosely bound tome with several pages almost falling from the spine. "is a copy of the record made of finding the tunnels and his surprise and confusion at finding such freshly created underground structures. If anyone would know that they were not part of the city, it would be Hephaesion."

"So that means the tunnels were created by someone else. You believe they were made by Cyprin?" Rist asked.

"That's precisely what I believe to be true." Totra-Dal said nodding excitedly. "And there's more. Hephaesion continued down the tunnels a great way, mapping as many as he could. If you take all of the known tunnels and trace back their origin…" Totra-Dal traced his finger along several of the tunnels bringing them all back to a single point on the map.

"They lead right into the heart of Olympus." Rist concluded.

"Precisely" Totra-Dal declared with a note of triumph.

"That is masterful work. You best be careful or you will turn into one of the queen's best scholars, Master Totra-Dal."

Totra-Dal guffawed.

"Me? No, no. This was all I could do to keep myself from going mad in here. I spend most days alone with my own thoughts. When that became too much to bear, I begged the queen for some way to keep my mind occupied. She gave me access to their historical records, and I poured myself into the histories."

Totra-Dal took a long swig and drained the last of whatever had been in his goblet.

"I didn't even mean to find any of this. I don't normally enjoy languishing in the past but after meeting Darien and being embroiled in the cycles events, I thought it would be interesting to dive into how it all got started. Then I stumbled upon Hephaesion's records. Shortly thereafter I heard that Darien had been taken and the importance was immediately apparent to me."

"Does Marenya know?" Rist asked.

"No," Totra-Dal admitted. "I've requested an audience. Still waiting."

"I will ensure she hears of this," Rist said, standing. "This cannot be ignored."

Totra-Dal inclined his head. "I'd appreciate that."

Rist studied him for a moment, then added, "And after you recover? What do you intend to do?"

Totra-Dal leaned back in his chair, exhaling through his nose. "Oh, I imagine I'll return to roaming. I'm not one to stay cooped up in one place for long. I need to move, and the Marauder's life is suited to that purpose."

Rist let out a quiet chuckle. "Do you think the Queen will take kindly to you returning to raiding her trade caravans? Especially now that she has all of your people in one place where they pose no direct threat?"

"She can't keep us here," Totra-Dal said with certainty. "She owes us a debt for aiding in the city's defense. Besides, our numbers were so diminished in the battle that we'll be little more than scolitips to her."

"Scolitips?" Rist asked.

"You know, scolitips—tiny insects that swarm and feed on any poor soul unfortunate enough to attract them."

Rist tilted his head. "I am… unfamiliar."

Totra-Dal smirked. "Consider yourself lucky. They're horrible"

Rist gave a small nod. "I thank you for your time." He turned toward the door but hesitated, glancing back at the broad figure seated before him. "If you should change your mind, Farkland Reach could benefit from a man of your intellect and ability. I have a feeling that a life here would bring Atreya a greater future."

For the first time in their conversation, Totra-Dal's expression hardened. His emotions shifted—firm, unmoving. When he spoke again, his voice had lost its warmth.

"Thank you, Master Rist. I enjoyed your company."

Rist held his gaze for a beat longer, then inclined his head in farewell. He stepped through the doorway, letting it close behind him, and made his way through the dim halls of the castle. Tomorrow, they would leave. He allowed himself one last moment of solitude in his quarters before his form would once again be confined beneath the folds of his robes for the journey ahead.

# Chapter 5: The Master's Valley

Darien found consciousness through a murky haze of headache and dizziness. He opened his eyes to see his surroundings and quickly closed them again as the pain in his head grew to a level that made him feel he would lose whatever was left in his stomach. He instead laid back and tried to listen to his surroundings through the pain in his head, which had begun to subside. He heard only the sounds of nature. A light rustle of wind through trees, the sounds of birds in the distance, and a small gush of running water breaking over small objects like rocks in a stream. The sounds were peaceful and allowed Darien to gain a sense of calm before he finally tried to open his eyes again.

Darien squinted at the light which seeped through his barely open lids, allowing his eyes time to adjust to the environment around him. Able to do that without too much discomfort, he pushed himself up onto his elbows and glanced around at the room he found himself in. Everything seemed to be made from nature itself. The room was made from wood, though none of it seemed to be carved or cut. The room seemed to have been made from the tree itself. It was as though someone had taken the centaur's deference to nature and expanded upon the idea. In one corner of the room sat a washbasin with pull cords similar to that he had found in Fenway Keep. On the other side of the room was the bed he found himself lying upon, made from some soft cloth stuffed with firm but comfortable material.

Darien swung his legs over the side of the bed and sat up, giving the pain in his head time to subside after the sudden movement.

*Where am I?*

Finally, when he felt stable enough, Darien stood up and made his way to the curtain that separated the room from the rest of the area beyond. Pulling back the heavy cloth, a wash of daylight poured onto him, and he threw his hand up to shield his sensitive eyes. When his eyes adjusted, he realized he was looking at what looked like an entryway to a house.

There was a front entrance which separated the room from the outside world by another heavy cloth, like the one between the room he had awoken in and this one. Darien moved into the room marveling at the natural look everything had. This room, like the one before, seemed to have been grown out of the very tree itself, as if someone had shaped nature to suit their needs.

Darien found himself distracted by his fascination with the home, and he went from room to room, marveling at the beauty and wonder of the place he found himself in. As he came out of the third room he had been exploring, he began to get the feeling that he was being watched. He instinctively reached for his sword at his waist and realized it wasn't there. Was this where Tahmer had him captive? No, Tahmer had gone somewhere else, but then who was watching him? *Whyn! Where was Whyn?* Darien was sure he had seen his master's face before losing consciousness. Hurrying out of the room he came into the front entryway to the house and moved towards the front door only to see that a figure was standing there in the doorway.

"Hello, Darien." Said a familiar voice.

Darien stared, mouth agape, at the man in front of him. How was it possible? Darien took several tentative steps forward, unsure if he could believe what he was seeing.

"Is it… are you… are you really here?" Darien stammered.

Whyn gave his usual friendly smile.

"Yes, I am really here. Welcome to my home." Whyn said, gesturing to the space around him. "Though I have prepared it to be your home while you're here. I'll be staying elsewhere to give you some privacy."

"What? While I'm here? Where am I? Am I back at The Academy?" Darien's mind whirled. Had everything about Olympus been nothing more than a dream? Was he somewhere in the forest around The Academy where Whyn called home?

"No, you're not back at The Academy." Whyn allowed a sad smile to cross his face. "You are very much still in Olympus."

"Wait." Darien stood up straight. "How do you know about Olympus?"

"There is a lot that I know which you do not, Darien. But I promise all that will be revealed in time. Come, let us sit and talk a while."

Whyn gestured into one of the room Darien had been exploring moments before. This room had a fireplace and two comfortable chairs topped by a skylight of semi-opaque material that diffused light through the entire room. Whyn sat and motioned for Darien to sit in the chair across from him. The chairs were woven from a strange material that appeared hard but which gave way like a cushion under his weight and supported him perfectly. Whyn spoke then, before Darien could even raise a question to the front of his mind.

"Darien, let me first say that I want to apologize, both for the future and for the past. I hid knowledge of Olympus from you while also trying to prepare you for the dangers you were going to find here. There is a great deal I wanted to teach you but I held myself back. That makes the nature of what we have to do that much harder, and it will make the road ahead of you more dangerous. I did it for my own selfish reasons, which I'll explain in time, but suffice it to say that I grew fond of you as I watched you grow up at The Academy."

Darien wasn't sure what Whyn was saying, but decided that it would probably be best to simply let him talk and ask questions after. If he knew anything of his master, it was that Whyn did not like to be interrupted.

"I'm sure you have questions, so many, many questions, as you always do. Before I let you ask them, though, I want to tell you that I will undoubtedly not give you all the answers you seek not out of a desire to keep you ignorant, far from it, but to protect you. Some information is dangerous if one learns it before they are ready. Does this make sense?"

Darien paused for a few seconds to consider.

"I—I think so. I'm not sure." Darien answered, feeling more confused than before they had sat down.

"It will become more clear over time. Suffice it to say that I will not answer all of the questions you are about to ask for you own good, but that all will be answered in the fullness of time. Now then, ask what questions you like, and I will answer what I may."

Whyn leaned back then, looking at him over his fingertips, which had come to rest on their counterparts in front of him. Darien searched his mind for what questions to start with and landed on the most obvious of them.

"Where are we?"

Whyn laughed then, a sound Darien had heard only a handful of times in his time studying under the swordsman.

"Starting with the practical as always, but not a bad way to start by any means. We are in what is known as the Valley of Nyseion, a very ancient and special place that has been long abandoned save for myself." Whyn's voice took on a touch of sadness as he finished.

"Master, that tells me the name of where we are, but it doesn't tell me where it is. Are we close to Farkland Reach or Taitron?" Darien asked, thinking of the little geography he knew from his stays with the trolls and the centaurs to the south of the grey city where he had first entered into Olympus.

"Oh no. Not near there at all, several days journey, perhaps even weeks from there. Though we may leave this place, those who don't know of it can never find it. All record of this place has been erased from the histories and there are other protections which prevent anyone from finding it."

"Protections?" Darien asked curiously.

"Yes, though we'll come to that later. Continue your questions, I assume you have more?"

Darien struggled internally with what direction to take. Finally settling on the next line of thought, he asked what seemed to him to be the most important question.

"Why are you here? Is there anyone else from The Academy here? How did you get here?" The questions began to pour out of Darien faster than he could stop them.

"So many at one time!" Whyn chuckled, "but fine questions all. I got here in the same manner that you did, through the transitions. Why I am here is a complicated question that I will answer at another time as the answer, by necessity, is a long one. Finally no, there is no one else from The Academy here. It is just you and I, I'm afraid."

Darien paused a few seconds to consider before continuing.

"You said you came through the transitions, but I was told that they only opened every fifty years to bring the Eldric to Olympus. So what do you have to do with the cycle?" Darien asked incredulously.

Whyn's head inclined towards him, causing him to look up from under his brow. Darien began to worry he had gone too far with his questioning before Whyn answered him in a slow, methodical tone.

"That is one of the questions I will not answer now. A piece of the answer is that I play a role in this cycle just as you do, though for now we play different parts."

"Parts?"

"Beyond that," Whyn answered with a gentle smile, "I cannot say more. Please continue with your questions."


Thinking, Darien racked his mind for more questions, but one rose above the rest.

"Who are you?"

Whyn cocked his head slightly. "How do you mean?"

Darien's frustration swelled. "I mean, who *are* you? I grew up training under you. You've been with me at The Academy for as long as I can remember, yet you seem to know so much more about Olympus than I did when I arrived. How? And what does any of this have to do with me?"

His voice had risen without him realizing, nearly reaching a shout. The room seemed to still in response, as if even the air had drawn back to observe. Whyn, however, remained unmoved, watching him with the same calm patience he always had. After a long moment, he brushed his palms together and leaned forward, elbows resting on his knees.

"Do you remember when I spoke of the secrets beneath The Academy?" Whyn asked softly.

The question caught Darien off guard. He frowned, searching his memory.

"That was... right before you offered me the teaching position, wasn't it? The day before I was brought here." The pieces clicked into place. "You mentioned something about secrets in the vaults."

"Precisely." Whyn stood and walked to a window, gazing out into the endless blue sky beyond. "Beneath The Academy are records long forgotten by the wider world, holding lost knowledge. Scrolls from the sacked Library of Alexandria, epics from Aeschylus and Homer once thought to be legend, histories buried beneath stone and time. Among them are documents preserved after the rise of the Dark One, detailing his severing of the ties between our worlds."

Whyn turned back to Darien, his eyes shadowed by something deeper, something old. Just as quickly as it appeared, it vanished.

"These secrets are known to only a handful at The Academy. Not even the full council has access to all of it. I was fortunate enough to gain that privilege. Within those texts are accounts of the Olympian civil war, the rise and fall of the last spellcasters, and the cycles that bring the Eldric here."

Darien sat in stunned silence. He had never known any of this existed.

Whyn continued, his voice steady, but his eyes unreadable. "The knowledge I uncovered at The Academy led me here. I have spent years studying what others dismissed as myth, piecing together the lost truths buried in forgotten histories. I knew there was more to Olympus than legend, and when the latest transitions opened, I found the path I had long been searching for."

Darien's breath caught in his throat. "Did… did you *know* I was going to come through the transitions? That I was one of the Eldric?"

Whyn met his gaze, just for a moment, before glancing away. He exhaled, walking back to his chair and sinking into it like the weight of his own words had pressed him down.

"Yes."

The single word landed like a hammer.

A fire ignited in Darien's chest, his emotions surging all at once. Anger. Confusion. Fear at what else had been kept from him. It spilled out before he could contain it.

"How?! How could you *not* tell me? How could you let this happen? Why offer me a job at The Academy when you *knew* it would be taken away from me? Was it some kind of sick joke?" His voice cracked, but he pressed on, his mind racing. "And Kara—what about *her*? You knew what this would do to her! You let me believe I had a future! That I had a *choice!*"

He realized he was on his feet, pacing, his hands clenched at his sides. He turned sharply back to Whyn, breath heavy, chest tight with betrayal. "You were the closest thing I ever had to a father. And you *lied* to me."

His voice dropped into something quieter, but no less powerful. "I trusted you."

The words hung between them, heavier than anything else he had said. Whyn's face remained impassive, but something *shifted*—a barely perceptible flicker, like a ripple across still water. Darien thought, for the briefest of moments, he saw pain.

Then, before he could be sure, he saw something else—a single tear tracing a slow path down Whyn's face.

Darien's fury faltered. The fire in his chest dimmed, replaced by something colder. He had never seen Whyn show vulnerability. It did not erase his anger. But for the first time, he saw his master as something more than an unshakable figure. He saw him as a man.

When Whyn finally spoke, his voice was steady, but his eyes remained on the floor. "You are right to be angry."

Darien swallowed, his throat tight.

Whyn exhaled. "I had my reasons for not telling you. If you will allow me, I will explain."

Darien hesitated, then gave a single, curt nod.

Whyn inclined his head slightly in thanks. "I do not blame you for being angry. I knew the cycles were beginning, but I did not know when. I estimated I had at least two more years—time to prepare you, to tell you *everything.* I offered you the teaching position because I thought it would keep you safe and allow me the opportunity to prepare you. To explain. It was never a trick."

Darien's jaw clenched.

"The fact that I miscalculated the timing of your transition is my own failure." Whyn continued, voice calm but laced with regret. "One of many. Some, perhaps, unforgivable."

He stood, gesturing toward the door. "Please, walk with me?"

It was a request, not an order.

Darien *wanted* to refuse. Just to spite him. But that was petty, and he was too drained to cling to it. He rose to his feet and followed Whyn through the entryway, stepping past the curtain into the open air.

The sight before him stole the breath from his lungs.

They stood on a raised platform, high above a valley so vibrant, so impossibly beautiful, that it didn't feel real. Waterfalls cascaded from the cliffs, their mist catching the sunlight in shimmering veils. A lake rested at the valley's heart, its surface reflecting the blue of the sky. The river feeding into it curled like silver thread, winding through meadows teeming with flowers in every color Darien had ever seen— and some he had not. The air was alive with the sound of rustling leaves, the distant calls of unseen creatures.

Overhead, something *massive* passed above them. Darien ducked instinctively, his arms rising to shield his head. He caught a flash of grey—then another, and another. His brain struggled to process what he was seeing until Whyn's voice cut through his astonishment.

"Ah. The Pegasus are returning."

Darien barely heard him. His eyes were fixed on the sky as the winged horses passed overhead, their vast wings cutting through the air with effortless grace. The way they moved, so fluid and powerful, left him momentarily breathless.

"The what?" Darien asked, his voice thick with astonishment.

"Pegasus," Whyn said. "You know them mostly as creatures from myth and legend, but they are very, very real. By no means kind animals, though. I recommend watching them from a distance." He started descending a set of stairs that, like the room they had just left, seemed seamlessly grown into the tree itself.

Darien followed, still drinking in the overwhelming beauty of his surroundings. The air was thick with life, with sounds that whispered of a world untouched by war. As they reached the bottom and began along a well-worn path, Darien's gaze fell upon the trunks of several massive trees, where strange orbs pulsed and glowed at steady intervals. Some emitted a deep violet hue, others a cold blue, and still others a burning red.

"What are those?" Darien asked, pointing.

"Hmm? Oh, those are filonial pods. Insect nests, similar to moths or butterflies, but they cluster together in colonies for shelter. They're harmless but provide a fine ambiance, don't you think?"

Darien nodded absently, his eyes lingering on the glowing formations as they passed. Every inch of this place seemed alive in a way he had never experienced before. The deeper they walked into the valley, the more details he absorbed, each more surreal than the last. It was almost too much to take in.

They emerged from the trees onto a meadow. Darien stopped in his tracks, his breath catching as he took in the landscape. The river wove through the field like liquid silver, cutting through wildflowers of every imaginable color. Butterflies, or creatures like them, flitted between the blossoms. At the meadow's center, atop a gently sloping hill, a lone tree stretched skyward, its massive branches casting long shadows over a stone table beneath it.

"Come, Darien," Whyn said, making his way up the hill.

Darien followed without question, too awestruck to feel any lingering resentment. He reached the top and found Whyn already seated at the stone table, gesturing for him to sit. The anger, the irritation that had simmered in Darien since their conversation began, felt suddenly distant—washed away by the sheer majesty of this place.

"I owe you a great many answers, Darien," Whyn said, his voice bringing Darien back to the present.

Their eyes met, and Darien noticed something unusual—Whyn's eyes, normally a sharp gray-blue, had darkened slightly. He frowned but dismissed it as a trick of the light.

"And you will have them in time," Whyn continued. "As I said before, I cannot give you all the answers now."

"To protect me, right?" Darien asked, feeling the sting of frustration creep back in.

"That's right," Whyn said.

"From what exactly?"

"From yourself. From me. From our enemy. And from the world at large."

Darien let out a sharp breath, a sound of disbelief. "That's a lot of protection."

Whyn didn't flinch at the mockery in his tone. "It is."

"That tells me who you're protecting me from," Darien said, his voice tight. "But what's the danger? Why do you need to protect me from myself?"

"You have been in Olympus for only a few months," Whyn said evenly. "Already, in that time, have you not faced your share of its dangers?"

Darien thought back—Cyprin's agents, the Marauders, the wraiths, the siege of Farkland Reach. He had nearly died more times than he cared to count. He exhaled sharply. "I guess."

"So I ask you—please trust me when I tell you that I hold back information to protect you. Yes, even from yourself."

Darien didn't respond. He made a small, noncommittal noise and let the subject drop.

"So what now, then?" he asked after a moment. "Why did you bring me here?"

"Now," Whyn said, leaning back, "you begin the next part of your training."

Darien frowned. "Training?"

"Training." Whyn's voice carried a kind of finality that left little room for argument. "You will take up a new kind of training, while still continuing to refine your swordsmanship. But in new and different ways."

Darien studied him. "What kind of training are we talking about?"

For the first time since arriving, Whyn smiled— not his usual, knowing smile, but something different. Something mischievous. The sight of it sent an odd shiver down Darien's spine.

"You will learn the same skills I learned as a child," Whyn said. "You will learn to bend the world to your will, to manipulate the forces around you, to command them as if they were an extension of yourself. You will learn what I was taught by my own teachers, and theirs before them—stretching back countless millennia."

The air around them seemed to still. The light filtering through the leaves flickered, as though the valley itself was listening.

Whyn's expression darkened just slightly, his voice dipping lower. "I will now begin to teach you the ancient skill of magic."

# Chapter 6: The World Revealed

Darien stared at Whyn for a long moment before laughter burst from his chest, unrestrained and full. The sound echoed across the valley, startling a herd of antlered creatures drinking from the river. Their heads snapped toward him, ears twitching in curiosity before they returned to the water.

Whyn, however, did not react. He simply sat, watching Darien clutch at his stomach as his laughter rolled into spasms.

"You…" Darien gasped between breaths, "You're going to teach *me* magic? *You* don't know magic! There's not even magic in Olympus except for Cyprin!"

He swung a leg over the stone bench, straddling it as he shook his head in disbelief. "You don't actually expect me to believe this, do you?"

Whyn remained impassive, though there was the faintest trace of amusement in his voice when he spoke. "Who told you that?"

Darien threw his hands in the air. "Everyone! *Literally* everyone who's ever told me about the cycles or magic says the same thing—Cyprin stole it! He took it from the people and hoarded it for himself. That's why the cycles are the only thing that can stop him."

Now it was Whyn's turn to laugh.

"Oh? *That's* what they say, is it?" He shook his head. "I hadn't realized how much the truth had been lost to time." He exhaled through his nose, looking at Darien with something that might have been pity. "No, magic was never stolen."

Darien frowned. "Then what happened to it?"

Whyn didn't answer immediately. Instead, he raised a hand and stretched out an empty palm. In an instant, a ball of white-hot flame burst into existence, hovering an inch above his hand. The fire crackled softly, impossibly bright, as if drawn from some unseen source. Whyn watched Darien carefully, giving him just enough time to process what he was seeing before his hands moved, expanding the flame outward until it was the size of a melon. Without hesitation, he thrust his palms forward, hurling the fireball toward Darien.

Darien barely had time to react before it struck him.

He flinched, throwing his arms up—but the fire passed through him harmlessly, leaving behind only a rush of warmth. He stumbled back, losing his balance, and landed hard on the ground, his legs still hooked over the stone bench.

"I *claim* nothing," Whyn said simply.

Darien clambered to his feet.

"What was that for?" He asked, feeling his anger rising again.

"Proof that what I say is true. Now, sit back down."

Darien hesitated and then sat slowly back down at the table.

"Now, as I said before, the understanding of what happened to the magic has been warped over time."

"Warped? What do you mean?"

"You see, the dark one didn't steal the magic from anyone. He hid it."

"He hid it? How?"

"Exactly." Whyn said, nodding. "You see, magic can't be 'stolen' or given. It simply exists as a result of a natural process for those who can tap into it. Magic can no more be stolen than gravity can be."

Darien stared back at Whyn, his curiosity peeked despite his distrust of his old teacher's slew of secrets.

"What do you mean?"

"You see, magic is simply the destruction of two fundamental building blocks of the universe, and then harnessing the energy from that destruction and directing it towards whatever purpose you set your mind to."

Darien stared back blankly.

"I see." Whyn sighed as he stood up, took a few paces away from the table and turned back around to face him. "How can I explain this simply? All around us, beyond the microscopic are particles, small bits of… well, what they're made of is not important, but suffice it to say that we are made up of atoms and atoms are made up of particles. Do you follow?"

Darien nodded. It made sense so far.

"Some of these particles have what we might consider opposites. Within atoms, you have protons with a positive charge, and electrons with a negative charge. Bring a proton to an electron and you have an entirely new creation, most often hydrogen will form."

Darien nodded again. It was sounding familiar from some lesson Professor Taren had given in his physics class.

"Now there are other interactions that happen," Whyn continued as he began to pace back and forth. "Our world is made up largely of matter. That's what atoms create when grouped together. But there is anti-matter, negative matter. When this anti-matter and matter come into contact with each other, it usually results in a cataclysmic burst of energy, disproportionate to the size of the matter or antimatter involved."

"And it's that energy you use to work magic?" Darien concluded quickly.

"No it's not, don't interrupt," chided Whyn. "There are similar reactions to matter and anti-matter that exist within the realm of the particles as well, namely that of aether, later renamed ether by later scholars on earth who tried to re-discover it, and anti-ether. These particles exist all around us. They help hold the universe together, though they are as inert as anything else. They don't exist within atoms, but separate from them, and separate from all other matter, and yet they act like a glue holding all things together. It is these that when brought together by one who has the ability to sense and manipulate them, that provide the source of all things that so many call 'magic'"

Darien sat in silence for several seconds as his brain tried to absorb the information Whyn had just thrown at him. He had to fight from breaking out into laughter again at what seemed like pure absurdity to him. Here was Master Whyn, the man who had trained him for his entire life, telling him about particles, and anti-particles, describing how magic worked. Magic. None of it made sense. He held back his laughter at the thought of another fireball hurled at his chest.

"So… if I got this right." Darien said slowly, "You have ether and anti-ether, and you put the two together to get energy and you use that to make magic?"

"Yes!" Whyn said clapping his hands together, "precisely that."

"So then, how do you get them to… hit each other or whatever?"

"Well, that is where the dark one's influence begins to take its toll. You must be able to sense them in order to manipulate them. Once you have honed your ability to sense the ethers, then you must master your ability to bring them together, and only then can you begin working to control them. What he was able to do through some twisted magic of his own invention was limit, and then restrict people's ability to sense the anti-ether. Without that, all spell casters could touch was the ether and their power faded."

Darien sat quietly for several seconds, thinking carefully before asking,

"So, if no one can sense the anti-ether, how can you use magic?"

Whyn considered Darien carefully before coming to sit down once more on the bench opposite the table they were sitting at.

"That is another answer that I will give you at a later time. Suffice it to say that one person was able to retain their ability to sense the anti-ether and I am... associated with them."

"So you're going to teach me how to sense the ethers?" Darien asked, finally relieved to be getting to the point of their conversation.

"No." Whyn said simply.

"What?" Darien almost shouted the question. Was this another thing Whyn was going to keep from him?

"I am not going to teach you how to sense the ethers because you already can. It simply needs to be revealed to you. That is what I will do."

Darien looked back at Whyn suspiciously.

"What you do you mean 'revealed' to me?"

"I will cast a spell that will remove the blinding effect from you. When that is done, the world of the ethers will be made open to you and you will begin to train with me on how to control your new power." Whyn's gaze hardened as he looked up at Darien from under his brow. "I have to warn you, though, not to test your ability to mix ether and anti-ether without my guidance, Darien. Power like this can be addictive and dangerous. You have to remember that you are causing fundamental building blocks of our universe to be destroyed. That does not come without consequence, and using this power can come with dire consequences if not done carefully."

"What kind of consequences?" Darien asked, apprehensive for the first time since their conversation began.

"For you? Death, dismemberment, disfigurement, a life of constant pain and anguish if you don't control yourself. For the world, it could mean being ruled by the dark one. If you were to cast a spell recklessly and injure or kill yourself or another, it could jeopardize everything that has been built these last three millennia in preparation to bring you here."

Darien shuddered internally at the thought of what could happen to him. Was magic even worth it? Whyn's warning wouldn't be taken lightly.

"I understand." Darien said with a note of steel in his voice that he barely recognized himself.

"Alright then." Whyn said simply as he rose to his feet and called after Darien to follow him. They walked into the middle of the field, the afternoon sun gently touching the tops of the trees and casting long shadows as evening began to fall in the valley.

"Stand there and please do not move." Whyn said, pointing at a rock jutting out from the field of tall grass. Darien did as he was asked and stood, feeling very self-conscious about what to do with his hands. Finally settling on crossing them as a chill, carried on a light breeze, brushed past them.

Whyn took several steps away from Darien and turned to face him. His face held an expression of deep concentration. Then Whyn's hands rose to the level of his chest and clasped as if holding a small sphere within them. A small speck of golden light appeared within and pulsed at regular intervals, almost like a heartbeat. Whyn's eyes never left Darien as his hands worked around the golden sphere of light. The pair of them stood staring at each other for what felt to Darien like five minutes, then ten, then fifteen. The sun was now only half visible over the tops of the trees and its light was quickly fading from the valley floor as shadows lengthened and the air became crisp and cool.

Finally, when the top of the sun had nearly disappeared over the tops of the trees, a vein appeared on Whyn's forehead, bulging from the extreme effort of achieving the goal he was working towards. The orb began to grow, like the fire had before it, under Whyn's direction. It grew to the same size as the white hot flame and with a shout of effort Whyn thrust the ball of golden light towards Darien, who had to work to keep himself from trying to dodge the perceived danger. The orb hit him, and unlike the flames Whyn had shot at him, he felt the impact and then spread of the projectile. The energy of the sphere spread over Darien, covering his skin in a layer of golden light that then seeped into his skin, being absorbed by his body. He gasped as the air entering his lungs felt thick and cold, as if he was now breathing water. Dropping to his knees, Darien struggled to breathe freely for several seconds before a sensation of warmth enveloped him, almost as if countering the oppressive cold from moments before. He took several long breaths and felt everything returning to normal.

Darien looked up from the ground, the panic in his eyes slowly fading as he searched for Whyn. Whyn wasn't there. Darien quickly stood, his legs shaking under his weight to see that Whyn had collapsed backward onto the earth. His eyes were closed and his expression was that of a deep sleep.

"Master? Master Whyn?!" Darien shouted, shaking the other's shoulder.

Whyn jerked and then sat quickly up, looking around confused for several seconds before his eyes met Darien's.

"It is done then." Whyn said.

"What's done? What did you do?"

"I removed from you the curse of blindness, Darien. You can now touch the ethers. Can't you see?" Whyn asked.

"See? See what? It's getting dark. I can't…" and then Darien realized he could see something.

"What…?" Darien began, but found himself lost in what he was seeing. No, seeing was the wrong word. There was nothing really there to see, it was more of a perception.

"What you are now able to view, though sight is not the best way to describe the ability, are the ethers all around you."

Darien barely heard Whyn as he swung his head around from side to side quickly, observing the radical shift in the world around him in awe. Whyn was right, the change really was a change in sense more than that of vision nothing was obscured by the ethers, and yet it surrounded everything.

"Darien." Whyn's voice made Darien jump, startled by its suddenness he turned his face to meet Whyn's. The expression on his face must have been one of fear because Whyn's turned to one of compassion.

"It can't hurt you. It was always there you simply lacked the ability to perceive it. I think we have done enough for today. I have shifted the understanding of your life as far as I'm willing to at one time." Whyn pushed himself back up into a standing position and extended his hand to Darien, who accepted and was raised to his own feet. "You've taken your first steps into a larger world, Darien. You have many more ahead of you, and the hardest are still ahead, but you've begun and that is the first step."

Darien followed Whyn back to the tree house in silence, seeing the beauty around him as before but feeling that it was not somehow subdued by the presence of the ethers. It was there even when his eyes closed, like a ringing in the ear that won't go away no matter how many times it's poked and prodded. They climbed the tall stairs and Darien entered the cabin past Whyn, who held the heavy curtain aside.

"This will be where you stay during your time in the valley. I will not be far from here and will come for you at dawn."

"You're leaving?" Darien asked quickly, grabbing Whyn's forearm.

Whyn smiled gently. "I thought you might like some time alone, but I can stay a while if you wish. I know how unsettling first realizing the presence of the ethers can be. Would you like me to stay?"

"I... I think so." Darien replied, unsure himself what he wanted. The day to this point had been such a rollercoaster of emotion for him. His shock at realizing that Whyn was in Olympus, anger at finding what Whyn had kept from him, the guilt at yelling at the man who had done so much for him, finding out he was a spellcaster, and then being shown the ethers.

"So much has happened so quickly. From the second I came into Olympus I've been thrown into something that I never asked for and didn't want. And here I am finding out that there's even more happening that I don't understand."

Whyn walked into the room they had occupied earlier, with Darien close behind. With the snap of his fingers, and a flash of light a fire roared into existence in the fireplace, giving the room a soft, warm glow.

"You have my sympathy, Darien. But please believe me when I say that this is who you are. This was always meant to be your mantle of responsibility. I am in part to blame for it being thrust onto you so early, but you have done well."

"Thanks." Darien said grudgingly as he fell into the chair he had been sitting in earlier that day. To him, it seemed like it had been weeks since he stood here yelling at his teacher. "Why me?" Darien asked no one in particular. "Why does it have to be me? I didn't know anything about this place. I didn't want anything to do with the cycles, with Cyprin, or magic, or any of it. Why couldn't it be someone else? I just wanted to try and find a way home. That's the only reason I even said I'd help with any of it, and now I found my way into a conflict for the freedom of the worlds." Darien sighed deeply and asked again. "Why me?"

Darien hadn't expected an answer but the fact that Whyn said nothing at all made him look at the old man sitting across from him, light from the flames dancing across the face drawn into a tight expression.

"You know, don't you? You know why me." It was less a question than a statement of fact.

Whyn didn't turn to look at Darien at first, simply stared into the fire before slowly shifting his gaze to meet Darien's eyes.

"I do." He said simply.

"But you're not going to tell me, are you?" Darien asked hopelessly, feeling he already knew the answer.

"I will tell you, but not today. That answer lies somewhere in your future, but would only serve as a distraction to you now."

"Let me guess, we're gonna get to Olympus, need some kind of magical key and the answer will be that 'I'm the key' or something like that?" Darien asked mockingly, thinking back to the stories and books he had read during his long summers alone at The Academy.

Whyn smiled and chuckled.

"I can promise you that it won't be as cliché as that."

"Good. I hate cliché." Said Darien, allowing the subject to drop, knowing he wouldn't get anything more.

The two of them sat in silence and listened as the fire crackled away in front of them. After several minutes of enjoying the silence and trying to ignore the ethers he still felt around him.

"Do you ever get used it?" Darien asked, finally breaking the silence.

"To what?"

"That!" Darien said, waving his hands all around. "The ethers, they never go away?"

"They were always there, and always will be. As for whether you get used to them or not, you do. I don't know this from experience as they were always there for me, but I know from others who grew to notice them or were granted the ability through magic, not unlike the kind I used on you, that they came to feel a sense of comfort in knowing that the ethers were there. Once you start to use them, they'll become almost like a companion you miss when it's not there."

Silence fell again as Darien watched the ethers float through the room for several minutes, trying to get used to the strange sensation of knowing they existed.

"What happened to you after you hit me with that golden ball thing? Does that always happen after you use magic?" Darien asked after watching a particularly small cloud of ether float through the room and pass through the far wall. The strange part was that he could still 'see' the ether through the wall until it floated past the limits of his perception.

"The spell I cast on you to remove the blinding spell placed on the world was one of my own making. As such, it lacks the… safety of tried and true spells. It also requires a great deal of energy to cast. I've been working on the spell for a long time and have only cast it once before with the same result. Do not ask who it was as I know you are about to, I'll not say, but it worked then as it did now. That is all that matters."

Darien inwardly rolled his eyes as the fact that yet another secret was being kept from him, but decided that he wouldn't press it too far.

"You can make spells?" Darien asked, deciding to move the conversation forward.

Whyn considered carefully before answering, speaking in a slow, deliberate tone.

"It is possible to create your own spells, but it is not recommended. Spells are cast using certain mental structures, which I'll go over more when we begin your formal training. Suffice it to say that typically, someone learning magic tends to gravitate towards one type of power. Electricity, water, fire, ice, and air are the primary conduits that people usually choose to channel their magic. It's easier to control and build on one mental structure than to try and manipulate them all. Once you know that mental structure and system of thought, you channel the energy of the ether-anti-ether reaction through it and produce results."

"So you push energy through your mind?" Darien asked, trying to understand the complicated tapestry of explanation Whyn was explaining.

"You push the energy through your body, but you control how that energy moves through you with your mind. It's like consciously slowing your heartbeat through breathing. You can control an inner process by means of concentrating on a desired result." Whyn answered, clearly enjoying teaching Darien this new information.

"So using electricity is safe, but removing this blinding spell isn't? What makes it so different?"

"Always digging deeper, aren't you? I think I'll answer this question and then suggest that we turn to another topic, or call it a completed day. You've been through a lot and have much more ahead. Is that agreed?"

Darien nodded in response. Whyn seemed satisfied and continued.

"Using any kind of magic has its dangers. It is never entirely safe to channel the ether energy through your body. There is always the risk of creating too large of a reaction and having a larger than desired result or using too little and failing to achieve the desired reaction. With the established schools of magic, those that I listed before, so much practice and trial and error has been put into its study that the pool of knowledge to draw from is large enough to teach the practice and achieve the desired results with reliable success."

Whyn raised a hand and with a flipping motion and a whoosh of sound, Darien saw a small blue orb appear out of the corner of his eye, and another appear in Whyn's hand. The cup that had been on the table had disappeared and reappeared, held in Whyn's hand. With another flick of his empty hand, the cup filled with a steaming liquid. From a pouch at his belt, he removed a pinch of some dried substance and sprinkled it into his cup.

"You see? The transitions can be created and manipulated by using a combination of air, and a few other minor schools of magic paired together. Water can be created from the air around us. All we need is to tap into energy of the ethers to cause these things to happen. When you know how these things are done, doing them is simply a matter of practice and we have countless millennia of practice from those who came before."

Whyn sipped at his drink before setting it down on a small side table next to the chair, steam still rising from the surface of the hot liquid within.

"The spell I used to release you from the dark ones blinding did two things. It opened your senses to the ether, but also released the curse from you simultaneously. There are a few other minor effects included, but those will become relevant and show themselves in time. This spell used no known schools of magic, instead relying entirely on the pure energy created from the ether reaction and intention of the person casting the spell, namely myself. There are no structures, mental or otherwise, that I could put the magic through. This kind of magic is incredibly dangerous, as there is usually little precedent for each individual spell. The result of one not practiced and tested meticulously could be catastrophic. Does that answer your question?"

Darien nodded, realizing that the world of magic was going to prove to be more complicated than anything he had learned so far. A yawn racked through him then, unbidden and uncontrollable. The level of his exhaustion hit him then and he realized precisely how tired he really was. Just then he realized he hadn't eaten since his arrival in the valley.

"Master, why don't I feel hungry?" Darien asked before realizing that he had overstepped his agreement to limit his questions.

"Oh, that. While in this valley, you will not need food or water. You can take them in, of course, but the valley itself will maintain you. I myself even grow a garden to enjoy food from time to time. Sleep will even be less needed, though you will still sleep regularly as you get accustomed to using magic and push your abilities. We will rest each night, but sleep will not be as necessary as you will find outside the valley. Time passes differently here to. More quickly. From my calculations, and I admit that I may be wrong, a month here is akin to only two days, perhaps less, in the wider world."

"How?" Darien asked in disbelief.

"Magic." Whyn answered, simply taking another short sip of his tea. "Ancient magic put in place long before either of us came here. And I believe that is more answers than I agreed to give tonight."

Whyn stood then, taking the cup of tea with him to the door.

"I take my leave from you now, Darien. In the morning we begin the next step in your journey."

With that, Whyn left Darien to be alone with his thoughts. He sat for several long minutes before finally surrendering to the cry of his body for rest made his way to the room he had woken up in only hours before and collapsed, mentally and physically spent, onto the bed.

# Chapter 7: The Lessons Begin

A whirl of noise surrounded him as he looked around. In front of him was a face. Hauntingly familiar, the face belonged to a body holding a sword, gesturing towards the edge of a cliff. Darien looked in his hand at his own sword. It was bloody and stained with the gore of battle, held ready between him and his opponent. There he saw a creature, beastly in manner and appearance, though still retaining some vestiges of what might have been human. The beast held Kara by the neck over an abyss, and below her, tongues of flame twisted and twirled, licking at the air, hoping to get a taste of their next meal. Without a word, the figure motioned to the creature, and Kara's body flew into empty space, her scream reaching Darien's ears as she cried his name.

*Darien! Darien! Darien…*

Darien sat up quickly and reached at the air in front of him trying to catch at the air where he had just seen Kara's body fly. Realizing that the vision was no longer there, he pushed his feet off the edge of the bed and began working to slow his breathing.

"It was just a dream." He said aloud to himself, unsure of what he hoped to gain by saying the words to the air around him.

He jumped as he 'saw' ether floating past him, forgetting for a moment about the events of the past day. Shaking off the unease, Darien placed his feet on the floor and saw a sword wrapped entirely in cloth hanging on a hook near the entrance to his room.

It was the sword! The sword that had been his reason for chasing Tahmer through the transition, and that he would use to open the gates to Mount Olympus. Excitedly, he grabbed it from its place on the wall and set it on the bed and began removing the bits of leather which kept the cloth in place. When he was done, he stepped back to look at the blade.

It was longer than his own by several inches, but otherwise shaped similarly. The sheath had intricate carvings and engravings running down one half of the cover, and was completely empty and smooth on the other. The blade widened slightly at the hilt, in which was set several stones of red, blue, and green colors, shining in rays of morning sun that streamed through the window. The handle was perfectly wrapped in find leather to enhance the grip and in the pommel a black stone with streaks of white streaking through the shiny black of its surface. Darien stared at the beauty of the blade for several seconds before reaching out and grasping hold of its handle. It fit his hand perfectly.

Darien drew the sword, feeling it leave its protective cover effortlessly. The blade was perfectly balanced, even more so than his own sword, and felt like an extension of his arm. He still favored his own sword that was back in Farkland Reach, but he could see himself favoring this blade in time. Darien strapped on the sword belt and returned the blade to its sheath. Walking out of the room, and then out the front door of his treehouse before winding his way down the stairs encircling his new home. Once at the floor of the valley, Darien began to search for a clearing suited for what he intended. When he found it, he drew the blade and began to methodically work through the various forms and battle poses as he had so many times before.

After a handful of poses were complete, Darien began to feel nauseous and dropped to his knees. Before he could react, a headache so powerful that it drove the thought of anything else from his mind racked his body causing him to release a scream of agony that echoed through the valley floor. He lie there writhing in pain for several minutes before the pain subsided to a level that allowed him to regain some sense of his surroundings. He realized he was back in his room in the tree house facing the wall on the opposite side from the door. He was curled into a ball on top of the blankets, the sword belt having been removed from his side.

"Are you awake?" Darien heard Whyn's voice ask softly.

"Unfortunately." His reply was little more than a whisper.

"I was unaware of your condition. When you are able, I need to know how you came to be afflicted by this…sickness." Whyn said, compassion filling his voice and giving Darien a sense of comfort he never thought would be possible to garner from Master Whyn.

Darien lay on the bed for several more long minutes before finally turning over to face Whyn and sitting up on the edge of the bed. The pain in his head still pounded.

"How long was I out for this time?" Darien asked.

"I'm not sure. I found you about fifteen minutes ago. I brought us here and have been waiting for you to recover ever since." Whyn answered.

Darien grunted in acknowledgement to indicate that he understood but said little else. Finally, when he felt like he was ready to talk, he responded. "It started after the battle of Farkland Reach. Cyprin's army attacked the city—"

"Forgive me for interrupting, but I know of the battle. You may skip the account of his army's assault."

"Okay," Darien nodded. "Well, during the battle, the wraiths came to help us. One of them…possessed me in a way, made me stronger. I don't know if we would have won without him. After he… left, I started getting these headaches whenever I worked too hard or did too much. Sometimes it wouldn't happen at all, other times it would happen if I lifted so much as a bucket the wrong way. The doctors said part of my mind died when the wraith left. Whatever happened, I don't know how I can be of much use to anyone like this."

Darien finished with a curse and punched the blankets next to him on the bed before looking up at Whyn and asking hopefully, "Can you help me?"

Whyn looked at him for several long seconds before he stood up and paced across the room and then back to his seat.

"What you did, letting that wraith possess you, was incredibly dangerous. Do you realize that you could have doomed all the worlds if it hadn't decided to leave?" Whyn said, angry for the first time since Darien had come to the valley.

"But I knew he wouldn't hurt me!" Darien pleaded. "He had been in my mind before."

"You were possessed more than once?!" Exclaimed Whyn, clearly taken aback.

"Well," Darien began, "twice before that, actually."

Whyn stared back at him in pure, unadulterated shock before falling down into his seat.

"You best tell me what happened and explain why you let one of their like into your mind. Damnit boy, how could you be so foolish!"

Darien stared back. He had never seen Whyn this angry before.

"I… I'm sorry. At the time, it seemed like the right thing to do."

Darien began to explain then exactly what had happened, first with Atreya, then at the caves, and finally a more detailed explanation of the wraith's assistance during the battle of Farkland Reach.

At the conclusion of his story, Whyn sat staring at him blankly for several seconds before exhaling quickly and saying in disbelief, "In all my time, both in my life and study of history, I have never heard of one like you, Darien. You have a disproportionate impact on the world around you and take risks greater than anything a person with a touch more knowledge would ever dare undertake."

"Is that a good thing?" Darien asked hesitantly.

"I'm not sure." Whyn said slowly. "Regardless, it is what it is. You seem to not understand the risk you took by allowing not only one, but two of their kind access to one of the Eldric, not to mention you who was to learn magic, though you could have no way of knowing that at the time I suppose." Whyn looked off into space considering something in the privacy of his own mind.

Darien watched quietly for several long seconds before asking quietly, "Can you help me?"

Whyn's eyes dashed to meet Darien's and what was left of the anger seemed to vanish.

"It's not that simple," Whyn sighed. "I wish I could simply tell you yes, but I've seen nothing like this before and it goes beyond dangerous. If I attempt to devise a spell to solve the problem, it could very well end up changing you. Dealing with the mind is dangerous and tricky work."

Darien fell back onto his bed and watched as a particularly large cloud of ether floated past where he had just been sitting until it went past the wall of his room, and floated away past the limits of his senses.

"So I'm stuck doing nothing then," he said, feeling hope leave him as quickly as the idea had come to his mind.

Whyn's lack of an answer made him sit up quickly.

"What is it?" Darien asked at seeing the thoughtful expression on Whyn's face.

"Well," Whyn began slowly, "it won't solve your problem entirely, but it could mitigate it. I could place a spell of warning on you, tapping into the processes that cause the headaches rather than eliminating them. You might still suffer the same problem, but you would be able to identify precisely what you're doing that is causing them and maybe limit the frequency of attacks."

"What's the downside?" Darien asked, skeptical now that a solution would present itself so easily.

"The downside is that it might not work. There is no record that I'm aware of that speaks of any damage like yours being suffered after wraith possession."

"I'm guessing not many of them survived to ask?" Darien asked with dark humor.

"Not many, no," Whyn said, though the humor seemed to be lost on him. "But we can try. I can't have you collapsing into fits while I teach you."

Darien nodded his agreement, and Whyn stood. Similar to when Whyn had released Cyprin's blinding spell, a golden sphere of light appeared between his hands, though this spell seemed to be done with far less effort. What caught Darien's attention this time though was the ether around Whyn. He could feel the energy coming from the intermingling of the two substances as they met, flashed briefly and then were absorbed into Whyn's body. After only a few seconds, the ball of light was pushed by his master and once again made contact with Darien, who felt nothing as it enveloped him.

"Did it work?" Darien asked, holding his hands up as if the answer were written on his palms.

"There is only one way we can be sure." Whyn answered and beckoned for Darien to follow as he grabbed the ancient sword from its place on the wall.

The two made their way back down the stairs and into the clearing where Darien had been practicing his forms. Whyn extended his arm, handing Darien the sword. He placed it around his waist with a feeling of apprehension. Whyn took several steps forward and turned to face Darien.

"Draw the sword." Whyn commanded, though not unkindly.

Darien took a deep breath and drew the sword, feeling again like it was an addition to his body and not some external object he was directing to a purpose. Darien took his ready stance and faced Whyn, grey eyes locked on his own.

"Now, do as you were before your attack. Let us see if the magic will serve its purpose."

Darien hesitated, but nodded before flowing seamlessly into the first of the rehearsed poses. This form was different than the one he had been practicing before, focused on holding poses to increase strength and stability rather than flowing from pose to pose to increase transitions during battles. Whyn watched as he crossed the blade slowly across his body, extending it straight out to the right and holding it outstretched in the air, pointed at some invisible target.

A buzz began to form in the back of his mind, almost like an itch. He felt a sense of something rising within him like a wave and quickly dropped out of the pose releasing his held breath. The wave began to recede, though the buzz lingered for several seconds longer.

"What happened?" Whyn asked.

Darien shook his head, trying to clear the buzz from his ears, but the sound was deeper than that and was beginning to fall away rapidly now.

"I'm not sure, I had this feeling of… rising? I'm not sure how to put it. And there was this sound. When I dropped the pose it all started to go away, but it didn't stop right away. The wave is gone but the buzzing… well it's gone now." Darien finished, realizing that everything had subsided.

"Do it again." Whyn answered back.

Darien nodded again, resuming his ready stance and resuming the same poses he had just ended with, moving through them and holding each for slightly longer than he was supposed to in order to push his limits. After a few of the poses flowed past the buzzing began again and the wave rose. Darien allowed it to rise slightly further than before and then dropped the pose he was in, holding the sword above his head in his right hand with his left tucked into his chest. Immediately the buzzing began to lessen, and the wave died back into the recesses of wherever they had come from.

"I think it worked." Darien said optimistically. "I can feel something happening, and when I stop it goes away."

"Good." Whyn said with a slight inclining of his head. "I want you to try to extend the amount of time you're able to exert yourself without causing an attack. Begin each day at sunrise by coming to this clearing and working through your regular series of poses. Do you understand?"

"Yeah." Darien answered.

"Darien. As at The Academy, you are to call me 'Sir', or 'Master.' It is a formality but one that stretches back longer than you would believe for the order of spellcasters and I would see it followed. Is that understood?" Whyn said. His words were firm but not harsh.

Darien nodded, "Yessir."

"Good, now for our first lesson, we are going to spar as we used to. Please take your position and ready yourself."

Darien felt happy to be getting ready to do something he was so familiar with. A number of times at The Academy he had come close to besting Whyn in their matches, even coming so close as to touch him twice out of the five allotted during a match. Taking a few steps away, he turned to face Whyn and assumed a ready position that would give him the most flexibility, something he needed when facing such a dynamic opponent as Whyn.

"Begin when you're ready."

Darien looked back at Whyn confused and came out of his pose. Whyn's sword was still firmly in its sheath. Everything that Whyn had taught him up to now had said that both were to draw their swords before any sparring match. Doing otherwise would give one party an unfair advantage over the other. Whyn must have noticed this look of confusion and surmised what was in Darien's mind.

"I know what I've taught you in the past. That adhered to the rules of The Academy. Those rules do not apply when dealing with life or death. Begin when you are ready."

Darien nodded to show his understanding and, pushing the fear of the oncoming headache aside, lowered into a ready stance. He estimated the distance between them to be no more than ten feet, a distance he could cross quickly enough and, hopefully, incapacitate or touch Whyn before he could even draw his blade. Steeling himself Darien tried not to show any indication of his potential movement and then, rushing forward, he swung his blade in an attempt to lade a touch on Whyn's shoulder, a move that would decapitate the man if not carefully controlled. He crossed the distance quickly, faster than he had thought he would initially and then he felt his blade tapped aside and he ran past where Whyn had stood only moments before.

Darien turned to look at his opponent, who was now turned the opposite direction facing Darien, hands still resting comfortably clasped in front of him. Whyn's sword was nowhere to be seen, but Darien had clearly felt the press of another blade parrying his blow.

"What was that?" Darien asked.

"What was what?" Whyn answered.

"I—you—I mean, I felt you hit my sword with yours."

"I did."

"But—" Darien stammered back "You couldn't have. That was too fast."

Whyn raised an eyebrow. "Was it now?"

Darien watched as a blur of motion flashed past him, faster than his eyes would allow him to perceive. Afterwards he was able to piece everything together, but in the moment all that was perceptible was a flash of motion.

Whyn drew his sword and, in an impressive display, worked in through no fewer than five different poses of one of the more complicated series of forms that Darien had ever learned at The Academy. He saw enough to recognize it though and felt his jaw go slack in astonishment at the speed Whyn had mastery over.

"I have taught you most of the necessary skills of swordsmanship. Those are skills you will absolutely need as your journey to the mountain nears its end and your battle with the dark one draws nearer, and they are skills we will maintain constantly here. But so too will your need to infuse what you already know with the new skill of magic."

"So you did that with magic?" Darien asked curiously.

"Precisely. And I wanted to demonstrate that the magic I teach you as we train here can be used not just to light fires or push air or objects around, but to enhance your own abilities, not unlike what the wraith did during your battle at Farkland Reach." Whyn began walking down the path and Darien ran after him, sheathing the jeweled sword as he caught up with his master.

"You have gained the ability to sense the ethers, you can see them, you can feel them, and now it's time that you learn how to manipulate them. We'll begin by teaching you to move one of the ethers, then the other, and finally bringing the two together to form the source of your magical abilities."

Whyn guided Darien through the trees until he came to a small circle of bare ground that allowed them to see the deep blue of the sky overhead. In the center of the clearing was a rock that jutted out of the forest floor and was flat on its top. Whyn stood next to it and gestured for Darien to take a seat on the hard surface.

"After you finish your poses in the morning, assuming that you have not triggered an attack, you will                    come                    here."
"What am I going to do here?" Darien asked before quickly adding, "Master."

Whyn allowed a quick smile to tick at the corner of his mouth at Darien's slip.

"Here you will begin manipulating the ethers. This is where you will master your manipulation of the essence of our universe and direct it to fulfill whatever purpose you set it towards."

Darien looked around. The clearing somehow fell short of some unrealized expectation. He didn't know what exactly he would have wanted to be different but he know that a rock in the middle of some trees was not where, had he been asked, he would have expected to master something, that up until just one day before, had been so absurd as magic. Inwardly, Darien felt a rise of incredulity which was tempered by the thought at what he had seen Whyn do. Whatever disbelief he held seemed insignificant by the thought of what seemed possible.

"Darien?" Whyn said abruptly, making him jump.

"Huh?"

"You must not allow your mind to wander, particularly not while you practice here. Discipline yourself. Concentrate on the present moment. Doing otherwise could be catastrophic, even when manipulating only one of the ethers you run the risk of contacting its opposite and forcing the two together. That would be nothing but dangerous for you now. I can't impress upon you the seriousness with which you must take this."

"I'm sorry Master, I won't let it happen again." Darien answered apologetically.

"Good. Now close your eyes. Yes, now feel the ethers. They're everywhere and should be familiar to you by now."

Darien reached out with his senses, feeling the ethers floating all around him, ghostly feelings of a presence, as if the ethers himself were looking back at him feeling their presence.

"I feel them." Darien said.

"Good. Now, notice their subtleties. Focus your attention on one batch of ether and push into it. Tell me what you feel." Whyn said in a whisper near his right ear.

Darien felt a particularly large group of ethers hovering nearby and focused his attention on it. The ether seemed to stop moving altogether, as if his very act of observing it alone and prevented it from moving any further.

"I've got one. It stopped moving." Darien said quietly.

"Good, I see the cloud you have. When you observe ether you change how it behaves. The fact that you can stop a cloud of ether shows great promise. Push into it, probe deeper, and tell me what you see."

Darien took a deep breath and tried to mentally push into the cloud. Nothing changed, but he kept trying, feeling himself test this new sense, almost like moving a hand that had fallen asleep. It felt unwieldy at first, but with each push grew more adept. Despite feeling as though he had gained more control over his new ability, he was gaining now ground in terms of pushing deeper into the ether. After several moments of no success, he opened his eyes and sighed in exasperation.

"Nothing's happening. What am I supposed to be doing?"

"Close your eyes," Whyn said sternly. "Keep pushing."

Darien took a deep breath and closed his eyes again, reaching out for the ether he had been pushing into. It was gone and so he searched for another cloud. He worked his way past several until he found a smaller clump passing through the clearing. As he focused his attention on it, the cloud slowed to a stop and he began pushing on the edges. This time he was able to feel a defined boundary, almost like running his mind along the surface of a balloon but not pushing hard enough to pop it.

"Push harder," Whyn's voice whispered.

Darien did so, pushing into the edge of the ether until finally, with an audible gasp, he broke through. He allowed his sense to open up into the cloud, feeling the edges from the inside this time.

"Good," Whyn said, his voice excited but calm. "Now, what do you feel?"

Darien extended his sense of feeling to the edge of the cloud and realized he couldn't feel the hold he had made. It was as though he was trapped inside the ether cloud.

"I'm stuck." Darien said, as a feeling of panic began to spring up into him.

"No. Stay calm." Whyn said quickly. "You are not stuck. You are simply exploring the ether. Breathe, Darien."

He attempted to fight back the panic and was moderately successful. Darien let out a slow controlled breath through his clenched jaw and felt his muscles tremble from the adrenaline spike.

"Okay, okay I'm calm."

"No, you're not. Take deeper breaths and relax. You can't go further unless you relax," said Whyn.

Darien did as he was instructed, taking several deep breaths, feeling his jaw loosen and he allowed himself time to simply exist within the ether and sit. Finally Whyn seemed pleased and instructed him further.

"Now, you are within an ether cloud, or a node as it's referred to. Within nodes are either ether or anti-ether. As you felt, each is self-contained even when penetrated by a spellcaster. What you are in now is ether and is usually the easier of the two for beginners to penetrate. Spend time here, get used to the feeling of the node. When you feel comfortable, push through the lining of the node and return to yourself here. After that, reach out and enter a new node, being careful only to enter one node at a time."

"How will I know which nodes are anti-ether?" Darien asked, curious to know what the counterpart felt like.

"You'll know simply by sensing the anti-ether that it is different. Anti-ether is far more resilient to the mind and is…how can I describe it? I will say it has 'bumps' on it. Stay away from those for now. If the exterior of the node is smooth, enter it, explore it, and when you've mastered that, tell me and we can move on to the other ether."

"Yes Master." Darien answered, his eyes still closed and his mind still within the edge of the ether.

He heard the crunch of the forest floor receding away from him. Then he heard Whyn's voice from much further away.

"When you have studied the ether for what you feel is a sufficient amount of time, come to the meadow where we spoke yesterday. It is further along the path which brought you here. There we will continue your lessons and you will dive even further into the world of magic."

Darien nodded and pulled out of the ether he had been in and opened his eyes. Taking a deep breath, he closed his eyes again, and pushed forward in search of a new node pushing into it, in an effort to better understand its nature, and master this new skill.

# Chapter 8: The Journey Continues

Rist sat atop his horse, gazing at the scenery all around him as Airlyn and Breyman rode ahead of him side by side. They had no way of knowing about his ability to sense emotions—and he wasn't ready to reveal that secret to these two newcomers who had just joined the Eldric, who were now only three. Why he hadn't shared this information with them was due to the fact that he simply didn't like Airlyn. She irritated him. Though somehow she had become close with the giant Lystran, and he suspected that should he tell Breyman of his abilities, Airlyn would surely hear about it shortly. It probably wasn't good to keep secrets from these members of their makeshift team, but it was what he had decided to do, for better or worse. At least for now.

"How much further are we traveling today?" Airlyn called back to Rist from her mount.

She was already irritated at him, and they hadn't even spoken in over an hour. She was always so quick to jump into negative emotion that even talking to her was grinding to his own stability.

Rist looked up at the sun, and then unfurled a map that he had been given by the queen's own cartographer. He spent a few seconds making a few mental calculations, in part because he needed to, and in part because he knew it would annoy the long-faced elf.

"Well?" she asked, turning almost completely around in her saddle.

"I'd say two more hours if we are to maintain our scheduled arrival at Minotatha roughly two weeks from now. We should arrive at the village by mid-day tomorrow."

"Is there no faster path?" Breyman asked in his rumbling voice.

"Sadly, no," Rist answered. "We are limited by the pass in the mountains. We could take a more direct route, but that would mean winding our way through relatively unknown lands, hoping to find an undiscovered pass through the mountains. There is likely nothing there but snow and cold to get us through."

"So, instead, we're going to cut our way through a forest?" Airlyn snipped back.

"You know there will be a path. Calm yourself," Breyman replied. "Caravans came through the pass as early as two months ago, according to the trolls. Nature cannot have reclaimed the land so quickly. There will be a way through the forest. From there, the road to Minotatha will be clear."

Airlyn let out a noise somewhere between acceptance and exasperation, but remained silent. The group rode on in relative silence. A few quiet phrases spoken back and forth between Breyman and Airlyn were all that marred their travel through the land west of the Troll city.

That night, they made camp near a grove of trees that would provide them a modicum of shelter from the winds that tore through the flat, vacant grasslands every night. This was their fourth night sleeping on the hard ground. Rist didn't mind. He didn't really sleep in the way his companions did, but it certainly did little to enhance Airlyn's mood. They sat quietly around the fire as water boiled in a solid metal pot hung from branches that Breyman had snapped from nearby trees. Rist had watched the Lystran carefully, noting how he had only taken branches from trees that were large enough to recover from losing a limb. Rist sensed an odd feeling of tenderness towards the trees coming from Breyman. He was almost apologetic as he gathered what he needed.

"Isn't there any way we can get there faster?" Airlyn asked, filling the silence between the snaps and pops of the fire.

"No." Rist answered flatly, not feeling in the mood to entertain Airlyn's testy disposition.

"No? That's all you're going to say, is no?" Airlyn asked heatedly.

"Yes," Rist said, not moving his face from the light of the fire.

"Well, that's unacceptable." Airlyn replied with a note of authority that Rist hadn't noticed before.

"Who are you?" Rist asked, curious about what made her feel she could be so demanding. He had an idea but wanted it confirmed.

"Who I am doesn't matter. What matters is getting answers." She responded back in a voice nearly as chilling as his own.

"I would beg to differ, elf." Rist replied coolly.

Airlyn stared into the inky blackness of Rist's hood. He could sense anger and frustration in her, but she held her tongue. After several moments of silence, Airlyn gave an exasperated sound and stood, making her way to the edge of camp just beyond the flickering light of the fire.

"What don't I know that I should?" Rist asked bluntly, turning his gaze toward Breyman.

"She is conflicted. I will not give you the fullness of her story. That is for her to tell as she sees fit. But she did not choose this path as willingly as others have." Breyman answered, staring at the point in space where they had lost sight of Airlyn.

"She was forced to come to Olympus? How is that possible?" Rist asked.

"No, not forced. I will tell no more. It is not my tale to tell." The deepness of Breyman's voice seemed to shake the tongues of fire.

Rist nodded and let the subject drop, deciding to move onto a new topic.

"What about you? What is your story?" Rist asked.

Breyman turned his cat-like face to Rist and stared silently for several seconds. His emotion was oddly calm, as if he were doing nothing more than studying some interesting bit of writing or sculpture.

"I was chosen as a young cub, along with one from each of the thirty clans, to be a candidate to come to Olympus. I trained for several years and rose above the rest. When this cycle came, I was chosen above all others and came to Olympus to keep evil locked away and protect my family, my clan, and my world."

Rist examined Breyman's emotions during his answer, seeing that same quiet calm that was so foreign to the people he had found in Olympus so far.

"The food is ready." Breyman said, cutting into Rist's thoughts. "Will you be having any?"

"No," Rist answered. "Thank you."

"You have not eaten since our journey began. Are you well?"

"Yes," Rist said, nodding. "I do not require sustenance in the same way that you do."

Breyman nodded his quiet acceptance without objection, which impressed Rist, and spooned two bowls full of the steaming liquid before rising to go in search of Airlyn. The two of them returned in silence and sat to eat their simple meal. When they were finished, they laid in their bed rolls and went to sleep without another word spoken among them.

The group got up and continued their journey with few words spoken among them. After a few long hours in the morning sun, Rist caught sight of a village rising over the horizon. Thatched rooftops of crude mud-brick houses slowly began to resolve themselves as they grew ever closer. Eventually small, two legged figures began to come into view and resolve into strange, half human figures not unlike the Chorrun, the centaur who had been so helpful to them before the battle of Farkland Reach. Something was different about these people, though. They were not as tall and walked only on two legs instead of four.

"Do we have a plan here?" Airlyn asked. Her voice lacked its usually annoyed tone, which pulled Rist out of his observations of the squat people they rode towards.

"Should we?" Rist asked.

"Given the dangers that Tahmer's presence suggests," Breyman said, "I think it best we reveal as little of the events that have befallen us in the past weeks."

"Agreed," Airlyn replied. "If these people know nothing of the battle, or of Darien's disappearance, let them live in peace and not arise suspicion of any other possible agents like Tahmer."

Rist shrugged his acceptance. It didn't make much difference given his own abilities, though the other two couldn't know that yet.

"I think these people are fauns, if what I can see is correct." Rist said.

"How can you know that from here?" Airlyn asked incredulously.

"Because," Rist replied coolly. "I came into Olympus just northeast of here and was able to find one to point me in the direction of the troll city. We traveled together for a few days before parting."

"Are they a friendly people?" Breyman asked.

"The one I traveled with was, though I think he was also frightened of me, which could have altered his mood." Rist said with a small chuckle.

Over the next hour the village grew larger, and their direct approach could no longer go unnoticed by the inhabitants of the small village. One of the fauns, a farmer by the implement he carried over his left shoulder, stared at them from a distance for several seconds before dropping his instrument and running into the village, his voice carried by the soft wind towards Rist and the others. The words could not be made out, but they were either excited, or frightened. Rist hoped it was not the latter. They were still too far away for him to feel any of the emotion from the squat peoples.

As they reached the edge of the village, Rist began to feel that the emotions of the people. They were excited, anxious, and eager. Most simply seemed to want to gain a glimpse of these newcomers, but a few seemed to want something more. Conversation? No, it was more purposeful than that, but there was a strange hesitancy that was over the entire village. Rist tried with every tool his mind was equipped with to gather more information, but it was too vague a notion that the fauns were dwelling on for him to gain any further insight. The group continued and Rist kept his mind keenly focused on any further variation of feeling.

They passed the outer edge of the village and came onto a small road that seemed to encircle the village. The paths and homes appeared to be made from a series of concentric circles, with farms and shops on the outer edge, and homes lining the inner rings. They crossed through four rings of buildings before running into the first lone faun. It had a bare chest of a man like Chorrun, however horns protruded from its temples on either side, and it stood on two squat, fur covered legs. The figure looked up at them, mouth wide in evident surprise at these strangers coming into the village unannounced.

"Hello." Rist said, trying to keep his icy tone to a minimum, though he still thought he saw a shiver run down the short frame.

"Oh my, is it that time already?" Came the concerned reply.

"What time would that be?" Breyman's voice rumbled.

The short figure's eyes dashed quickly to the large figure, made even larger by his position on the enormous horse carrying his weight.

"Oh, oh please forgive me, you gave me such a scare!" The voice went from concerned to apologetic. "Please, please, come! Come! We must let everyone know that you've arrived!"

"It seems we've been expected." Rist said, turning his head to look at the others.

"Apparently so," Airlyn answered slowly as she dismounted and led her horse after the squat fellow.

Rist and Breyman dismounted as well and followed the squat man through the last few rings of homes and other buildings before coming into a clearing in the middle of the village. At its center was a large covered area that stood a few feet above the surrounding ground. Rist saw a small handful of fauns standing on the platform. These seemed to Rist, based on their confident minds and position above the others, to be the leaders of the village. Around the circle were small open-air shops, a smith, small stables, a butcher shop, and various others. Three wells for drinking water were spread around, just outside the large pavilion at the center.

Rist and the others continued their journey towards the center of the village as onlookers gazed up at him with a mix of terror and excitement, at

Breyman with awe at his height, and at Airlyn with amazement at her long, striking, angular features. The group finally made their way to the pavilion and stood before the three fauns. The man in the center stepped forward and gestured with open arms to the scenery around them.

"Welcome to our home!" came the cry from his voice. A mix of excitement and anxiety tinged the announcement that sent the crowd around him into a cacophony of cheers and excited whistles.

"I hope your journey here from our friends in Farkland Reach was uneventful. I pray that you find rest and comfort while you stay here. We are honored to invite such distinguished guests as The Eldric! But…" the fauns voice became concerned and curious, "I count one missing from your number."

The unasked question sent the village into silence as the crowd realized that the one who spoke for them was right. Rist felt a wave of curiosity and anxiety run through the throng of people there.

"We hope to rejoin with our friend later. He was pulled to another task." Rist explained, hoping that the simpleness of the answer would suffice. Airlyn and Breyman shot their eyes briefly at Rist before nodding their agreement.

The man looked at them quizzically, clearly not understanding, but thankfully allowed the subject to pass without further inquiry.

"Ah, well then, we will have to make do with the three of you!" he continued. "My name is Jaleq. Welcome to our little home. This is the village of Arcadium, where we Fauns live. Well, some of us anyway, those who haven't made their way to the western cities. Tell us, do you have news from Farkland Reach? How is our friend King Aghemnon?"

The group remained silent for several seconds before Breyman decided to break the silence. "Master Jaleq, we are more than willing to provide you with news from the cities east of here, but we would appreciate a brief respite first. If that is not too much to ask."

The people around looked unhappy with the request, clearly wanting to hear what these people of such importance had to say.

"Of course," Jaleq answered hesitantly, clearly disappointed. "Follow me, please. We will take you to our inn, where you may each have a room. You can rest there, and we shall have a feast tonight in your honor."

The trio nodded their appreciation and moved to follow Jaleq through the cramped, crowded streets. The people parted, muttering their disappointment at the lack of news, and curiosity about the missing member of their company flowing through them, and past Rist's mind. Just as they entered the first ring of buildings outside of the town's center, a faun, young by his features and lack of a full curve of his horns, came and offered to attend to their horses.

"They will be well fed and cared for. Ready for you to continue your travels to the west whenever you should have need of them." Came the timid voice of the young faun.

"Thank you," Breyman said, the depth of his voice causing the boy's eyes to widen.

The three passed the reins of their horses to him and watched as the horses rounded the corner of a building a few doors down.

"Alrus is a good boy," Jaleq said proudly. "Works for Master Duntus down at the stables. Kid has a knack for horses. Well, unicorns anyway, but they tend to be more temperamental. My mother always said, 'If you can tame a unicorn, you can master a horse.'"

The group continued their walk through the compact dirt roads. The paths were so worn from the continued travel by the fauns and other travelers that almost no dust rose from the ground as they walked. After a short time of walking in silence, the only sound coming from their group was the faint thud of their footsteps against the path. They came to one of the only buildings in the village with more than one floor.

"Welcome to our home! Well, our home and place of business. A faun has to make a living, doesn't he?" Jaleq said with an air of excitement and a chuckle, clearly amused by himself.

A small plain looking female faun eyed them from behind the counter. Rist could feel some emotion coming from her, but it seemed to be a mix of anxiety, fear, and hope intertwined. She watched apprehensively as they entered, almost appearing to decide between welcoming them or running out the door.

"Tindra! Tindra please, get our guests something to drink. They must be parched from the journey." Jaleq said.

# Chapter 9: The Desperate Plea

The scent of warm bread and herbs filled the small home, a contrast to the quiet tension in the air. The room was modest but well-kept, its wooden beams and stone hearth giving off a welcoming warmth. Rist sat at the simple wooden table, his hood still drawn, though his gaze was fixed beyond the immediate surroundings. He could feel the weight of unspoken words pressing in on the room.

Jaleq, ever jovial, forced a smile as he ladled stew into bowls. "It's not right, Tindra," he said lightly, though his eyes flickered with worry. "They are not here for us. Their path is set, and we shouldn't burden them with our troubles."

Tindra, standing near the doorway, wrung her hands together. Her expression wavered between hesitation and despair. "Jaleq, I can't just stand by. Arven... she's slipping away. The neighbors have already lost Brynn. She doesn't have much time."

Rist, sensing the turmoil before him, finally spoke. "Your daughter is ill." It was not a question.

Jaleq's smile faltered, but he nodded. "Yes, but it's nothing for warriors like you to trouble yourselves with. We will manage." His voice held its usual warmth, but it was stretched thin, barely concealing the fear underneath.

Tindra turned away from her husband and looked directly at Rist. "She was bitten by an echidnian viper two days ago, she and her friend. At first, we thought they would recover, but Brynn passed last night and now Arven… she hasn't woken since last night. She barely breathes." Her voice cracked, and she pressed a trembling hand to her mouth. "The apothecary says there's a plant, a blue-veined thistle, that can counteract the venom. But it only grows in the marshes around the lake at the center of the forest. We're forbidden by the Peronia from entering and so…"

Rist studied the woman before him as she trailed off. Desperation radiated from her, a mother clinging to the last embers of hope. Jaleq, however, still wore his mask of reassurance, though the worry in his mind betrayed him.

"It's not their concern," Jaleq added quickly. "We don't ask for charity. This is our problem to solve."

Tindra turned sharply. "She will die, Jaleq!" she snapped, the emotion finally breaking free. "I don't care about propriety or what's proper. If they can help, then we must ask."

The room fell silent. Rist let the moment stretch, watching the conflicting emotions play out between husband and wife. Airlyn spoke for them, though Rist thought they would all be in agreement.

"Where exactly can this plant be found?"

The group left early the next morning, having spent their night looking at various maps, and even drawings in the dirt where maps were unavailable in the sparse belongings of the people in Arcadium. The lake in the forest looked to be about two days' journey, followed by whatever time it would take to actually find the herb. The group consisted of Rist, Airlyn, Breyman, and Jaleq, who had insisted on coming along with the group as something of a guide. He would be the one to point out the plant they needed.

At one point during the night, while the group was finalizing the route they would take to the forest lake, Airlyn had stepped away and into Arven's room. Rist had followed several minutes later, feeling the same empathy coming from Airlyn as he had before. He stood beyond the doorway, his black robes keeping him from view in the deep shadows of the home that had fallen almost entirely into darkness save for the scant moonlight of Olympus' smaller moon.

Airlyn sat at the edge of the girl's bed, holding the tiny hand in her own. From Airlyn's lips emanated a sweet melody, the words of which Rist could not make out. As with the trolls' funeral ceremony in their city, it appeared that whatever magic allowed them to communicate did not function the same way for song. The notes flowed through the air like droplets of water dancing on waves of wind. The song was so warm and pleasing, that is if Rist had possessed the ability he thought he might have been moved to tears.

Taking a step forward, Rist allowed Airlyn to know that he was there. The melody faded as she turned to him, her face wet with soft tears.

"What troubles you, elf?" Rist asked quietly.

"I-what-how long have you been standing there?" Airlyn asked in an embarrassed and somewhat angry whisper.

"Only a moment."

Airlyn stared at him for a few seconds, as if she wanted to challenge him to admit he had been there longer, but that faded, and she looked back to Arven's sleeping face.

"She shouldn't be alone." Airlyn said simply.

Rist nodded and left without another word, knowing from what emotions he could feel from Airlyn that there was little else she would, or maybe even could, say right now.

Just as the sun was beginning to set on the first night of their trip into the thickly wooded forest, the group found a small area sheltered by a small grove of trees to make camp. The Eldric of them sat and ate quietly for several long minutes before Jaleq broke the silence.

"I have to thank you all. I didn't expect you to be willing to divert your journey to help a single family in a small village like ours. Seeking the help of The Eldric is considered taboo by so many, as your work is so important to keep Cyprin from the lands. That was why I didn't want Tindra to bring it up to you. It seemed… small compared with who and what you are. Please don't think that I do not care for my daughter."

"We are like you," Breyman answered. "We have lives, family, a past, and a future. As brief as the latter may be. We understand your need."

"Why did you agree to help? If I may be so bold to ask." Jaleq posed tentatively.

Rist and Breyman both glanced at each other before turning their attention onto Airlyn, who stared deeply into the fire before standing and walking away from the group deeper into the small stand of trees surrounding them.

"Do not mind her. She is…complicated." Rist explained to the puzzled Jaleq. "If I may ask, what do you do in Arcadium? The village seems so small, you must spend most of your time subsistence living?"

"Oh no, no master Rist." Jaleq chuckled. "We fauns take care of these lands between the village and the forest. There are herds of unicorn here that we monitor and sometimes use for our own purposes in the village. You have caught us in our off season, but at the peak of harvest or planting, and much else you would have seen no fewer than twenty of the beautiful creatures put to various purposes throughout the village."

"Unicorns?" Rist asked. "I am unfamiliar with the creature."

"Horses! Horses, Master Rist. Though they have a long, spiraled horn stemming from their heads. In fact, one of the problems we have stems from the place you are headed to, Minotatha. That is, I presume where you'll be headed after you go through the pass west of here?"

"It is." Breyman rumbled.

"What kind of problems are you having?" Rist asked.

"Bah," Jaleq said with disgust. "Those scaled beasts hunt the unicorns for their horns. Believe it prolongs their life or some such nonsense."

"We'll have a talk with them about it when we arrive." Rist said.

"Ah, well, if you can sway the Peronia from anything, I'd have it be that. They cause us no end of trouble. Their trapping and hunting have almost become a rite of passage."

"Have you not tried speaking with them?" Breyman asked.

"Us?" Jaleq asked. "They want nothing to do with us. Whenever we speak with one of them, we are treated as little better than their quarry. I spoke with one once and felt lucky he didn't decide to take my own hide as a trophy back to his people."

From there, talk turned to idle chatter about the nature of the landscape, the southern trees, and question about their lives to this point.

"What of you, dark one? I heard whispers and tales of your kin on my world, but little solid fact has remained over the years." Breyman asked in a lull during the conversation.

Rist knew this question would come at some point. He had spent a significant amount of mental energy trying to decide how much of himself and of his people to reveal. There were so few of them left. What secrets there were should be strictly guarded. Though with his purpose in Olympus, and the fate that awaited them drawing closer each day, there was little harm in divulging a little.

"I am the last of —" Rist stopped abruptly as he heard Airlyn's voice shout out of the dark.

The trio hesitated only an instant to confirm what they had heard, and then Rist and Breyman were up and bolting towards where they had heard the voice call out, Jaleq calling after them from the edge of the fire. Rist reached out with his senses and felt Airlyn's mind, laced with a calm coldness that he associated only with combat. There was another there too, their mind likewise focused.

"This way." Rist shouted, and he ran into the darkness, Breyman close behind.

After several quick steps, they reached the pair. Airlyn and a dark robed figure stood locked in a now silent battle. Both held weapons, Airlyn her dagger from her boot and the other a long knife. Each was trying to gain the upper hand, and neither could, which was impressive for Airlyn, as the other was nearly twice her size. The conflict was severely interrupted when Breyman rushed past Rist and with a large clawed fist, struck the hooded figure across the face giving Airlyn the opening she needed to finish the fight, she reached out with her dagger attempting to thrust it into the chest of her opponent but they sidestepped the blow and staggered away trying to regain a sense of the situation. Looking around, the figure saw they were outmatched and drew their arm back to throw the knife at Airlyn, thereby winning the fight with at least one of the opponents before them.

Quicker than anyone saw with their eye, Rist reached into his robes and withdrew a small piece of metal, sharpened to a point and tipped on one end with bright green and yellow fletching. With the flick of his hand and swish of his black robes, Rist hurled the small glint of metal towards their attacker, burying the bolt in the man's chest, just as he had with Tahmer's head in the duel with Darien. Airlyn stepped back in surprise at the sight of the robed figure attempting to throw their weapon at her and lost her footing. She fell to the ground and collapsed at roughly the same moment that her opponent had.

Rist ran forward to Airlyn and extended a black-gloved hand to the elf who had fallen onto her back, though much more gently than whoever it was she had been fighting had. She hesitated a second before pushing herself up, ignoring Rist's offer of help. He sighed and turned his attention quickly back to where Breyman was standing over Airlyn's opponent, clutching at the bolt which was still nestled in the other's chest. It was clear he would not survive the wound.

Breyman, Rist, and Airlyn stood around the figure cast down into the dirt, amazingly in the tumble their hood still remained up, obscuring their face. Breyman reached down and withdrew it, revealing the scaled, snake-like face protruding from the shadow of the cloak.

"Name yourself!" Airlyn snapped. "Who and what are you?"

The reptilian figure hissed back at her before looking over and catching sight of the size of Breyman, cutting off the hiss just as quickly as he had begun it.

"I asked you a question." Airlyn snarled.

"I am Niraloth, sssson of Borinoth." Came the answer as a tongue flicked out to taste the air.

Rist felt revulsion flow through Airlyn as she watched the tongue dart through a small opening at the front of the slightly elongated mouth.

"What are you doing here, Niraloth?" Breyman asked with a calm that belied the rage Rist felt inside of him at his assault on Airlyn.

"I wasssssss hunting."

"Hunting what?"

"The only thing worth hunting in these vile east lands," Niraloth said with the hint of a hiss that always seemed to be just under the surface of his voice.

"He's hunting the unicorns that the fauns tend to." Rist said from behind Airlyn.

She stared back at her captive and gave a shudder.

"What are you?" She asked.

"I am Peronian, can you not tell?" Niraloth said, clearly annoyed by the question.

"And why is it you attacked me?" Airlyn demanded.

"You were disturbing my traps. No one can interfere with the hunt. To do so is punishable by death."

"Are you a fool?" Rist said, intentionally making his voice as cold as possible in an attempt to break the smug, arrogant demeanor of the man in front of him. "Do you know who you just tried to kill?"

"It does… it does not matter. No one can disturb the hunt!" Niraloth shouted as pain racked his body.

"You just tried to kill a member of The Eldric, you simpleton," Rist hissed. "Would you be so stupid as to doom your world and our own to attack so blindly when the cycle was so near?"

A look of shock and indignation cross Niraloth's scaled face.

"You? You are The Eldric? But… but why are you here in the forest?" Niraloth let out a cry of pain as his wound took its toll.

"Why we are here is no business of yours," Airlyn spat.

"You… you will not live long when my people hear of this," Niraloth said, now struggling to breathe.

"We shall see," Breyman asked before turning and walking out of the clearing, with Airlyn close behind.

Rist stood looking at the fallen man whose life had expended itself with its last breath only moments before. He reached down and gently closed the scaled eyes as he removed his bolt and followed after his companions.

Rist walked into the circle of camp to find Airlyn and Breyman standing at the perimeter, waiting for him to arrive. He continued past where they stood, turning his dark hood to Airlyn as he passed.

"You're welcome," He said, in a whisper that only Airlyn could hear.

He watched a look of annoyed anger cross her face and he walked towards where he saw Jaleq standing looking in the direction of where they had run to.

"Is everything okay?" the faun asked.

"You have one less hunter in your lands," Rist said, not bothering the keep the ice from his voice.

"You… you killed a Peronian?" Jaleq asked in a frightened tone.

Airlyn nodded as she came into camp.

"To be more specific, he attacked me and got what he deserved." Airlyn said venomously.

Jaleq's mouth fell open in astonishment before he came to his senses and he asked his next question.

"Why would he attack you?"

"I would ask one of them," Airlyn said, gesturing to Breyman and Rist. "They seem to know more about it than I do. I just saw a bit of metal on the ground in a game trail and wondered what it was. When I bent down to inspect it, he came out of the stand of brush and attacked me."

"It seems she interfered with his hunt." Breyman said.

"Oh… oh this is not good. When he doesn't return, and they come looking for him, they're going to come to us for answers!" Jaleq said.

"Then you tell them the truth." Airlyn snapped. "That he jeopardized the entire world. He risked reducing our already small number from three to two!"

Rist turned his head to look at Airlyn, who saw that she had said too much, but Jaleq hadn't seemed to notice.

"You don't understand. When we don't have the right answers, they will kill one of us as 'penance.' It's happened before."

"That won't happen," Rist said. "That I will promise you. When we arrive at Minotatha, all will be explained. That man can't have been due back for some time. We will arrive before his hunt was supposed to end and deal with the situation, as well as deal with the hunt itself."

"We have our own business to attend to now, Jaleq," Breyman rumbled. "Keep your mind with us. We will need you when we enter the forest."

This seemed to mollify Jaleq to some degree, who nodded.

"Okay... okay. I suppose there isn't much left we can do about it now, anyway. We have our own work here. You're right."

Rist informed them that he would be keeping watch for the night so that the rest of them could regain as much strength as they could for the following day when they would be entering the forest. The three laid down on their bed rolls as Rist added another log to the fire, using a longer branch to turn the logs that had been burned on one side to the other, giving the flame new surfaces to spit its roiling flames at. Once he was satisfied that the fire would burn for an adequate amount of time before needing to be tended to once more, he turned his attention outward to keep watch over their camp with all his senses.

The next morning the sun rose and began to chase the smaller of Olympus' two moons across the sky. At the first break of the morning rays of light, Rist abandoned his watch and began to make preparations for the group to continue their journey through the forest. They came upon the lake about midday and set up a small camp at its edge.

Rist remained observant as they spread out to search for the blue-veined thistle, his senses always probing beyond what his eyes could see. He felt Airlyn's presence drifting farther from the others, her emotions tinged with determination and, beneath it, something harder to define—perhaps the need to prove herself.

He followed her path from a distance, letting her be, but keeping her within the range of his perception. As he sifted through the marshy undergrowth himself, a sudden ripple of alarm shot through his senses. Airlyn.

He moved quickly, reaching the edge of a sinkhole just in time to see her struggling, her leg pinned beneath a collapsed section of earth.

"Hold on," Breyman's voice came from nearby as he lumbered into view, already assessing the situation. Rist remained above, his mind sharp as he monitored the growing tension in Airlyn's posture.

She tried to shift but winced, muttering a curse. "Just hurry up," she said through gritted teeth.

Breyman crouched, using his immense strength to lift the heavy stone trapping her. As soon as she was free, a new sensation jolted through Rist's awareness—a predator's intent.

"Move!" Rist called, but the warning came just as a hiss erupted from the underbrush.

A snake lunged from the underbrush, its fangs sinking deep into Breyman's forearm before he could react. The beast slithered away before he could retaliate, disappearing into the shadows.

Breyman stumbled, gripping his arm as the pain shot through him. Jaleq, arriving at the commotion, paled at the sight. "By the gods," he muttered, rushing forward. "That was an echidnian Vviper… the same kind that bit Arven."

Rist felt the surge of pain ripple through the warrior's being, the slow burn of the viper's venom creeping through his veins. They had found the herb needed to save Arven, but now Breyman needed saving too.

# Chapter 10: The Unraveled Balance

The stillness of the valley surrounded Darien as he sat cross-legged on the cool stone, his hands resting on his knees, palms upward. The morning air was crisp, the sky a pale blue canvas streaked with wisps of clouds that drifted lazily overhead. This was his meditation space, the same secluded outcrop where Whyn had first shown him the ethers. He had been able to feel them ever since, an ever-present hum at the edge of his perception. Today, he would attempt something new.

Closing his eyes, he exhaled slowly, reaching inward. The ethers responded to his intent, the way they always did, yet remained elusive to his control. Ether was smooth, a current that moved with an almost liquid grace. Anti-ether was jagged, shifting unpredictably like a river filled with broken ice. He had grasped at them before, but never together, never with the ability to hold them both at once.

The goal was simple in theory—to make them touch, to push into both at the same time. But as he reached out, they resisted, repelling each other like magnets of the same polarity. Frustration bubbled up inside him. He knew they could be merged; Whyn had made that clear. But knowing and doing were very different things.

Gritting his teeth, Darien forced his breathing to steady, pressing his awareness into the energies again. His head began to ache, a familiar, dull pressure settling behind his temples. He ignored it. Slowly, carefully, he willed his mind to hold both forces at once. The sensation was strange, like stretching two separate muscles that had never been used in tandem. Ether flowed eagerly into his grasp, but anti-ether resisted, spiking against his control.

For a brief moment, he succeeded.

A flicker. A shift.

For the first time, Darien felt both within his reach. The energies crackled against each other, neither merging nor dispersing, simply existing together within the confines of his will. A jolt ran through his body, sending a shiver down his spine. His breath caught, and then—

Pain.

A sharp pulse shot through his chest, radiating outward. His old wound, the remnants of the wraith possession, burned like a fresh brand against his ribs. His concentration snapped, and the ethers tore apart, sending a shockwave through his limbs. He gasped and doubled over, his hands pressing against the stone beneath him for stability. He could feel the warning signs—his heart hammering, the dizziness creeping in.

And then… it stopped.

Whyn's alarm. The safeguard his master had placed on him held firm, preventing the episode from fully consuming him. The pain ebbed, leaving behind only exhaustion. Darien sat back, wiping sweat from his forehead. He had done it. Not perfectly, not even well, but he had touched both ethers at once. That was more than he had ever managed before.

His lips curled into a grin. He needed to tell Whyn.

Pushing himself to his feet, Darien steadied his breathing and turned toward the path leading back to the stone halls of the valley's inner sanctum. He walked quickly, his mind racing ahead, already anticipating his master's reaction. Whyn would be pleased. He had to be.

When he entered the chamber, Whyn was already waiting, arms folded across his chest, his expression unreadable. The older man studied Darien carefully, and before the young warrior could even speak, Whyn simply said, "You pushed into both."

Darien blinked. "I—yes, I did! I managed to hold them at the same time, just for a moment."

Whyn gave the faintest nod. "Good." He reached and took a sip from his carved wooden mug. Coils of warm steam billowing up from its surface as the liquid flowed between Whyn's lips.

Darien waited for more. Some praise, some acknowledgment of what this meant. But Whyn's expression remained composed, his approval measured. The silence stretched, and Darien felt his excitement begin to cool into disappointed frustration. "That's it? Just 'good'?"

Whyn took another long, slow sip of his tea before exhaling softly, the silence seeming to drag on between them. "You've taken the first step. But do not mistake a first step for the journey itself." He turned, moving toward a nearby shelf where ancient tomes lined the stone walls. "Control will not come quickly. And if you move too fast, you will undo yourself before you even begin."

Darien clenched his jaw but said nothing. He had learned to expect this. Whyn's methods were always the same—teach through restraint, let knowledge come slowly, deliberately. It made sense, but it was maddening. Couldn't he show some kind of enthusiasm or excitement at the progress of his students?

Whyn stood and walked to a shelf of books. He perused them in an almost disinterested manner before selecting one, flipping through its pages before glancing back at Darien.

"Darien, I've seen this eagerness before. We have much to do and little time to do it in. What I would wish to teach in years I must teach to you in weeks and months. But that does not mean we should forgo the basics of control. You have no idea the potential power you're using."

Whyn sighed, clearly seeing in Darien's face the arrogance of youthful determination. He wanted more.

"Since you are so eager, I will give you something to do. You will continue your practice as before, but this time with a more structured approach. A goal." Whyn shook his head at Darien's excited expression. "No. You will not force the ethers together; there are still steps before that you must take. You will learn to hold them in balance first. Once you can do that, we will discuss the next step."

Darien inhaled deeply, pushing down the frustration. "Fine."

Whyn smirked slightly, as if he could see Darien's internal struggle plainly. "You're progressing faster than I expected. But do not mistake speed for mastery."

Darien nodded, letting his pride drip away. Whyn had never steered him wrong in any of their lessons before. It was due to Whyn's teachings that Darien was even here and alive. He tried to let go of his ego, of his impatience, but he was finding it harder than he would have liked.

For the next few weeks, Darien's days became a relentless cycle of repetition and frustration. He woke at dawn, stretching his muscles with precise, deliberate movements, mindful of his injury and stopping before the ringing in his ears became too much. He would then move through his forms, using the bejeweled sword of The Eldric, having no other weapon at his disposal. The weapon felt like a natural extension of himself, perfectly balanced. It surprised him, given its age, how well it had been made.

Then he made his way to the meditation outcrop, settling onto the stone and closing his eyes. The ethers were there, always just out of reach. He would stretch toward them, testing their resistance, his mind working tirelessly to find a way through the invisible barrier keeping them apart. Some days, he felt progress—a tiny shift, a momentary stillness when both energies hovered, just barely held in balance. But then, always, they would slip from his grasp. Sometimes he would have a repeat of success and push into one or the other of the ethers, but the excitement of that success would pull him away from focus and prevent him from being able to connect the other without losing his hold on the original conquest.

Hours would pass before his stomach reminded him to eat. He would trudge back to the valley, forcing food down quickly, then return to his training. Whyn offered little feedback during their meals, but he offered some small words of encouragement when he would see the younger mans confidence wane.

Darien's frustration grew. He was building endurance, sharpening his senses, but the result still felt the same. He was running in place, getting stronger, but going nowhere.

Days bleed into weeks and he had finally been able to push into the ethers a handful of times. But just as he would find himself feeling balance, the control would shift away. The ethers would continue their monotonous push through the space around him. It was especially disconcerting when an ether cloud he was focused on shifted paths and made its way through Darien himself. He could never feel it, but the strangeness of knowing it was there was enough to make him shiver sometimes.

Finally, after weeks of little more progress besides what he had made before, frustration overcame his willingness to restrain himself. Impatience that had been building for weeks, frustration at the wall of circumspect and ethereal information that Whyn seemed to be keeping behind a thin veil of smug knowledge overrode any sense of caution he had left.

This time, he would not stop at balance. He would push forward. He would merge them, even if he could not hold them in balance. They *would* do as he willed.

He steadied his breathing, focused, and pressed his will into the ethers. The smooth current of ether flowed readily into his grasp, while the jagged chaos of anti-ether resisted, shifting erratically like broken shards of glass against his control. Sweat formed at his temple as he exerted more focus, pushing them together, willing them to interact.

The first touch was a shock. A violent clash of energies rippled through him, like colliding tides fighting for dominance. The space between them warped, a trembling, unstable core forming in the center of his vision. A single ember ignited, flickering wildly, hungry for direction.

Darien gasped as the ember became a spark, then flared into a ball of fire the size of his fist that hovered before him, spinning in place like a miniature star. For a heartbeat, he marveled at it. He had done it. He had merged them.

Then, the fire expanded. The balance unraveled, the ether pulling more and more into itself. The flames darkened, twisting violently, feeding off the energy surrounding him. He felt the pull increase, a ravenous hunger in the magic, drawing on the very fabric of the valley's air.

Panic took hold. He tried to withdraw, to sever the connection, but the energy had gained its own momentum, spiraling beyond his control. Ethers clashed together like moths drawn to a flame, the heat reaching his face and becoming unbearable. He couldn't move. The fire burned higher, hotter, devouring everything in its reach. His pulse pounded, his breath came in ragged gasps. He had gone too far.

Then a figure appeared at the edge of the clearing, gold light emanating from his hands as Darien felt a shift in the chain reaction he had caused. Ethers slowed their descent towards the singularity of power Darien had created before coming to a complete halt.

The fire twisted and began to flicker. Darien felt the shift instantly—Whyn's mastery weaving through the chaos, forcing the elements into submission. But the strain showed. Whyn's body tensed, his breathing quickened. The fire collapsed inward, snuffed out in an instant.

Then, Whyn turned to Darien, frustration and anger on his face. Whyn staggered. His face went slack and his knees buckled. Before Darien could react, his master crumpled to the ground, unconscious from the sheer effort it had taken to stop the disaster than Darien had almost wrought.

Darien clambered over to his fallen master, guilt washing over him like a tidal wave.

*What have I done?*

Whyn lay crumpled on the ground, looking broken. His breathing was calm and measured though, and Darien breathed a sigh of relief.

Gathering the last of his strength, which had been greatly diminished by the task of attempting to control the chain reaction of flames he had conjured, Darien pulled Whyn over his shoulders and began to carry him, step by step, slowly towards his master's home.

Each step felt like it took an eternity, progress hampered by the constant buzz of alarm in his ears. Darien had to move agonizingly slowly through the worn path between his clearing and the stairway to Whyn's house.

The stairs!

Darien wasn't sure he would be able to make it up the stairs. He steeled himself. He had to. This was his fault. One by one. Heartbeat by heartbeat, he pushed his way up through the naturally grown staircase of his master's abode. The sun, at near midday when he had started his journey was setting behind the mountains that rimmed the peaceful valley as he entered the naturally made peace of Whyn's bed room. Darien lay Whyn down on the comfortable looking mattress and turned to find a rag, with which he could drop some water between his master's lips.

That turn was the last motion his body, his mind would allow. The constant ringing in his mind had turned to a deafening roar as he collapsed to the ground, writhing in silent agony. His injury pulling him down into something that resembled sleep, but gave no rest.

# Chapter 11: The Wounded Mentor

Darien woke with a raw, metallic taste coating his tongue, a dull throbbing at the back of his head making it hard to focus. His lips were cracked, and when he licked them, he felt the crusted remnants of blood. The night before was a haze, exhaustion and strain pulling him under as soon as he'd collapsed onto the wooden floor of Whyn's home. He pushed himself upright with shaking arms, wincing at the stiffness in his shoulders. His body felt foreign—slow, heavy.

A groan from the bed cut through the haze of his thoughts, and he twisted toward it. Whyn lay still, his breathing shallow, his skin ashen beneath the morning light filtering through the window. The sight of him sent a deep pang of guilt through Darien's chest. He had done this. His arrogance, his impatience—it had cost them both dearly. The best he could do now was keep Whyn alive.

Darien forced himself up, ignoring the aches that rippled through him. His legs protested, but he staggered forward, kneeling beside the bed. He poured water from a nearby jug, pressing the rim of the cup to Whyn's lips. It took a few attempts before the older man reflexively swallowed. It wasn't much, but it was enough to keep him from slipping further away.

The hours stretched unbearably long. Darien had nothing to do but sit in silence, and silence, he found, was worse than pain. The cabin was eerily still—no footsteps, no voice to fill the space. He busied himself with whatever he could—adjusting Whyn's blankets, reheating broth he could barely get the man to swallow, rinsing cloths in cool water and pressing them to his forehead. But the small tasks never took long, and the silence always returned.

When the weight of it became unbearable, he began to move.

He wandered through Whyn's house in a way he never had before—not as a guest, but as someone searching for something he couldn't name. He started with the main room, already familiar, then found himself in Whyn's study. Shelves lined the walls, heavy with books and scrolls. Darien picked one at random, opening it, only to find symbols he couldn't decipher. He frowned, setting it aside and trying another. The script was likely Olveery. The same language he had heard sung during the funeral rites in Farkland Reach. He could recognize it now, but reading it was another matter entirely.

Frustration flared. There was knowledge here, but it was beyond his reach. He picked up another book, one written in the language he could understand, but hesitated. He had already overstepped enough.

Exploring Whyn's home while the man lay unconscious felt wrong. He shut the book and left it where he found it. Another time, maybe.

By the time he returned to Whyn's bedside, the sun had shifted lower in the sky. He sat down heavily, exhaustion pressing into his bones, but sleep wouldn't come. Instead, he stared at the floorboards, jaw clenched. He had rushed forward, eager to prove himself, and it had nearly cost them everything. And now, the only person who could guide him was lying motionless, while he was left to stumble through the aftermath alone.

The first night passed in a restless half-sleep, his body forcing itself into uneasy naps while he jolted awake at every shift of Whyn's breathing. The second day was much the same. He fed Whyn what little he could, kept the fire burning low, and stepped outside only when the walls felt like they were closing in. The valley stretched endlessly before him, and he stood at the edge of the porch, watching the world below move on as if nothing had happened.

By the eighth day, his restlessness grew unbearable. His body, despite its soreness, ached for movement. He started slow—breathing exercises, focusing on his balance. His sword was untouched at his side, but he couldn't bring himself to channel magic. His body knew how to move, knew the drills, but his mind recoiled from the idea of tapping into something deeper. He wasn't afraid of training itself—just what lay beneath it.

Instead, he focused on the basics. Strength, precision. His footwork, his stance. He took careful, deliberate steps through forms he had long mastered, testing himself without overextending. When his muscles burned, he stopped, breathing deeply through the exertion. The magic could wait.

The days stretched on. Whyn remained still. Darien continued his training, piece by piece, rebuilding himself from the ground up. He carved small markers into the wood of the porch, counting the days that passed. When he wasn't training, he read from Whyn's collection of books, skimming titles, reading sections here and there. He tended to the garden at the back of the house, pulling weeds and making sure the small patches of herbs Whyn had grown didn't wither. Anything to keep his mind moving, to keep the doubt at bay.

By the seventh day, Whyn stirred for the first time. Darien nearly dropped the water jug when he heard the hoarse inhale, saw the slight twitch of fingers. He rushed to his side, pressing a hand lightly to Whyn's shoulder.

"Master Whyn?" His voice was rough from disuse.

The older man didn't respond at first, his face twitching slightly in discomfort. Darien held his breath, waiting, until finally, Whyn's eyelids cracked open. His gaze was unfocused, flickering briefly across the ceiling before settling on Darien.

A slow, strained exhale left him. His lips barely moved, but Darien could make out the word he rasped.

"Water."

Darien scrambled to get the cup, holding it to Whyn's lips. The older man drank in slow, measured sips, and for the first time in days, Darien allowed himself a sliver of relief.

Whyn had fallen asleep again not long after drinking the water, but this time, Darien could tell it was real sleep, not the fragile, unconscious stillness of before. He sat by the bed for a long while, just watching Whyn's breathing, steady now, reassuring in its rhythm. The weight in his chest hadn't fully lifted, but it had loosened. The man would recover. Slowly, perhaps, but he would recover.

When Whyn woke again, it was midday. He blinked at the ceiling for a long moment before turning his gaze to Darien. His voice was stronger this time, but still rough. "How long?"

Darien hesitated. "A little over a week."

Whyn's brow furrowed, but not in the way Darien expected. He wasn't shocked that he had collapsed—there was something else about the passage of time that had unsettled him. He exhaled sharply, closing his eyes for a beat before speaking again.

"What have you been doing?"

Darien exhaled, rubbing the back of his neck. "Taking care of the place. Reading. Training—physical, not magic." He said the last part quietly.

Whyn opened his eyes again, and this time, Darien could see the disappointment there. "So much time wasted."

Darien tensed. He had expected that reaction, but it still stung. He clenched his jaw, forcing himself to meet Whyn's gaze. "I was trying to keep you alive."

"And you did." Whyn's voice softened, but his eyes remained sharp. "But that doesn't mean the world stopped moving." He shifted slightly, testing his strength, before letting out a slow breath. "We'll fix it."

The next few weeks fell into a pattern. Darien still maintained the home, but now with Whyn's quiet instruction. He cleaned, cooked, chopped wood, maintained the house—small, grounding tasks that gave structure to the long days.

Every morning, Whyn handed him a book to read. The subjects were carefully chosen. Some recounted great battles, but not the ones Darien had expected. They spoke of figures he had never heard of—Anax, the ruler whose kingdom vanished from the land with no explanation; Polybotes, a warrior whose war against an unnamed enemy left the earth cracked in his wake; Iphitus, a seer who saw an empire's fall and was cast away for his visions. Others were more practical— treatises on the fundamentals of ether manipulation, early writings on how practitioners had once approached magic as a craft rather than an art, even speculative studies on whether the elements themselves had patterns that could be harnessed. Some books delved into philosophy, proposing theories on the nature of power, how it could be wielded responsibly, and whether discipline or instinct played a greater role in mastery. Darien didn't know why Whyn had chosen these particular stories and lessons, and Whyn never explained. He just told Darien to read.

Between readings, Darien resumed training. He moved through familiar physical exercises, regaining strength, sharpening his reflexes. Yet every time he thought about magic, about reaching for the ether, something in him recoiled. He wasn't ready.

Whyn let him have that time. He said nothing about it. Until, one morning, after breakfast, he simply stated, "It's time."

Darien set his cup down, fingers tightening around the rim.

They stepped outside.

Darien stood in the open clearing behind the house, heart pounding. The last time he had reached for fire, it had ended in disaster. He had lost control. He had hurt himself and nearly killed Whyn. The memory was sharp and heavy in his chest, his fingers twitching at his sides.

Whyn saw the hesitation and didn't ignore it. "I'm here this time," he said, his voice calm but firm. "It won't happen again."

Darien swallowed hard. But could sense a trickle of the ethers energy funneling its way into Whyn. He was using it to restore himself, give himself energy in the case of an emergency. This made Darien feel both better and worse. At least they were more prepared this time.

He let out a slow breath and extended his hands. The ether was there like always—he could feel it, like threads woven into the very air. But that wasn't enough. He pushed deeper, stretching his awareness beyond the surface where the ether shimmered and wove itself into the fabric of the world. He knew the anti-ether was there, its opposite force, repelling and pulling in equal measure. He had felt it before, when he lost control. He had to break through that barrier, force the two together, merge them as one. His breath slowed as he reached further, his skin tingling with the shift in energy, the tension in the air tightening like a drawn bowstring.

The world around him changed. The air warmed, heavy with potential. He could smell something faintly burnt, though nothing had caught fire yet. His skin tingled, his heartbeat steady but fast.

He focused and the ether pulsed in response. A flicker. A spark.

This time, he didn't recoil. The flame curled in his palm, small, controlled. It swayed with the wind but didn't falter. It felt... steady. Not wild, not overwhelming, but alive, there in his hand. He could feel the energy of the ether and anti-ether flowing as they merged, annihilated each other providing the energy through their destruction to fuel his magic.

He exhaled, letting it fade, the warmth still lingering in his fingertips.

Whyn studied him for a long moment, then nodded. "Good."

Darien flexed his fingers, feeling the residual energy. It was different this time. He had done it. Not by force, not by accident, but with understanding and control.

A thought surfaced—something that had lingered in his mind since he started reading those strange histories. "Can magic be infused into weapons?"

Whyn glanced at him, considering the question. "Yes. But it isn't simple. The flame must not just coat the weapon—it must bond with it. A blade of fire is not simply a sword with flames. It is an extension of its wielder, of the magic itself."

Darien nodded slowly, a grin spreading across his face. "A flaming sword."

Whyn's lips twitched, the closest thing to amusement Darien had seen in weeks. "Perhaps."

Darien turned the idea over in his mind as they headed back inside. He had found control. Now, he had to learn what to do with it.

Darien exhaled and let his hands drop to his sides. The tension still clung to him, the fear lingering even though he had done it—properly, safely. But he needed answers. He turned to Whyn, the weight of unspoken questions pressing down on him.

"What happened?" Darien asked finally. "Why did you collapse? Was it my magic? Was it something else?"

Whyn looked at him, unreadable as ever, then turned on his heel. For a moment, Darien thought he was walking away, dismissing him, but then Whyn glanced over his shoulder. "Are you coming?"

Darien hesitated, then followed. They stepped onto the porch overlooking the valley; the sun continuing its slow climb into the sky. The air was crisp, the colors of late morning sun beams shining through the clouds reflected on the river and grass lands stretching ahead. Darien sat beside Whyn, watching the world wake below them.

For the first time, he saw it—saw the energy of the ethers flowing toward Whyn, seeping into him like threads of golden light. It wasn't healing in the way Darien had expected, but something deeper, something sustaining. Yet, beneath that, he noticed something else: Whyn looked older. More tired. The magic restored his vitality, but it couldn't stop time from claiming its due.

Whyn exhaled slowly, his gaze lost somewhere in the valley. "It gets harder, you know. Pulling on the ether. Every time I do, it takes more effort. As I get older, the power dims. It happens to all of us. It's part of the passing of time."

Darien looked at his master with silent patience, knowing that more answers would come if he allowed it.

"That is why I collapsed Darien, because the magic and strength that it took was greater than the scope of the magic I can control. Merging the ethers is the beginning, but being able to control that merge, that powerful thread of energy that results, it can take a toll over time."

Whyn noticed Darien's look of concern.

"Oh it's nothing you'll have to worry about, not any time soon anyway. And the toll isn't so great that it's not manageable. But over time magic gets just a little… harder. The longer the time and the more you use it, the greater the toll and the more distant the ethers feel."

Darien frowned. "But I thought—magic can keep you strong. Doesn't it?"

Whyn gave him a sidelong glance. "Strength, yes. But not forever. Magic doesn't stop the body from aging. The more you wield it, the more it asks of you. Eventually, it takes more than it gives. And the more sudden and acute the magic, like controlling your cascade—"

"What's a cascade?" Darien cut in.

"It's the word magicians used for magic that got out of control, the way yours did. Now don't interrupt. Controlling your cascade was a highly acute, energy intensive thing to do. It was more than my reserves could handle, even drawing on the ether the energy to feed my body."

They sat in silence for a while, the quiet filled only by the occasional rustle of wind through the trees.

Darien's mind spun with questions, ones that he felt pressing against him, demanding to be asked.

"What exactly happened to me?" he asked finally. "When I lost control. I could feel something tearing through me—was that the ether, or was it something else?"

Whyn sighed, rubbing his hands together. "That was the breaking point. The moment when the ether and anti-ether collided without direction. The power didn't know where to go, so it tried to consume you instead. You're lucky you survived it. If you had tried to hold it any longer…"

He let the thought trail off, and Darien swallowed hard. "So, if I lose control—"

"It could kill you." Whyn didn't sugarcoat it. "Or worse. There are fates beyond death when it comes to magic."

Darien sat with that for a moment, staring down at his hands. The weight of what he was learning settled deep in his chest, but so did something else—a determination to understand, to wield this power with the precision it demanded.

"Then I'll learn."

Whyn nodded, his gaze still on the valley. "That's the only choice that matters."

By the following day, Whyn was looking like his old self. His body had recuperated enough that Darien no longer saw ether flowing into him. Whatever work he had been doing with the magic was done. Whyn guided Darien down to the training circle for what Darien thought was to be another meditation lesson. To his surprise Whyn had something else in mind.

"Darien, you have already seen by my use of the ethers that you can channel their energy to fuel and speed up your bodily processes. Healing, for example, can be greatly increased simply by giving your body more energy."

Whyn stepped forward with a knife in his hand and sliced his finger. Darien lurched forward to stop him but paused as he sensed ether flowing into Whyn again, but this time flowing directly into this finger. He watched as the wound stitched itself together.

"Cells need energy. When your cells have the energy they need, they can do amazing things. Take metabolism of your own body's calories out of the mix and you can speed up the healing of nearly any wound."

Darien stared at Whyn's finger which, moments ago had been dripping blood, the skin now fused together so cleanly there wasn't even a scar.

"But the rest of you needs energy as well. So what happens if you give your body more energy than is needed?"

Darien shook his head. "I don't know."

Whyn looked disappointed, "Think, Darien. What did I just show you?"

Darien let the question bounce around in his mind. Whyn had given his cells more energy than they needed to perform their natural functions. They had done their jobs more quickly. Did that mean—

"Does that mean I can move faster if I use magic?"

"Precisely," said Whyn, a smile of pride at his pupil's grasp of the complexities.

"Think of the advantage that gives you in a fight against normal, average soldiers," Whyn said as he took a step back towards the entrance to the clearing. "Being able to span the distance…" Whyn stepped forward once, and nearly instantly closed the gap between himself and Darien, moving as a blur of motion through the space between them.

"…in an instant. Draw your sword faster than they can even think to knock an arrow."

Darien looked down, seeing the blade of the same knife pressed to his stomach, the movement having been so fast, Darien had barely sensed the ether being used to create the unnatural speed that Whyn yielded.

"So if I find myself facing another magician, someone like Tahmer, or even Cyprin, they'll be able to move that fast?"

Whyn nodded. "Possibly faster, depending on how quickly they can channel the ethers. This is why your training is so important. You're dealing with enemies who have had three millennia to hone their skills."

"But," Darien started remembering something Whyn had said the day before, "You said that as you get older the magic gets harder to access, to use. If Cyprin is three thousand years old, why doesn't that count against him?"

Whyn took a moment before answering, considering something before he said,

"Cyprin is entombed by magic. He does not age as you might. He is released every fifty years, and usually not for very long. Even if it were for a full year of life every fifty, and it's typically much, much less than that, it would only add sixty years onto his lifespan."

"But you're not that old. Why are you having problems with magic, but Cyprin wouldn't be?"

Whyn smiled and then gave a chuckle.

"Darien, don't let looks deceive you. I use magic, I always have, even on earth when at the academy. Don't you think that it's possible that I'm older than I appear?"

This gave Darien pause. But then the obvious question arose.

"How old are you, then?"

"Manners boy!" Whyn said in a half harsh, half humorous tone. "I'm old enough to have problems. With magic. Let it rest that I'm older than I appear. But you're forgetting one other thing in relation to the dark creature that awaits you on that cursed mountain. It's the magic he wields. He will use any method of power he can find to extend his life, to continue living, and to gain more power for himself."

Whyn looked off into the distance as if remembering something.

"He will do whatever it takes, do anything, say anything to increase his power. Even if that means extending his life by… unnatural processes."

Whyn's eyes returned to Darien's.

"The dark one will have ways of magic you haven't even dreamed of yet. That is why this training we do is so important. Now back to the matter at hand, and enough distracting questions."

Darien began to protest, but Whyn cut him off.

"I know you want more answers. But for now, be content with the ones you have. Now, in order to use magic to increase your speed, you need a steady flow of ether. I want you to begin by…"

Whyn then began coaching Darien through the precise steps to funnel the magic into his body. The sensation was a wonderful feeling. Their lesson drove on into the evening as the sun set as Whyn began in earnest, teaching Darien the finer points of controlling the ethers and his new found magic.

# Chapter 12: The Marauders Resolve

The council chamber reeked of incense and stale words. Evatra stepped inside, silent but brimming with barely contained frustration as the nobles and military commanders argued over maps and logistics. The long stone table was cluttered with parchment, lists of names, potential search routes, and a series of plans that all led nowhere. They had been at this for hours, possibly days, and still, no action had been taken.

Queen Marenya sat at the head of the table, her expression unreadable, though Evatra caught the tightness in her shoulders, the way her fingers tapped against the table's edge in impatience. Without her husband, the late King Aghemnon, to hold order, the court had devolved into self-interest and hesitation.

"We've debated this enough," one noble barked, slamming his palm onto the table. "We must send an expedition to the eastern cliffs immediately. If the tunnels—"

"And waste time if he's not there?" another snapped. "We should be combing the northern valleys!"

"We don't have the numbers to do both. And what if Cyprin's forces are still lingering? This needs to be precise—"

"What of the maps Totra-Dal uncovered?" another noble interjected. "We could use them to guide our search."

A scoff followed. "The Marauder again? We've been over this. He cannot be trusted."

Evatra stepped to the side, leaning against the stone wall, watching them argue. They had noticed her entrance but did not acknowledge her outright. That was fine—she had no interest in their politics, in their ceaseless power plays. They spoke in circles, more interested in positioning themselves than solving the problem. Darien was missing. He needed to be found. And they were doing nothing.

Marenya exhaled sharply, standing abruptly. "Enough. This meeting is adjourned. I have hopes that we can reach a decision soon. Or all our fates may be decided by our inaction." The Queen's voice cut through the noise, and the nobles fell silent, exchanging glances before murmuring amongst themselves as they left the chamber.

Evatra remained as the others filtered out, watching Marenya rub her temples. When they were alone, the Queen let out a heavy breath and motioned for Evatra to follow. "Come. Walk with me."

They stepped into the corridor, the cool stone walls lined with tapestries depicting Farkland Reach's past victories and its lineage. Servants passed them hurriedly, carrying ledgers and scrolls, whispering among themselves about taxation, trade routes, and the grain supply.

Marenya led Evatra to a balcony overlooking the city. The rooftops of Farkland Reach stretched out before them, smoke curling from chimneys, merchants haggling in the streets below, children darting between stalls. Beyond the city walls, golden fields swayed under the afternoon light, and in the far distance, the silhouette of the mountains loomed.

"They think the city runs itself," Marenya murmured, nodding toward the bustling streets. "Every day, new demands. Repairs, disputes between merchants, soldiers needing supplies. My husband handled this with ease. I... find it exhausting."

Evatra smirked slightly. "Politics isn't as glorious as battle."

"No, it is not. But it decides who holds the swords." Marenya gestured downward. "What use is a grand army if it is poorly supplied? If its commanders bicker rather than lead? If the crown does not hold them to purpose? That is what my court fails to understand."

Evatra frowned, watching the Queen carefully. "And where does that leave Darien?"

Marenya stopped, gripping the stone railing. "Stuck between indecision and political vanity."

Evatra sighed, running a hand over her face. "It's maddening. He risked everything for this city, and they can't even agree on how to bring him back. If it were one of them—"

"They would be launching expeditions already." Marenya's lips pressed into a thin line. "I know."

Evatra studied her for a moment. "And you? How are you holding up?"

Marenya hesitated, then exhaled deeply. "Not well. My husband was better at this. He could cut through their nonsense, make them listen. I... they see me as a widow playing at leadership. And now there are offers—" she scoffed, shaking her head. "Some of the nobles have suggested I remarry, find a new king."

Evatra's expression darkened. "That's disgusting."

Marenya let out a dry laugh. "Isn't it? As if my grief is an inconvenience to be solved through another political union. As if my husband's death was just a shift in power and not the loss of the only man I truly loved."

Evatra hesitated before placing a hand on the Queen's shoulder. "You don't have to let them decide that for you."

"I know," Marenya whispered, voice thick with emotion. "But it is a fight I don't have the strength for. Not yet."

They stood there for a moment, the silence between them heavy with understanding. Then, Marenya turned to Evatra. "You are here because I trust you."

Evatra nodded. "Then trust me when I say—I have to leave."

Marenya's gaze sharpened. "What do you mean?"

"Totra-Dal has found something, you know of it, just as the fools in there do. Old tunnels, mapped centuries ago, leading beneath the mountains. They were built by an ancient builder long before Cyprin's rise. They may lead toward where Darien was taken." Evatra's voice was steady, but there was urgency in it. "I can't stand here and wait for them to make up their minds. I have to go."

Marenya studied her for a long moment before nodding. "If you can ensure the marauders hold to their word—no raiding, no hostilities,—then I will grant you whatever you need for your task. But I need assurances, Evatra."

Evatra exhaled. "Consider it done."

Evatra climbed the narrow, spiraling staircase leading to Totra-Dal's quarters. The stone steps were uneven, worn by years of use, and the air carried the faint scent of smoke and aged parchment. As she neared the top, she heard the unmistakable sound of laughter—boisterous and full-bodied, echoing off the stone walls.

She stepped through the heavy wooden door to find Totra-Dal sprawled in a cushioned chair, a goblet in one hand and a half-finished plate of roasted meat beside him. His grin was broad as he spotted her. "Evatra! And here I was, thinking you'd forgotten all about me now that you're an important woman among the nobles."

Evatra smirked, crossing her arms. "Hardly. I figured I'd let you enjoy your wine and laziness for a while before imposing my self on you."

Totra-Dal chuckled, motioning for her to sit. "Ah, you wound me. This is not laziness, my dear. This is well-earned leisure. A man nearly dies, and the least he deserves is a comfortable chair and good drink. Besides, it's not just any wine—this was a gift from the Queen herself."

She raised an eyebrow. "Marenya must be feeling generous. Or perhaps she's trying to keep you occupied so you stay out of trouble."

He laughed heartily, taking a deep sip from his goblet. "Both, I suspect. But come, tell me—what brings you to my humble living quarters? I doubt it's just to exchange pleasantries."

Evatra exhaled, she didn't quite see what was so humble about the opulently ordained room. She steadied herself before leaning forward. "I came to talk about the marauders."

The lightheartedness in Totra-Dal's face faded slightly. He set his goblet down with deliberate care. "What about them?"

She hesitated, then met his gaze. "I want to give them back to you. You're awake, alert, healed. They need their leader."

For a rare moment, Totra-Dal was silent. He studied her, his usual jovial demeanor slipping into something more measured. Then, instead of answering directly, he leaned forward, resting his elbows on his knees. "You've done well with them, haven't you? I hear the marauders respect you. Some might say you've found your place among them."

Evatra narrowed her eyes. "What are you saying?"

He swirled the wine in his goblet, contemplating. "Change is inevitable. Maybe it's their time for something new. Maybe it's yours."

Her expression darkened with suspicion. "You don't want them back."

Totra-Dal sighed, rubbing a hand over his face before leaning back into his chair. "Evatra, I appreciate that you think of me, but you misunderstand. I'm not taking them back."

Her brow furrowed. "What? Of course you are. You led them for years. They listen to you. You built them into something more than just scattered raiders."

He gave a small, rueful smile. "And now they need something else. Someone else."

She shook her head. "No. You fought to keep them together, and now that they're looking to you, you want to just—what? Walk away?"

Totra-Dal sighed again, rubbing a hand over his face before meeting her gaze. "I've taken on a new role, Evatra. I'm staying here, as an advisor to the Queen. My daughter needs a safe life. Farkland Reach gives her that. I can't drag her through the wilds anymore."

Evatra sat back, digesting his words. She knew how much Atreya meant to him, but she hadn't expected this. She wasn't sure if she felt disappointed, betrayed, or just exhausted.

Finally, she muttered, "Then who leads them?"

Totra-Dal shrugged, pouring himself another drink. "Not my problem anymore."

Evatra's fists clenched. "Not your—? You think you can just say that and be done with it?"

He exhaled, rubbing his temple. "I think I've earned the right to step away. I gave years of my life keeping them together, keeping them from turning into the kind of beasts people expect them to be. And you? You took them farther than I ever did. Maybe you should consider that."

She scoffed, standing abruptly. "You're a coward. You built them, shaped them, and now you want to just sit in your tower and drink while they fend for themselves?"

Totra-Dal's eyes darkened slightly, his jovial mask slipping for a moment. "Careful, Evatra. I won't be called a coward by anyone. Not even you."

She took a deep breath, grounding herself. This wasn't helping. "I'm leaving."

He blinked. "What?"

"I'm leaving," she repeated, firmer this time. "I'm going after Darien."

Totra-Dal set his goblet down with an audible thud. "You can't. It's suicide."

Evatra met his gaze, her stance unwavering. "You can't stop me."

Totra-Dal studied her for long moments, his gaze unreadable. Then, slowly, he exhaled and leaned back into his chair. "You let your emotions drive you too much, Evatra. I've seen it before. You throw yourself headfirst into danger for those you care about, and it nearly kills you every time."

She clenched her jaw, but after a moment, she nodded. "Maybe. But this isn't about me. It's about Darien. And if you won't lead the marauders, we need to decide who will."

Totra-Dal sighed, rubbing at his temple before nodding. "You're right about that. We can't leave them leaderless."

She crossed her arms. "Then let's figure it out."

He scoffed. "Fine. What about Vorgath? He's experienced."

She shook her head. "Too reckless. He enjoys fighting too much. He'll burn through whatever goodwill the marauders have earned. What about Rashka?"

"She's got the loyalty, but she lacks the tactical mind... Groth?"

Evatra wrinkled her nose. "You want the marauders to follow a goblin who can't even hold his liquor?"

Totra-Dal chuckled. "Fair point."

They continued tossing out names, each rejected for one flaw or another, until finally, Evatra sighed. "What about Drak?"

Totra-Dal tapped a finger against his goblet, considering. "Drak... he's got the respect of the marauders. He's pragmatic. He listens."

"And he doesn't get caught up in petty fights like some of the others," Evatra added.

Totra-Dal nodded slowly. "Drak might just be the best option we have."

Evatra let out a breath. "Then that's settled. Now, I need your help."

Totra-Dal raised an eyebrow, his fingers drumming idly against his goblet. "Oh? I thought you just said you were leaving. What could you possibly need from me now?"

She exhaled sharply, folding her arms. "I need to know where to start looking for Darien. You've spent more time studying those old tunnels than anyone else. If there's even a hint of where he might be, you're the one who can find it."

Totra-Dal leaned back, stroking his beard as he considered her words. "So that's it, then? You want to march into the dark and unknown, following a trail of old stories and crumbling maps?"

Evatra didn't waver. "Yes. And you're going to help me do it."

A grin crept onto his face. "You always were a stubborn one." He stood, grabbing a thick roll of parchment from a nearby table and unfurling it across the desk. "Alright then, let's see what we can piece together."

He began pointing at locations, tracing faded paths with a calloused finger. "Now, this… this is where the last recorded transition, save for those in the cycles obviously, happened—at least according to these records. If Darien's been taken anywhere that's not inside the mountain itself, he might have gone through here… but, see, this passage here— according to the scouts over the last century or so it's collapsed. So that means…"

Evatra moved through the market streets of Farkland Reach, her steps lighter than she expected. The conversation with Drak had gone smoother than anticipated, and now that she was no longer bound to the marauders, there was a strange weight lifted from her shoulders. And yet, something else had taken its place—a quiet emptiness. She had always been a wanderer, a fighter on the fringes of civilization. Even now, she wasn't one of these people. She wasn't truly a citizen of Farkland Reach. Perhaps she never would be. But for now, she was simply the one going after Darien.

The city was alive with the usual bustle of merchants calling out their wares, the scent of roasting meat mingling with the sharp tang of metal from the blacksmiths' forges. The trolls of Farkland Reach moved in a steady rhythm, their long strides parting through the smaller goblins who darted between stalls, bartering with fervent energy. Cyclopes lumbered through the streets, their hulking forms slow and steady as they carried massive crates of supplies from one end of the market to the other.

She stopped by a stall selling dried meats, running a hand over the rough-wrapped packages before selecting a few. The vendor, a goblin with skin the color of moss and sharp yellowed teeth, regarded her curiously.

"Didn't take you for the settling type," he said, handing over her purchase. It disturbed her that she was so easily recognizable to people. She was glad to be leaving soon.

She smirked. "I'm not. Just passing through."

The goblin snorted. "Aren't we all?"

She tucked the package into her satchel and moved on, weaving her way through the throng of bodies. The weight of the past few weeks pressed against her, but there was something freeing in knowing that, come morning, she would be back on the road. The city had its comforts, but it wasn't her home. She wasn't sure she even had one.

As she neared the stables, the din of the market faded behind her, replaced by the earthy scent of hay and the steady sounds of horses shifting in their stalls. The stable boy, a lanky young troll with perpetually wind-tousled hair, looked up as she approached.

"Got your supplies ready, just as the Queen ordered," he said, gesturing to the carefully packed saddlebags resting against a wooden post. "Fresh water skins, rations, extra blankets, and flint. Everything you asked for."

Evatra gave him a nod of appreciation. "You've done good work."

The boy beamed, his tusks barely peeking from beneath his lips. "You heading out alone?"

She opened her mouth to answer, but a shadow shifted at the edge of the stable. She turned sharply, hand instinctively brushing the hilt of her knife.

A hulking figure stepped forward from the dimness, moving with deliberate slowness, as if mindful of the space he occupied. He was a cyclops, but far larger than any Evatra had ever seen, towering even over his kin. His form bore the telltale signs of one of the creatures the wraiths had inhabited—

something once part of Cyprin's dark army, now freed, though not unchanged. His single eye, a burning shade of deep amber, gleamed with something ancient, something dangerous. His skin was a mottled mix of grays and deep blue, thick and scarred like the surface of a weathered stone.

"You are leaving to find Darien," the creature said, his voice a deep rumble.

Evatra did not confirm it, nor did she deny it. Instead, she simply met his gaze, her hand resting lightly against her belt. "And what's it to you?"

The creature took a step closer, slow and deliberate. "I would come with you."

She raised a brow. "And why would I take you along?"

His shoulders shifted slightly, something unreadable in his expression. "Because I want vengeance. On Cyprin. On the ones who imprisoned me and my kin. The cycle turns, but I see fractures in its pattern. I see a chance that this time, it may truly end."

Evatra studied him. There was no deceit in his voice, no hesitation in his purpose, but she wasn't sure what he meant by his last statement. Regardless, he wasn't asking for her trust, but for a chance to fight. She understood that kind of desire.

"What's your name?" she asked.

He hesitated only briefly before answering. "Cycnus."

The name rang with old power, though whether it was his true name or one he had taken for himself, she couldn't say.

"Alright, Cycnus," she said, measuring her words. "Tell me something—if it comes down to it, if this doesn't end the way you hope, will you still fight? Will you still see it through?"

His gaze held steady. "Vengeance does not end when the battle is over. If I fall, I fall fighting. That is all that matters."

She considered that for a long moment before finally nodding. "Fine. You ride with me. But make no mistake—I'm not here to carry you. You keep up, you pull your weight. If you become a liability, I'll leave you behind. And if you betray me, I'll make you wish that had stayed a wraith. Understood?"

Cycnus inclined his head slightly. "Understood."

Evatra turned back to the stable boy. "Add another set of supplies. We leave at first light."

The boy hesitated, then hurried to his task, glancing at Cycnus warily as he worked. Evatra tightened the strap of her satchel and looked back at the looming figure beside her.

Vengeance could be a powerful ally.

# Chapter 13: The Burdened Past

Rist studied the people and culture around him with interested intensity. The faun village was shaped from the valley itself, not placed on top of it. There were no roads, no square-cut foundations, no structures that looked as if they didn't belong. Instead, the village was molded into the land, its buildings carved into the natural stone formations and grassy knolls that scattered the quaint little town.

Homes were built into the sides of the rock, their entrances framed by carefully placed wooden supports, their interiors hollowed out over generations of work. Stone pathways wound between them, worn smooth from centuries of footsteps. Reinforced terraces jutted from the valley slopes, connected by narrow staircases that led up to higher levels. Some buildings sat lower, nestled between massive boulders where the stone had fractured over time, leaving gaps just wide enough to be enclosed with stacked timber and packed earth.

Wooden awnings jutted out from some of the entrances, shading doorways from the heat of the midday sun. Along the paths, woven baskets of dried herbs and medicinal roots were placed in neat rows, their earthy scent blending with the faint smokiness that clung to the air from distant hearths. Water trickled through a network of carved channels that guided it down the valley walls, collecting in stone basins placed at the center of the terraces, where fauns stopped to wash their hands or drink before returning to their work.

Nothing here was accidental. The village was built for survival, designed to withstand the elements rather than defy them.

The fauns, for their part, seemed to be centered and adapted to their existence as well. Their emotions remained steady as they had carried Breyman inside. There was no hesitation in the way they moved, no wasted motion. Even as the apothecary examined the girl, there was no urgency, no sharp edges to their movements. Their confidence settled into the space like a stone placed carefully into an open hand. They knew she would recover.

Breyman was another matter.

His body wasn't responding to their medicine the way hers did. The fauns had never treated a Lystran before, and their methods—refined over generations to suit their own physiology—weren't as effective on him. His metabolism processed the herbs differently, his body rejecting some remedies outright, others taking longer to work. The healers adjusted, testing new combinations, watching closely, but the uncertainty remained.

Rist could feel it in the way they spoke to each other in measured, hushed tones, their usual confidence fractured at the edges. They were doing everything they could, but they didn't know if it would be enough. They labored diligently, however. Knowing that should the Lystran fall, it could spell doom for their entire world.

Airlyn spent her time waiting for their answers. The rest of their time after bringing him back she stood outside the apothecary door, silent and brooding as ever. She tapped her fingers on her arms in rhythmic patterns, the color of her emotions tinged with complexities that Rist couldn't quite pick apart. There was something… deeper, but he wasn't sure what it was.

By the second day, Airlyn had stopped waiting by the healer's door. She hadn't gone far, but she never stayed in one place for long. She drifted through the village, always near people but never with them. It was like she wanted to be distracted by their existence, but her feelings never went far from Breyman and his battle with the viper's venom in his veins.

Rist once saw her near one of the stone staircases, watching as a group of fauns worked to repair the beams that lined a terrace. They moved with the same quiet efficiency they always did—one placing a support in position, another fastening it in place, a third already measuring the next. Their work continued without pause, without tension, as if nothing had changed.

The rhythmic sound of wooden mallets tapping against stone mixed with the distant murmur of conversation, the occasional scrape of tools against rock.

Smoke curled from an open hearth near the gathering hall, where a faun elder sat weaving thin strips of dried bark into rope, her hands moving with the careful ease of someone who had done the task a thousand times before.

Airlyn stood with her arms crossed, posture stiff, her gaze moving over them without truly watching. It wasn't curiosity. She wasn't trying to understand their process or their way of life. She was just there. Not moving forward. Not standing still.

By the third day, she was simply gone. Rist had noticed her absence before he even looked for her. He extended his heightened senses into the village, letting the emotions around him come into focus. The fauns remained steady, their work uninterrupted. The healers inside still carried a low hum of tension, their uncertainty pressing at the edges of their otherwise calm presence.

She wasn't there… then where was she?

Reaching further, he widened his awareness, feeling the slow rhythm of the land beyond the village. The animals in the forest flickered with instinct—small pulses of movement, caution, hunger. Everything in balance, their emotions untroubled save for the constant fear of daily survival in the wilds.

Then—something sharp. A presence outside the village. Frustration, curling inward. Contained, but restless. He followed it.

Down past the last of the faun homes, beyond the terraces, he found her at the river. She stood on the bank, boots sinking into the loose gravel, her body wound tight. The water moved steadily past her, its rhythm unbothered, but her movements were tense, controlled. She was skipping stones across the surface of the water.

No, he realized as he watched. There was no skipping. She was throwing the stones into the water. No grace or elegance that it took to get the stones to skim across the surface. Pitching them with a hidden, but still restrained, ferocity.

The first hit the water with a sharp slap, breaking the surface before vanishing beneath it. The second struck the far bank, disappearing into the mud. She picked up another, rolling it between her fingers before launching it across the river with the same force.

She didn't acknowledge him, though he could tell she knew of his presence. Rist waited, allowing silence to fill the space between them as he stood stoically.

"Knock it off," she muttered as annoyance filled her mind and tone.

He didn't move. "Knock what off?"

She threw another stone with a greater flicker of irritation. "You know what."

She finally looked at him, and for a moment, he thought she might say something else. Instead, she exhaled sharply, pressing her fingers to her temples before dragging her hand down over her face.

"You're watching me. You've been watching me ever since we got back. I can tell where you are, you know. You're not subtle."

Rist cocked his head beneath his hood, adopting a curious and attentive position.

"You're infuriating. You know that?"

Rist simply nodded. "Darien felt the same about me. It... can be unsettling for others."

Airlyn paused and studied him for several moments before he felt something in her inner workings settle and shift into place. She had decided something.

"You ever feel like every time you let someone in, something bad happens?"

It wasn't a real question, and so Rist didn't answer.

She let out a quiet scoff, shaking her head. "Back home... I had people. Friends, when I was younger."

She wasn't just telling him. She was pulling the memory into focus, forcing herself to relive it.

"I had a special friend in particular. We were so close. We did everything together."

The words carried weight, pressing down between them. She flexed her fingers, gripping another stone but not throwing it. "She was careful. Always thinking ahead. I wasn't."

She let out a slow breath, watching the river but not really seeing it.

"One day, we decided to go off on an adventure together. There were cliffs past the city walls. If you climbed high enough, you could see past the valley, all the way to the sea. I'd been there before, so I knew the paths. The view was..."

She swallowed, her voice catching as emotion smacked her with the force of a boulder falling from high atop a cliff into an ocean below. "She hadn't seen it and I wanted to show her. But she didn't want to go." The next words were thinner, the sharp edges of them breaking. "I 'convinced' her to. I forced the issue."

The air around her changed. Rist felt the weight of it as she spoke, the way her emotions started to collapse inward, tightening like a trap of memory that refuses to let its quarry retreat.

"The view didn't disappoint. We stood there for what must have been an hour, watching the green western waves crash over the beaches. We were almost back down when the rain hit. Sudden storms weren't uncommon that time of year… but we were young. Too sure of ourselves. Well, I was anyway."

She curled her fingers into her sleeve, her body tensing as if bracing for impact.

"The ground gave out. The cliff face fell off into nothingness on the side of the road leading back to her parents' house. Neither of us saw it coming."

Her voice cracked. Just once.

"There was someone else there." The memory slammed into her before she could stop it. "I didn't even know he was watching us. Some scout, a guard—I don't know. But when we fell, he was there."

She took a breath, sharp and uneven. Like the words had physically struck her.

"He caught me first." Her jaw clenched. "She was reaching for him when... when she fell."

Disgust twisted in her voice, layered beneath exhaustion. It wasn't just grief. It was anger. At herself. At the moment. At the fact that she was saying it out loud.

"They found her body the next day. I—"

She exhaled, pressing her thumb against the inside of her palm like she could push the memory away.

"I can still hear her mother crying. I can still hear the sobs as she saw her daughter's grave."

Rist let the silence settle before speaking.

"It wasn't because of you," he said simply. "No one could have known the ground was unstable."

She looked up at him, unsure whether he was talking about their recent endeavor through the forest, or her past childhood memories. Perhaps it had been both.

"I decided from that day forward," she continued, letting the reassurance he had attempted to provide wash away, "that I would atone for my sins. I decided that-"

"Master Rist!, Lady Airlyn! Where are you?"

A voice called from the city. Rist pushed his senses towards the voice, searching for any sign of danger. But instead what he found was reassurance, confidence. They had good news.

"Over here," Airlyn cried back, her tone urgent. She was clearly worried about the same thing. Had the village been attacked or something worse? Rist knew better.

A faun ran up to them, breathing hard, resting his hands on his thighs.

"Master Breyman, he awakens! Please come quickly. The healers are asking for you."

Rist and Airlyn followed the squat little man back towards the village and towards the apothecary where Breyman had been spending his time being seen. They entered the dimly lit room.

Breyman stirred, his breathing still uneven but steadier than it had been the day before. Rist stood at the edge of the room, watching as Airlyn hovered near his bedside, her hands curled into fists at her sides. He could feel the storm of emotions inside her—guilt, frustration, relief, all layered over something she hadn't yet decided how to name.

She shifted, glancing toward Breyman as his eyes fluttered open, then immediately looked away as if she hadn't been waiting.

"You're awake," she said, voice low.

Breyman let out a slow breath, adjusting slightly against the bedding beneath him. "So it would seem." His voice was rough but stable, a weary smirk forming at the edges of his lips.

Airlyn hesitated before speaking again. "I'm sorry I got you hurt. That's twice now you've had two have had to save me. I—"

Breyman's gaze softened, and he shook his head cutting into her speech. "You couldn't have known about the viper, Airlyn. None of us could."

She didn't look convinced. "It wasn't supposed to happen like that. We were all searching together—I just—"

"Airlyn," Breyman said, cutting her off again, "I'm still here. Don't trouble yourself with it."

Rist remained silent, watching as Airlyn processed his words. Her emotions didn't immediately settle, but something in her shifted. He could feel the knot of guilt loosening—just slightly.

Despite how long it took for the venom to work through his body, Breyman's strength returned quickly once he was awake. The next day, he was already sitting up, speaking in full sentences, and by the afternoon, he was on his feet. His body still bore the weight of his ordeal, but it was clear that whatever battle had been waged inside him was over.

The following day, he was outside, moving through the village as if he had never been laid low at all. Rist and Airlyn found him playing a game with a group of faun children, their laughter ringing through the air as he chased them in a mock battle, their wooden sticks clashing against each other. Watching him, it was hard to believe he had been unconscious only two days ago. His recovery was nothing short of remarkable, though Rist could still sense the lingering stiffness in his movements, the way he caught his breath when he thought no one was looking.

On the morning of their departure, Jaleq and Tindra gathered with them at the village's entrance along with a small gathering of fauns, including Arven, their daughter, who was now nearly fully recovered from her ordeal with the viper's venom. Rist could feel her emotions, the weight of the loss of her friend weight heavy on her. Just as Airlyn's past weighed heavily on her.

The assembled crowd was not large, but their presence carried meaning. These were citizens of Olympus, standing together to see off those who had risked themselves to save just one life—a small act in the grander struggle to save the world, but no less significant to those who had witnessed it firsthand.

"You did a great service for us," Jaleq said, his deep voice carrying the weight of unspoken gratitude. "We owe you more than thanks."

Tindra stepped forward, offering a small, knowing smile. "You saved our daughter and risked yourselves, and much much more, to ensure her safety. That is no small thing."

Before anyone could respond, Arven stepped forward, her small frame trembling slightly under the weight of the moment. Her gaze flicked toward Airlyn, uncertain at first, but then she seemed to gather courage from the silent support of the fauns around her. She clutched something in her small hands—a bundle of woven grass and wildflowers, carefully tied together with a thin piece of twine.

Without a word, she stepped closer and held it out to Airlyn.

Airlyn hesitated, blinking as if uncertain what to do. Slowly, she reached out and took the small offering, her fingers brushing against the girl's.

Then, to everyone's surprise, the girl threw her arms around Airlyn in a tight, sudden hug.

Rist felt the wave of emotion hit Airlyn before she even registered it herself. The tightly wound grief and guilt that had held her together cracked, just for a moment. She stiffened, hands hovering awkwardly at her sides, but didn't pull away.

The girl whispered something too soft for Rist to hear, but whatever it was, it made Airlyn's throat tighten. She gave a slow nod before finally resting a hesitant hand on the child's back.

Rist knelt down to come to the same eyeline of the little girl, though he had no eyes for her to look back into, only the inky blackness of the depths of his cloak.

"What has happened has happened." Rist began speaking to her, but also in part to Airlyn. "Learn from it, grow from it, and mourn those who are no longer here. But living with it, means living with it. Do not let the tragedies of life stop you from becoming who you are meant to be, young one."

The girl's face, first showing discomfort and fear, changed to a hard acknowledgement. Airlyn's eyes locked on Rist as he stood back to his full height, her knowing look one that he didn't wish to let her know that he had noticed. After a few moments, the girl stepped back and offered a shy smile before hurrying back to her parents, turning to face them. Her eyes were tight, as if holding back tears.

Jaleq cleared his throat. "We have gathered supplies for your journey. You will need them on the road to Minotatha."

Tindra gestured toward the packs resting near the door. "Weapons, food, medicine—whatever we could provide."

Breyman exhaled, glancing at Airlyn. "I suppose that means we're moving on, then."

Airlyn didn't immediately answer. She looked down at the woven bundle in her hands, her thumb tracing over the fragile stems, before nodding once.

"Yes."

Without another word, they gathered their things and prepared to leave the village behind, stepping onto the road that would take them to the Peronian city of Minotatha.

# Chapter 14: The Serpent Court

The journey to Minotatha began under an open sky, the morning sun painting the valley in gold as they left the faun village behind, their horses moving at an easy trot along the well-worn road that had carried them from Farkland Reach. The terrain stretched wide before them, rolling into endless fields of tall grass that swayed with the wind like the slow breath of the world itself.

Their first day was spent navigating the valleys, where the land rose and fell in steady undulations. Rocky outcroppings jutted from the hillsides, breaking the monotony of the grasslands, while streams trickled through narrow crevices, their waters carving pathways that had existed for generations. The air was crisp, carrying the scent of fresh earth and the occasional wildflower that dotted the plains.

By midday, the sun bore down on them, and their steady pace slowed. The road, though clear, was beginning to show signs of the land's transition. The packed dirt had softened, patches of marsh grass creeping closer to its edges. They paused briefly, consulting their map to confirm the direction. The road still led true, but the terrain was beginning to shift beneath them. It was Breyman who suggested a break, gesturing toward a nearby stream that had widened into a small lake. The water shimmered under the sunlight, clear enough to see the smooth stones beneath the surface. Airlyn hesitated at first, watching as Breyman knelt by the shore, cupping his hands to drink before turning with a mischievous grin and splashing water in her direction. She barely dodged, shooting him a glare that softened when he laughed.

Rist, silent as ever, remained mounted on his horse, watching them from the shore. He had no desire to join them, no interest in the water. It was an unnecessary indulgence, something that held no function for him. Instead, he took quiet enjoyment in their amusement, observing as Breyman disappeared beneath the surface, resurfacing with an exclamation of delight. Airlyn hesitated at first, but before she could turn away, Breyman lunged from the water, grabbing her wrist and pulling her in with a triumphant grin. She hit the water with a sharp splash, sputtering as she surfaced, glaring at him with a mix of irritation and reluctant amusement.

Rist remained where he was, unmoved, as Airlyn called out to him, but he simply tilted his head, the closest he came to acknowledgment. It was only when Breyman waded in further, encouraging Airlyn to follow, that she rolled her eyes and gave in, stepping back into the water.

Rist stood next to his horse, watching the two of them splash and play about in the water. He felt it was a waste of time, but the release of tension he felt coming from them was enough to convince him that this slight detour was worth the minor delay.

That night, as they gathered around a fire, the landscape had begun to change. The rolling valleys gave way to flatter plains, the tall grasses parting only for the occasional grove of trees. The wind carried the scent of damp soil now, a hint of the wetlands that lay ahead. They sat in a loose circle, the fire casting flickering shadows against the night.

Breyman, ever the quiet presence, tended to his horse's saddle, checking the weight of the supplies loaded within the bags. The fauns had prepared them well—dried meats, medicinal herbs, and extra water skins carefully packed alongside additional weaponry. Finally, he turned, stretching his arms behind him. "So, what were your worlds like?"

Airlyn poked at the fire with a stick, watching the embers rise. "Different. Stricter. I spent most of my time training, preparing for this."

Breyman gave her a look. "No fun at all?"

Airlyn sighed amusedly. "Depends on your definition of fun. But no, not really since I was a child."

Rist, who had been quiet since their time at the lake, finally spoke. "Mine was quieter."

Breyman turned to him, clearly intrigued. "Quieter how?"

Rist tilted his head slightly, as if considering. "Less… chaotic. More order. We had consensus."

Breyman huffed a laugh. "Sounds boring."

Rist didn't respond immediately, but there was something deliberate in the way he shifted his posture. "Not boring. Just… a different kind of existence."

Airlyn scoffed. "Sounds the same to me."

They spent the rest of the evening exchanging pieces of their pasts, trading stories that, while different in detail, still carried the same undercurrent of struggle and survival. Airlyn spoke of her training, of the long hours spent honing her skills. Breyman countered with tales of his people, of their traditions and the importance of honor in Lystran culture. Rist offered little but listened, his presence steady, absorbing everything without judgment.

By the time the fire burned low, they were no longer just traveling together. They were learning about each other.

By the second day, the grasslands began to change. The ground, once firm and dry, grew softer beneath their feet. Small pockets of water pooled in shallow dips, dark with silt. The groves of trees grew thicker, their roots tangling through the earth like veins, gnarled and twisted. The scent of damp moss and decaying wood filled the air, a stark contrast to the freshness of the valleys they had left behind.

They moved carefully, their steps measured as they adjusted to the shifting terrain. By nightfall, they camped on a raised patch of land, the distant sound of unseen creatures filling the air. The firelight barely pushed back the encroaching darkness, the humidity clinging to them like a second skin.

That night, after their laughter around the fire had died down, their conversation turned quieter, their words more thoughtful. It was Airlyn who eventually shifted the subject toward what they had been avoiding since leaving the faun village. "So what happens if we don't find him? Do we just keep pretending the Eldric can work with only three? His recklessness makes me wonder if this whole journey isn't pointless."

Rist, who had been watching the fire, spoke without looking at her. "We find the weapons. That is our task."

Airlyn scoffed. "Right. Because that makes up one of us recklessly endangering this whole process."

Rist bristled internally. "Darien made a decision to try to stop the sword from going with an agent of Cyprin to who knows where. What else would you have had him do? Let it go?"

Airlyn's voice sharpened as her temper flared, the ever-present undercurrent of frustration that defined her now boiling to the surface being conveyed in her tone.

"So you're okay with him having done that? You're okay with him being missing, possibly even dead, while we move along pretending like nothing is wrong?"

Breyman, ever the mediator, shook his head. "We have no way to search for him now. If we don't finish the rites, then nothing else will matter. The weapons are our priority."

Airlyn didn't argue, but her expression remained tight. The conversation lingered in the air even as silence settled around them, the weight of it pressing between them, creating a divide in the unity they had only barely begun to form.

On the third day, they entered the marshlands proper. The ground sucked at their boots, water pooling around their steps. The trees here were different—taller, their bark slick with moisture, their leaves hanging low and heavy. Vines draped from the branches, shifting as unseen creatures moved through them. The air was thick with the sounds of buzzing insects and distant calls of unknown animals.

Breyman wiped the sweat from his brow, glancing at Rist and Airlyn as they maneuvered their horses through the thickening marshland. The road was nearly swallowed here, its edges blurred by creeping waters and tangled roots. The sky, once vast and open, now seemed choked by the towering trees, their heavy canopies filtering the light into a hazy green. He exhaled, the damp heat settling into his fur giving him a somewhat mangey appearance. "Remind me again why we're headed to a city in the middle of all this?"

Airlyn smirked. "Because we're idiots."

Airlyn didn't argue, but her expression remained tight.

Rist sighed, growing tired of Airlyn's persistently present pessimism regarding their situation. "Because Minotatha holds what we need."

The ground sloped upward ahead, a ridge just beyond the thickest part of the swamp. They pressed on, the sight of their destination drawing them forward, the city of Minotatha waiting beyond the mist.

The first sign of Minotatha was not the towering walls or grand gates, but the scouts that emerged from the mist. They moved with the effortless grace of creatures born to the marsh, their scales shimmering faintly in the dim light filtering through the dense canopy above. The Peronia had found them long before the city was even in sight.

Rist sensed them before they revealed themselves—shapes gliding between the trees, their presence a ripple of watchful tension. When the first of them stepped onto the path, Airlyn reached for her weapon, but Breyman lifted a calming hand. The Peronia were wary, but not overtly hostile.

"You've losssst the road," one of them said, voice hissing slightly with the lilt of his people's accent. He was tall and lean, his skin a mottled green and brown, his slitted eyes unreadable. "We will correct your path."

Airlyn scowled. "I told you we should have stayed on my route."

No one responded, least of all Rist, who had long since grown tired of the argument. Instead, he extended his senses toward the lizardfolk, feeling the coiled distrust beneath their measured words. There was no welcome in their manner, only duty.

The scouts led them through a winding trail that soon merged with a more well-traveled path—packed dirt reinforced with wooden planks where the marsh threatened to reclaim it. Ruts from wagon wheels and deep hoof prints marked the route, evidence of trade and travel. It seemed they had veered from the intended road, straying into the wilder parts of the swamp where few dared to tread.

Minotatha revealed itself gradually, emerging from the mist like some great sleeping beast. Massive stone pillars rose from the waterlogged earth, their surfaces etched with intricate carvings worn smooth by time. Bridges of woven wood and vine stretched between elevated platforms, the city built up rather than out, rising above the marsh on reinforced stilts. Tall structures of carved stone and layered clay loomed in the distance, their rooftops adorned with curved spines and golden inlays that gleamed faintly even in the filtered light.

The city was alive with movement—Peronia gliding along the raised walkways, their scaled forms moving with effortless precision. Merchants barked offers in guttural tones, the scent of roasting meats and pungent spices thick in the humid air. Carts laden with goods were pulled by creatures adapted to the swamp, their broad feet keeping them from sinking into the mire. The roads leading in and out of the city were busy with trade, proving just how far they had strayed from the main path.

Rist felt the tension in the air, a subtle pressure beneath the daily life of the city. The wariness of the people extended beyond them, woven into the very fabric of Minotatha. These were not people given to trust, and their arrival had only tightened an already coiled thread.

"Something feels off here," Airlyn whispered to him, quiet enough to avoid being overheard. Rist simply nodded and kept walking forward, following the scouts.

They were led without pause through the winding streets; the scouts weaving through the throng of Peronia with ease. The crowds parted slightly as they passed, slitted eyes following their every move, murmurs rippling through the air.

They stopped before a grand structure, one of the largest they had seen—its entrance flanked by guards clad in dark leather armor reinforced with metal plating designed for mobility rather than brute defense.

They were ushered inside, past great stone archways into a vast, open chamber where the air was thick with the scent of damp stone and burning incense. As they stepped forward, the Peronia council watched them with unreadable expressions. A silence settled, heavy and expectant, before one of the seated figures finally spoke.

"You have traveled far to reach Minotatha. Allow myssssself, Boronoth, to welcome The Eldric to our hallssss. I ask you. What news do you bring from the world beyond our borderssss?" His voice carried an unhurried weight, his slitted gaze fixed on them.

Breyman exchanged a brief glance with Rist and Airlyn before answering. "Much has transpired. War has touched Farkland Reach. A great battle was fought there."

A ripple passed through the gathered Peronia, a flick of tails, a subtle shift in posture. Another council member, a female with dark green scales and gold-flecked eyes, spoke. "We knew of the battle at Farkland Reach two daysssss ago. We suspected it would come nearly a month passssst."

Airlyn frowned. "And did you send warning to Aghemnon?"

Boronoth scoffed, the sound deep and guttural. "Why would we? The affairssss of Farkland Reach hold no weight here. We do not bend our actions to the squabbles of otherssss."

Airlyn's jaw tightened, but she said nothing.

Another council member leaned forward, fingers tapping lightly against the armrest of his seat. "The weapon you seek, the bow you need to complete your ritual, is not of Minotatha. It was placed in our care long ago, a relic of the past when the cycles began. It is not ours to keep or to withhold. It belongs to the rites, to the ones who must wield it. And yet, you are not four."

A murmur passed through the chamber. Another councilor, their voice heavier with skepticism, asked, "It is true. I see only three before us, and only three were in the village of Arcadium. Where is your fourth? Why are you incomplete?"

Breyman shifted but held his composure. They had discussed this question at length on the first part of their journey. He recited their practiced answer, "Our fourth meets us at the southern sea. He was wounded in the battle at Farkland Reach and required time to recover. The rites state that the weapons must be claimed by the Eldric, but so long as it comes into the hands of one, it will reach all. The cycle will continue."

Silence stretched between them, heavy with unspoken suspicion. The Peronia did not like the answer, but they could not dispute it outright. Boronoth's gaze lingered, then he exhaled sharply through his nostrils. "It issss a risk to give over the bow while the Eldric remain fractured. But our role is to safeguard it, not dictate its use. Our duty ends when it is in your handssss."

The council fell into a moment of quiet deliberation, exchanging glances, some considering, others skeptical. Finally, one of the elder council members spoke. "The bow will be given to you, for that isssss our duty. We have no obligation beyond that."

Breyman gave a slow nod. "Then we request a place to stay for the night. We will take the bow and depart at first light."

There was a moment of silence before Boronoth gestured to one of the attendants at the side of the chamber. "Arrangementssss will be made."

But as the meeting seemed to reach its conclusion, Boronoth's gaze darkened slightly, his expression shifting. "Before you go… my sssson, Niraloth, set out on a hunt many days ago. It is unlike him to be gone so long without word. Have you by chance come across him in your travelssss?"

The air in the chamber tightened as all of their eyes turned to the three of them.

Breyman's ears flicked slightly. Airlyn stilled. Rist felt the shift beneath the surface, the undercurrent of something deeper than mere diplomacy. Corruption. Intrigue. A presence in the council that did not belong. But the greater threat, for now, was the outrage that was about to erupt.

"We must speak of his fate," Breyman said carefully.

Boronoth's expression did not change, but the tension in the room sharpened. "Sssspeak quickly, outsider."

And so they did.

By the time the words were finished, the council chamber was no longer a place of discussion but one of fury. Outrage rippled through the gathered Peronia, their anger seething like a storm held barely at bay. Voices rose, accusations spat.

"The Eldric have betrayed usssss."

"They are murderersss."

Boronoth rose from his seat, his expression dark with fury. "The death of a Peronian at your handsss is an affront we cannot overlook. You are not above the conssssequence of your actions, not even as members of the Eldric. Either you are expelled from Minotatha at onccce, or you are imprisoned to await judgment."

Murmurs spread through the chamber, some of the council shifting uneasily. Rist felt the tension rising, his senses attuned to the conflicting emotions in the room—fear, uncertainty, anger. But there was also hesitation. Many feared Boronoth, but they were not ruled by him alone.

"We are not here as enemies," Breyman said, his voice calm, measured. "We have followed the path set before us, seeking the weapons that will see Olympus saved. We did not wish for bloodshed, but neither could we stand idly by and allow threats against Arcadium to go unanswered."

A figure near the far end of the chamber leaned forward, his golden eyes narrowing. "And yet a Peronian liessss dead. Does thissss not concern you?"

"It concerns us deeply," Breyman admitted. His calm, low tones were useful in the tense situation, Rist thought in another life he would make a wonderful politician. "But we cannot undo what has happened. We can only move forward, fulfilling the duty that binds us all. Niraloth attacked a member of The Eldric. He did not do so knowingly, but we acted as we had to. Not just to save our lives, but for the lives of your world and our own."

Another councilor spoke up, this time an older Peronian with a regal bearing. "Boronoth, you let your grief blind you. You have long isolated ussss from the other nations, pushing us further into seclusion. We all mourn Niraloth, but this isss not the way. We cannot let one death unravel what has been set in motion for millennia."

Boronoth's nostrils flared, but he said nothing. His tail lashed once behind him, a clear sign of barely restrained rage. When no one else spoke in his defense, he exhaled sharply. "Then I will not ssssit in this chamber and allow my sssson's killers to be sheltered like honored guests. You have made your choice." His voice was venomous, filled with a promise of retribution.

Without another word, he turned sharply on his heel and stormed out of the chamber, his heavy footfalls echoing in the silence he left behind.

The room remained tense even after his departure, but the immediate threat had passed. One of the council members turned toward them. "We would advise you to remain within the capital for now. Boronoth will not stay quiet, and his wrath may stir others. You will be given quarters and a meal in the hall in your honor. It would be best if you were not seen until matters settle."

Rist exchanged a glance with Breyman and Airlyn. There was little choice in the matter.

The Peronian guide led them through winding corridors that opened onto a vast platform overlooking the city. The path was carved into the mountainside itself, twisting like the roots of an ancient tree, each step echoing against the polished stone beneath their boots. The air smelled of damp earth and burning oil, mingling with the faint metallic tang of something alchemical.

When they reached their quarters, a pair of Peronian attendants opened the heavy wooden doors, revealing the chambers within. The room was dim, illuminated only by lanterns of thick, slow-burning oil that cast undulating shadows along the intricately carved walls. The markings told stories of hunts, battles, and victories long past, their patterns blending seamlessly with the swirling designs of the reinforced wooden doors.

Rist stepped forward, trailing his fingers along one of the carved murals. The texture beneath his gloves was rough, uneven, like the echoes of something alive beneath his touch. Each mark told a story, and he turned to their guide, a Peronian named Zathrin, to ask about them.

Zathrin flicked his golden eyes toward the carvings, his tongue flicking briefly from between his lips. "Thessse walls hold the recordsss of our people. Every warrior, every hunt, every challenge that made us what we are." He gestured to one intricate carving of a Peronian figure standing before what looked like a colossal serpent. "Here, thisss one tells the tale of the firssst hunt. Our people were not always dominators of the swamps. There were othersss before us, creatures we had to conquer to call thisss place home. Thisss one, the World Fang, was the last of them. Its death marked the beginning of Minotatha's rise."

Rist studied the carving, understanding more about their hosts in that moment than through all their interactions so far. These were people who had shaped their history with claw and blood, their survival etched into the very walls of their home. The texture beneath his gloves was rough, uneven, like the echoes of something alive beneath his touch. Every symbol spoke of survival, of an unbroken lineage of warriors and hunters who had carved their stories into the stone itself. His gaze drifted to the bed— layered with thick woven mats and furs, practical for warmth but lacking any real comfort. A basin of still water sat in the corner, the surface occasionally disturbed by unseen currents, sending ripples that glowed faintly in the flickering light.

Breyman let out a low whistle as he set his pack down on the wooden stand beside his bed. "They may not like outsiders, but they certainly respect hospitality." Airlyn grunted in response, already running a hand over the reinforced wood of the door as if testing how easily it could be barred shut.

After settling in, they were summoned to the feast. The hall was filled with Peronians, some standing in clusters, others coiled comfortably on cushioned seats. As they took their places at the long banquet table, a Peronian councilor with emerald scales and a thick ridge along his brow addressed them directly.

"Outssiders rarely dine in our hallsss," he mused, his tone carrying neither welcome nor hostility. "It is a rare thing, but hospitality isss a law older than our city. You are guestsss, until tomorrow."

Breyman nodded, taking his seat carefully. "Your people have been most accommodating. We appreciate the welcome."

"It isss not always given so freely," another councilor said, his slitted gaze flicking toward the empty seat where Boronoth should have been. "Sssome of us would have preferred another outcccome."

Airlyn met his gaze with a raised brow, "And yet here we are," Her tone was almost playful.

The Peronian offered a slow nod before reaching for his goblet. "Yesss. Here you are. Let usss eat."

The table was adorned with plates of slick, glistening cuts of fish, coiled serpentine meats, and bowls of thick, gelatinous stew. The scent was strong, earthy and pungent. Breyman and Airlyn took careful bites, their expressions neutral but their pace slow, determined to be polite. Rist, however, merely observed. He had no need for food in the way they did, and even if he had, this would not be it. The textures alone—slimy, viscous—

held no appeal. He was glad that consumption was not something he required. Though he would need to restore himself soon.

As the night wore on, the sibilant speech of the Peronians filled the hall, their elongated "s" sounds slipping through conversations like reeds brushing against each other in the wind. At first, it was noticeable, a constant reminder of the alien nature of their hosts. But the more Rist listened, the more his mind adjusted, until the sound became nothing more than the natural cadence of speech, no different than the dialects of the other lands they had traveled through. Eventually, he ceased to notice it at all.

Between bites of their meal, the Peronians spoke of governance and trade, their hushed words tinged with cautious diplomacy. One councilor leaned toward another, murmuring about tensions with a neighboring city over contested hunting grounds. Another lamented the difficulties of maintaining proper supply routes through the marshlands.

"The trades with the westerners have grown… difficult," one of them admitted, his claws tapping against his goblet. "They demand more, yet offer less. We may need to reassess our terms."

"If Boronoth had his way," another councilor muttered, "we would abandon those trades entirely. He has no patience for their kind of politics."

Breyman listened intently, his brow furrowing slightly. "It sounds as though your city is at odds not just with outsiders, but within its own leadership."

The councilor regarded him for a long moment before inclining his head. "such is the way of all rulerships. Power is never held in equal hands." As the meal wound down, the Peronians returned to their conversations, the murmur of voices blending into the background. A servant approached and bowed slightly. "Your quarters have been prepared. You may retire when you wish."

Rist, Breyman, and Airlyn exchanged glances before standing. The Peronians offered no further words, only nods of acknowledgment as the three left the hall.

Back in their quarters, they settled in, the glow of the lanterns flickering against the walls. Airlyn leaned against the doorway, arms crossed. "So, what now?"

Breyman sat on the edge of his bed, exhaling. "We wait. Boronoth won't stay quiet. He may not have been able to turn the council against us tonight, but that doesn't mean he won't try something else."

"We should assume he will," Rist said. "And we should be ready."

Airlyn ran a hand through her hair. "Great. Another night of waiting. Love that."

Breyman offered a small smile. "Better than another fight."

Rist said nothing, stepping toward the window, peering out over the city. He remained still as the others spoke, his mind reaching outward, sensing the undercurrent of unease that still clung to Minotatha. He did not sleep like they did, and tonight, like every other, he would stand watch while they rested.

"Get some sleep," Breyman muttered as he lay back. "Tomorrow might be worse."

Airlyn sighed and turned toward her bed, but before closing her eyes, she shot Rist a glance. "Wake me if something happens."

Rist did not turn from the window. "I will."

As the meal wound down, the Peronians returned to their conversations, the murmur of voices blending into the background. A servant approached and bowed slightly. "Your quarters have been prepared. You may retire when you wish."

Rist, Breyman, and Airlyn exchanged glances before standing. The Peronians offered no further words, only nods of acknowledgment as the three left the hall.

Back in their quarters, they settled in, the glow of the lanterns flickering against the walls. Airlyn leaned against the doorway, arms crossed. "So, what now?"

Breyman sat on the edge of his bed, exhaling. "We wait. Boronoth won't stay quiet. He may not have been able to turn the council against us today, but I worry he may try something else."

"We should assume he will," Rist said. "Else they wouldn't have recommended that we stay here. And we should be ready."

Airlyn ran a hand through her hair. "Great. Another night of waiting. Love that."

Breyman offered a small smile. "Better than a fight."

"Says you."

Rist said nothing, stepping toward the window, peering out over the city. He remained still as the others spoke, his mind reaching outward, sensing the undercurrent of unease that still clung to Minotatha. He did not sleep like they did, and tonight, like every other, he would stand watch while they rested.

"Get some sleep," Breyman muttered as he lay back. "Tomorrow might be worse."

Airlyn sighed and turned toward her bed, but before closing her eyes, she shot Rist a glance. "Wake me if something happens."

Rist did not turn from the window. "I will."

# Chapter 15: The Hidden Trap

As the night deepened, Breyman and Airlyn eventually succumbed to sleep, but Rist remained where he was, unmoving, watching with his back to the wall and facing the window he had been standing at when the two had dozed off. He kept his vigil in the quiet darkness, listening to the rhythm of the city beyond, waiting.

The sound was faint, nearly lost in the hush of the night, but Rist heard it—a slight creak of wood. His gaze flicked toward the window just in time to see it shift open, a shadow slipping through. Rist felt the figure, there was intent, but the rest was somehow strangely muted as though his edges were blurred. He found this strangely fascinating, but had to put that aside.

The figure moved with trained efficiency, a blade gleaming in the moonlight as they advanced toward Airlyn's sleeping form. Rist waited, holding position until the right moment. The arm raised, dagger catching the reflection of the largest of Olympus' moons. He reacted instantly, crossing the space between them with a speed that sent his cloak whipping behind him. His hand caught the assassin's wrist mid-strike, twisting sharply. A grunt of pain followed, the knife clattering to the ground after betraying its owner.

The scuffle was brief, sharp movements exchanged in rapid succession. The assassin was skilled but had not accounted for Rist's speed and precision. A misstep on the assailant's part, a well-placed strike from Rist, and the struggle ended with the assassin's face pinned against the wall, one arm wrenched behind their back.

Airlyn jolted awake, her dagger in hand, eyes darting to the scene unfolding before her. Breyman was already on his feet, tense and ready for a fight.

"Who sent you?" Airlyn demanded, stepping closer, her voice sharp.

The assassin was breathing heavily, their body limp against Rist's unyielding grip before sliding limply to the stone floor. Blood seeped from a wound on their side, staining the dark fabric they wore. But their lips curled into something close to a smirk. "You are too late," the assassin rasped. "The cycle is shifting. The ones who stand in the way will be removed."

Airlyn's gaze hardened on the man as she knelt to look at him in his eyes. Her voice took on a strange softness, as if talking to a child.

"What does that mean? Who sent you?"

The assassin chuckled weakly. "Cyprin's reign will be restored. Plans that stretch back centuries are coming to fruition, and our lord will reward us for our service. We are everywhere. You cannot stop us. Kill one and another will rise."

They all exchanged worried looks.

"The end is coming," the assassin whispered.

And then his breath left him.

The journey back to the council chamber was tense, the weight of the assassin's attack pressing upon them like the thick stone walls of the Peronian stronghold. Though the assassin had died, the implications of his actions lingered, unspoken but deeply felt.

When they entered the chamber, the remaining council members were already waiting, their expressions unreadable. Airlyn wasted no time.

"A man tried to kill us!" she shouted, her voice reverberating off the stone walls. "An assassin, bold enough to strike against us in the heart of your city! And you sit here, silent?"

A ripple of unease spread through the council. One of the elders straightened in his chair, eyes dark with concern. "This is troubling, but it does not mean—"

"It means everything!" Airlyn cut in. "This was not some common criminal. He knew who we were. He was waiting for us. Who else knows? Who else has been watching?"

Breyman folded his arms, his massive form towering over the table. "The assassin did not act alone. Someone sent him. Someone with knowledge of our presence."

The council exchanged glances, hesitating, before one of them finally spoke. "We have reason to believe Boronoth may be involved."

Silence hung thick in the chamber. Rist turned his head slightly toward the speaker, absorbing the words. "And what exactly do you mean by that?"

The elder sighed. "For some time, we questioned his loyalties, especially considering his recent absences. We tried to keep eyes on him, but he moves carefully. We do not know where he has traveled to."

Airlyn's expression darkened. "So you locked us in here, not to protect us, but to keep us from interfering with whatever he's planning?"

The elder held up a hand. "We did what we thought necessary to maintain order. If Boronoth is truly conspiring against us, then our position is more fragile than we believed."

Another council member hesitated before speaking. "We have heard... whispers."

Airlyn scoffed. "Whispers? A man tried to gut us, and you call it whispers?"

The elder continued, unshaken. "Rumors of a cult—followers of Cyprin—growing in the shadows. Not just here in Peronia, but in other cities as well. We have no proof, no names, only murmurs among traders and scattered reports of disappearances."

Airlyn's glare was sharp as a blade. "And yet you said nothing? You chose silence over action?"

Another councilor shifted uncomfortably. "We did not wish to spread fear without certainty. Minotatha thrives on order. A panic could be as dangerous as an unseen enemy."

Airlyn stepped forward, hands clenched at her sides. "Well, now you have certainty. The assassin's blood is proof enough."

A heavy pause followed. Then, one of the council elders spoke, his voice firm. "If the cult exists within our city, then the bow must remain locked away. We cannot risk placing it in further danger."

Breyman's brow furrowed. "But that is exactly why we need it. To fight against threats like this."

Another council member shook her head. "Not while we are vulnerable. If Cyprin's followers truly walk among us, revealing the bow now would be folly."

The council elder sighed. "The weight on the scales has changed. If you wish to claim the bow, then the path forward is clear. Root out this cult. Remove the risk. Only then can we move the bow safely."

Rist turned his head toward them, his voice measured. "You didn't want us in the city before. You wanted us locked away until we were useful to you. But now that you need something, you're willing to give us more freedom? Convenient."

Airlyn's jaw tightened. "And if we refuse?"

The elder's voice was calm, unwavering. "Then the bow remains where it is. You may have come here seeking it, but you are not the first to demand something of us. Peronia does not barter with unknown dangers. Before you lecture us, know that we understand what is at stake with the cycles. And it is those stakes that put us all in agreement that the bow cannot be put in jeopardy."

Breyman let out a slow exhale, glancing at Rist and Airlyn. They could not simply take the bow by force. Doing so would turn the entire city against them. The council had backed them into a corner, and they knew it.

"We have no choice," Rist murmured. "If we want the bow, we do their work for them."

Silence settled over the chamber. The meaning was clear: the bow would remain hidden, and if the Eldric wished to claim it, they would first have to root out the cult themselves.

The days that followed were grueling. The trio moved through the city like ghosts, speaking with merchants, dock workers, and tavern keepers, listening for any trace of the cult's influence. They had little to show for their efforts.

They spent mornings planning, mapping out their next leads, afternoons in the streets, weaving between wary Peronians, and nights poring over any scraps of information they could find. Conversations led to dead ends, names to empty houses, and suspicion to nothing but whispers.

Breyman sighed. "We're missing something. The cult is here, but they're careful. Too careful. We need to make them come to us."

Rist turned his head slightly, listening to the city's pulse. "We should push harder. If we become enough of a problem, they won't be able to ignore us."

Their plan took shape—applying pressure, asking the right questions to the wrong people, forcing the cult's hand. It worked.

On the fifth day, they were directed to a prisoner, a man detained by the city guard for reasons unrelated to the cult. But the moment they stepped into his cell, Rist felt it—a presence, but blurred, obscured, as if something was shielding him. The prisoner refused to speak, his gaze unwavering, his silence absolute.

Rist kept the revelation to himself. He still hadn't told Airlyn or Breyman about his ability, and now wasn't the time. He took the amulet and stuck it within the deep dark folds of his cloak, slipping it into a leather pouch to prevent it from touching his being.

By the seventh day, exhaustion had set deep into their bones. The investigation felt endless, a cycle of questioning and dead ends. The city had its own rhythm, and they were struggling to find a foothold in it.

They sat at a small open-air eatery in the merchant quarter, watching the ebb and flow of the city around them. The streets were alive with the shouts of vendors, the clatter of hooves against cobblestone, and the laughter of children darting between stalls. The scent of roasting meats and spiced bread filled the air, mingling with the sharp tang of freshly tanned leather and the sweet aroma of fruit carts.

Airlyn rubbed her temples. "We can't go back to the council empty-handed again. They'll write us off as useless."

"We need a new approach," Breyman rumbled. "Every path we take leads back to silence."

Rist sat with deceptive ease, his posture relaxed as he observed the market around them. "People know something. But they're afraid."

Breyman nodded. "We need to show them they can trust us."

A moment of silence settled between them, interrupted only by the din of the city. Airlyn took a slow breath, letting the sounds wash over her. "We've pushed so hard. Maybe we need to stop forcing our way in. Maybe we need to listen more."

Breyman leaned forward slightly. "So we stop chasing and start watching?"

"Something like that," Airlyn murmured.

Before another word could be spoken, Rist stiffened. First two blurred outlines. Then five. Then a dozen. His head tilted slightly.

"Get ready," he said quietly.

The first attack came fast. A blade flashed, aimed for Airlyn's throat. She moved with precise efficiency, twisting away and countering in one fluid motion. Her sword was an extension of herself, swift and unrelenting, cutting down the first attacker in a single, lethal stroke.

Breyman was a wall of brute force, his axe cleaving through the air with terrifying momentum. He fought with heavy, deliberate strikes, each swing meant to break through defenses and leave nothing standing.

Rist moved in the gaps, his dagger flicking out with surgical precision. A crossbow bolt fired, striking an attacker between the ribs. He was a shadow, a whisper of movement between the chaos.

The fight spilled into the streets. Airlyn danced between foes, her movements sharp and economical, countering aggression with ruthless efficiency. Breyman tore through opponents like a battering ram, his sheer size and strength forcing their enemies to give way.

Rist kept his distance, striking from the periphery. A flick of his wrist sent another bolt into a lunging cultist's leg. Another, a clean cut to the throat. He never wasted movement, never overcommitted.

They were winning—but the cultists kept coming.

The attackers began to retreat, vanishing into the narrow alleys. Without hesitation, the trio gave chase, their boots hammering against the stone as they pursued their fleeing foes into the tunnels beneath the city.

The passages twisted and turned, leading them deeper into the unknown. Rist slowed his pace, his head tilting slightly as he focused on the dim shapes shifting ahead. Something was wrong. The blurred outlines he had sensed before were no longer scattered—now they were gathering, clustering in pockets of waiting silence. He turned his head toward the others, his voice low.

"They're ahead of us. More than before."

Airlyn shot him a sharp look. "And you know this how?"

Rist hesitated only for a second. "I can feel them. Not like before, not emotions exactly. Just their presence. It's… clouded, as if something is blocking me, but I know they're there."

Airlyn's expression darkened. "And when exactly were you going to tell us about this ability?"

Breyman shifted, his grip tightening around his axe. "Now's not the time, Airlyn. If he can sense them, he can lead us through."

Airlyn didn't back down. "So what else have you been keeping from us, Rist? How much have you been reading us this whole time?"

Rist's voice was calm, measured. "This isn't about you. This is about surviving what's waiting ahead."

Breyman exhaled sharply. "Enough. Airlyn, you'll get your answers later. For now, we follow Rist's lead."

Airlyn clenched her jaw but nodded. "Fine. But we're not done with this."

Rist took the lead, his steps carefully placed. The air was thick with damp, the scent of rot and something older than the city itself clinging to the walls. Their torches flickered, casting twisting shadows that made the tunnels feel smaller, more suffocating. Water dripped somewhere in the distance, each drop echoing unnaturally loud in the stillness.

They moved forward, their breathing quiet, their footsteps controlled. The passage narrowed, funneling them toward a waiting darkness. Rist felt it again—a gathering of blurred shapes just beyond the dim glow of their eyeline. The three continued cautiously forward as they stepped into an open chamber.

Torches flared to life, casting jagged shadows along the damp stone walls. The chamber was wide, its ceiling lost to darkness, and the air was thick with the scent of stagnant water and cold stone. Boronoth stood opposite them, his posture at ease but his presence suffocating. He took a step forward, the sound of his boots echoing in the silence.

"You took your time," Boronoth said, his voice carrying across the chamber like a rumble of distant thunder. "But it doesn't matter. It was always going to end here."

Airlyn shifted her stance, sword raised, her glare unwavering. "This isn't how this ends, Boronoth. We're not finished yet."

Boronoth smiled, slow and deliberate, before a small chuckle. "No, you're finished. You just haven't realized it yet." He let the words settle, watching their reactions carefully before continuing. "You've been led in circles, chasing shadows, thinking you still had a chance to claim what was never meant for you."

Breyman's jaw clenched. "Then this was all a farce."

"A necessary one," Boronoth admitted. "To keep you occupied, to keep you running in circles while we removed you from the equation. My plan was to simply kill you. But plans change. You stopped my assassin." His expression darkened, and for a moment, there was something raw in his gaze. "I would have liked to kill you myself. Especially you, Rist. After what you did to my son."

Rist said nothing, his head tilted ever so slightly. He was watching, listening, waiting.

"But," Boronoth continued, his hissing tone icy and filled with malice, "that privilege has been denied to me. I have orders to bring you to Olympus. Cyprin wishes to meet you himself."

Airlyn's grip on her blade tightened. "We're not going anywhere with you."

Boronoth laughed loudly then, a deep, humorless sound filled with hisses and scrapes of his people's tongue grating against their ears. "You can struggle all you want. But this has been over for days."

He gestured, and from the shadows along the chamber walls, crossbowmen stepped forward, their weapons already trained on the three of them. The steel tips gleamed in the flickering torchlight.

"You should know," Boronoth said, "Cyprin has been preparing for this possibility. The amulet you found—it was his design. A precaution against you, Master Rist."

Rist felt the cold claw of unease curl around his being. He reached out with his senses—and found nothing. No emotions, no blurred outlines, nothing but a void where there should have been presence. He tested the other aspects of his abilities, the ones he had rarely spoken of and had yet to use. They, too, escaped him.

Boronoth smiled as understanding settled over Rist's features. "Yes. He knows what you are. Even the things your kind would rather keep secret. He is who gave us the ability to shield our emotions from you. Frustrating to be restricted to only your own mind, isn't it? Like the rest of us?"

If he could have, Rist would have shivered.

Airlyn took a step forward. "We won't be pawns in this."

Boronoth sighed, as if growing bored of their conversation. "You don't have a choice."

Airlyn's eyes darted between the bolts aimed at them and Boronoth. Breyman rolled his shoulders, a muscle in his jaw twitching. Rist's mind raced, but the suffocating absence in his awareness made it impossible to see the way forward. The lack of feeling was oppressively distracting.

Boronoth took another slow step forward, his expression shifting from amusement to something colder, more calculating. "Do you understand now? You were never meant to succeed. The council strung you along like puppets while we ensured your failure. While you asked your questions and chased shadows, we had already won."

Airlyn's fingers flexed around the grip of her sword, her eyes burning with defiance. "You can gloat all you want, but we're not going with you."

Boronoth  rolled his eyes and chuckled, slow and deliberate. "You are, though. You always were. Whether you walk willingly or are dragged unconscious makes no difference to me." He lifted a hand, and the crossbowmen took a step closer, their bolts gleaming.

Breyman tensed but didn't move. He was calculating, waiting, but there was no escape. Not now.

Boronoth withdrew something from his belt at last— a transition orb, identical to the one Tahmer had used to spirit away Darien and the sword, its smooth surface pulsing faintly. He cupped it in the leather pouch that had contained it. A barrier against the orbs ability to transport the user to wherever the orb lead to. "There's no shame in accepting the inevitable." He sneered as he extended it toward them. "Touch it."

The silence stretched, thick and suffocating.

The smooth sphere pulsed faintly in his grip. "You can fight, but you know how this ends."

None of them moved.

Boronoth stepped closer, extending the orb. "Touch. It."

Silence. They were stuck. They had no choice. If they fought, they would be cut down by the bolts of Boronoth's crossbows and Olympus would be doomed. If they went wherever Boronoth was trying to take them, they may find some way to escape. However unlikely that might seem.

At least we may be reunited with Darien

Rist thought to himself before each of them moved forward.

On Boronoth's count, they placed their hands against the sphere.

The world vanished in a swirl of blue light.

# Chapter 16: The Ravine Edge

Darien could no longer be sure of how long he had truly been in the valley. By his own reckoning, a month had passed, but he knew better. Time flowed differently here, stretched and compressed in ways that defied his understanding. He had learned to let go of such concerns. It was pointless to measure the days when they melted together so seamlessly.

Eating had long since become unnecessary. He no longer felt hunger gnawing at him, though thirst was another matter. Drinking remained a pleasure too refreshing to surrender, the cool water like liquid clarity as it slid down his throat. He had grown comfortable with the ebb and flow of magic within him, using it instinctively now. He could enhance his movements with speed, summon flames to warm the cool evenings, and call forth water when he needed it. Each spell felt more natural, as if his body had always known how to wield this power and only now remembered.

His injury rarely troubled him anymore. The old pain and the convulsions that once plagued him had dulled to a whisper at the edge of his awareness. When he felt it rising, he had learned to pull back—dial down his intensity and allow himself to recover without being forced to stop completely. He had mastered control, a balance between power and restraint.

But restraint was not in his nature. Not truly. As his mastery grew, so too did his curiosity. He tested the boundaries of his abilities, sometimes diving into spells and techniques he should not have. Often, he would pose questions to Whyn—questions that earned him nothing but a disapproving shake of the head.

"You're not ready for that yet."

"Why not?"

Whyn would never answer directly, only shift the subject and push him into a different vein of study, one more suited to his current studies. Darien accepted this at first, but the more it happened, the more it grated at him. He felt something stirring beneath the surface of his lessons, something deliberately hidden from him.

His studies broadened in unexpected ways. He read of spellcasters of old—wielders of immense power, those who had shaped the world with their gifts. Yet their names were conspicuously absent, their identities erased from history. Only their deeds remained. The more he read, the more familiar their stories became, echoes of something he had learned at The Academy, half-forgotten lessons whispering in his mind. But when he tried to place them, they slipped through his grasp like mist.

"Magicians in the past would usually spend time focusing in on single branches of magic." Whyn said one day to him as Darien had bend fire between his fingers, his focus that day on control and precision and finer control over the stream of energy.

"Why? There's so many uses, why pick one?" Darien asked incredulously.

"It's a matter of focus and ability. Some magicians do better with various forms of magic. Fire, Water, Air, Speed, Lightning, even using the ethers to alter people's perceptions or thoughts. Some simply had abilities that were stronger in areas than others."

"So, eventually I'll have to focus on one type of magic?" Darien asked, mildly disappointed.

Whyn hesitated, "Not necessarily, no."

Darien looked back at his mentor apprehensively.

Whyn took some steps around him, monitoring his progress, using his own power to prod and influence the flames twisting their way through Darien's fingers.

"A select number of magicians were especially gifted. They were able to expand past a single subject and learn not just control, but mastery over a wide variety of subjects."

"Was Cyprin one of those people?"

Whyn looked at him sharply, some expression on his face that Darien couldn't read. Like he had been wounded somehow.

After several long silent seconds, "He was."

Darien allowed the silence to continue as he moved the flames into a spiral pattern in front of him, allowing the flame to start from the center and work its way out, maintaining the flow of fire in its wake and growing the spiral larger with each second.

"As was Whytaren, the one who cast the spell three millennia ago to imprison Cyprin. Their break was one of the single greatest tragedies in history."

"What happened?" Darien asked.

His master sat himself with his back against the tree, observing the control his pupil had with quiet pride.

"The histories aren't clear. But the fallout was what has caused the cycles. Clearly, Cyprin turned away from working with his allies and friends as part of the schools of magic and turned instead to gaining as much power as he could. The details are not recorded anywhere that I am aware of."

"I wonder why?" Darien asked, but it was only half a question. He didn't expect an answer, and didn't get one.

Whyn moved on, "To address your most immediate question, whether you'll have to choose a path, that isn't yet obvious to me. You seem to have the inate ability to control multiple types of magic but," Whyn gestured to Darien's spiral which was now reaching almost 10 feet wide, "You seem to have found a preference for flame."

Darien smiled and released his control of the ethers which healed the rifts he had made in the cloud of each and continued their invisible journey through the universe.

"Fire is just...cool."

Darien smiled at the word play.

Whyn nodded with a slight uptick in the corner of his mouth, "However, I have also seen you have proficiency with several other forms of magic. Your speed abilities, that is quickening your movements in relation to the world, seem particularly strong. You still have much improvement to make, however your progress and dedication to the tasks helps us speed along this process."

"Why is that?"

"Why is what?"

Darien reached down to pick at the grass as he sat across from Whyn in the grass.

"Why can I just...do magic so easily?"

Whyn stayed quiet for several moments.

"You know?" Asked Darien.

"No. No one can know. Often it comes from lineage but that is not always the case, and some children of magicians can't do magic at all. And your parents-"

Whyn stopped, but it was too late.

Darien pressed further. "But do you know who my parents were?"

Whyn hesitated, then relented, his voice measured and neutral. "Your mother was a kind and gentle soul. She carried a quiet strength that few noticed at first, but it was there in everything she did. She was ill, long before she ever realized. By the time she knew, it was too late."

Darien remained silent, watching Whyn carefully.

"Your father was a foolish man," Whyn's harshness sur-prised Darien. The juxtaposition of his tone with how he described Darien's mother was almost shocking, but his tone softened as he continued. "Your father was... different. He was determined, ambitious in ways that made him restless. But when he met your mother, all of that seemed to settle. She gave him purpose beyond himself, something he had never known before." Whyn's tone did not waver, did not betray anything as before beyond simple recitation of fact. "Their love was... unexpected. They were never meant to be together, though neither of them knew it. And when she died, he unraveled. The world no longer made sense to him without her in it."

Darien frowned, his fingers pressing into the grass beneath him. "So he just left me?"

Whyn inclined his head slightly. "He made a choice. Perhaps not a perfect one, but one he thought was best. He took you somewhere he believed you could have a future. The Academy was known to him, a place of knowledge and discipline, a place where you would be safe." He paused. "A place where you would not have to live in the shadow of what he had lost."

Darien studied his face, searching for something deeper, but Whyn's expression remained unreadable. "And he never came back?"

Whyn shook his head. "He let go of you the moment he left you there. Not because he didn't care, but because he feared what he would become if he held on."

Something twisted inside Darien, but he forced himself to exhale slowly. "And you knew all this?"

Whyn met his gaze evenly. "I know many things, Darien, and now, so do you. Think of who and what you have discovered me to be since coming to this valley. Is it really so hard to believe I would have these answers?"

Darien shook his head. He supposed not.

"Do you know where he is? Is he alive?"

Whyn's expression was unreadable for a long moment before he finally spoke. "If I did, I would tell you," he said carefully. "But following your mother's death, your father became a man who did not wish to be found. He sought out places beyond the reach of others, places where few could follow. If he still lives, I suspect he remains in such a place now."

Silence hovered over them for many long minutes as Darien sat with this new found information. The information twisted into his brain, finding ways into his identity as he had never thought it would when he dreamed of who his parents had been. He was him, and their identity didn't change that. But somehow it did. The information filled a small hole that had been in him, but not completely.

He examined that bit of himself then, allowing introspection to take over. What was missing? What didn't he know?

It doesn't change who I am, he decided consciously. But my past still helps me to know myself. Just as I'm learning the past of this world.

He sat in silence a little longer before simply saying.

"Thank you."

Whyn took the compliment in silence, simply enjoying the task of weaving the grass together as he made the last few weaves to his basket, setting it on his palm to examine the work.

"I think that is enough for today," Whyn said, standing and beginning the walk to his home. "Are you coming?"

Darien sat still for a moment, looking at the basket Whyn had left in the imprint his body that had taken his place in the grass.

"I think I'm going to stay a while, if that's okay with you, Master?"

Whyn said nothing, simply looking at Darien for several seconds, before nodding and walking away.

The next morning, their training began anew. Darien had spent the night in solitary thought about their conversation the day before. But as Whyn had pointed out to him numerous times, there were simply more important tasks at hand. The fate of worlds rested on his success at his studies.

He threw himself into them with even more reckless abandon, absorbing information at a prodigious rate. He found one book that taught him how to twist the ethers into such a pattern that it allowed him to slow the perception of time around him, while he could continue to think at a faster pace. He used this to his advantage every evening to read until his eyes watered. Whyn had entered his room one evening to see him at work. Darien ended the spell and looked up. Whyn simply nodded, approval at Darien's focus evident in his expressions.

Every now and then, he still would pick up a text that Whyn would immediately take away. "Not that one," he would say, replacing it with something else. At first, Darien accepted this too. But now, each book taken from him felt like a secret being withheld, a door slammed shut before he could glimpse what lay beyond.

The days, the weeks—perhaps even the months—bled together. His studies consumed him. Magic was no longer something he did; it was something he was. Information was simply absorbed and retained.

"It's time you learned other forms of magic," Whyn said one morning, setting aside their usual lessons. in form and precision. "You've come far, but magic is more than fire, water, and speed. It's more than force and control. There are subtler arts, and it is time you began to understand them."

Darien listened intently as Whyn spoke of the transitions. The movement of objects through space, of bending distance to one's will. The theory behind the transitions fascinated him—how one could step from one place to another in an instant, as if the space between had never existed. He was also taught the art of seeing across distances, of focusing his mind to view things and people from afar.

These lessons filled him with excitement, but also with questions. If he could move objects through space, could he one day move himself? If he could look upon the world from afar, could he one day see beyond this valley? And if the transitions that Darien could make would take one from world to world… what did that truly mean for him and his ability to return home after all this was completed?

He did not ask these questions aloud. He knew what Whyn's answer would be.

"You're not ready for that yet."

But Darien was beginning to think otherwise.

The morning mist curled low through the valley, wrapping around the tall grass in lazy tendrils. Darien stood outside Whyn's dwelling, rolling his shoulders as the cool air settled on his skin. Today, something was different. There was an expectancy in the way Whyn watched him, a deliberateness to the stillness between them.

"You've grown comfortable," Whyn said at last, breaking the silence. His voice carried across the clearing, calm and measured.

Darien smirked. "Isn't that the point?"

Whyn ignored the comment. "There is a task for you today." He motioned toward the tree line at the valley's edge. "You will venture into the valley, following a path that I have made for you to retrieve something for me."

Darien turned toward the trees, his pulse quickening with anticipation. He had ventured into them before, but never with purpose. "What am I looking for?"

Whyn's lips twitched in something that wasn't quite a smile. "A token. You'll know it when you find it. Use your magic to find it, but be mindful of how you use it."

Darien exhaled, nodding. Darien flexed his fingers, rolling his shoulders as he stepped forward. He cast a glance at Whyn, but his teacher's expression remained unreadable. There was no further instruction, no reassurance—just expectation. Darien let out a slow breath and focused, reaching out with his magic, letting it pulse of exploratory energy wind outward like a ripple across still water. The valley whispered back to him, hidden traces of energy threading through the land like unseen roots.

Darien stepped forward, following a path he had never taken before. The valley stretched ahead, familiar yet unknown. He walked in silence, the rhythmic crunch of his boots against the earth filling the air. As he moved, the landscape shifted subtly. The trees here were thicker, their bark darker and ridged, their leaves broader. Strange flowers dotted the underbrush—deep violet petals curling at the edges, luminescent blue veins running through their stems. He bent to inspect one, running his fingers along its surface, feeling the cool, waxy texture.

The sound of trickling water caught his ear, drawing him deeper into the valley. A thin stream cut through the forest, carving a path through moss-covered stones. He crouched beside it, dipping his fingers into the water, relishing the chill. The sensation grounded him, a reminder that he was far from the lessons inside Whyn's dwelling.

Then, like the first faint breath of wind before a storm, he felt it through his magic that was searching the grassy . A pulse.

Not a sound, not a sight—something in the ethers shifted, tugging at him, subtle but insistent. He straightened, his breath steadying as he reached out with his magic. The pulse flickered again, like a ripple across still water, leading him further in.

His steps grew lighter as he followed, his mind sharpening to the sensation guiding him forward. The valley, once still, now felt like it was humming around him, a presence unseen but undeniable. He had no name for what he was feeling, only that it was *there*—pulling him onward.

Then the valley changed. The air grew thick, heavier. The trees twisted closer together, their gnarled roots pushing through the earth in chaotic knots. The sense of openness was gone, replaced with an oppressive silence that pressed against his senses.. He reached out with his magic, threading it through the valley, searching. It was difficult at first—like trying to grasp mist—but soon he began to pick up traces, faint signatures hidden beneath the layers of nature. He moved carefully, stepping over roots and pushing through the thick brush while allowing his senses to expand.

Darien pressed forward, weaving his way through the trees, feeling the shift in the ethers around him. He stepped carefully, his eyes scanning the path ahead, when suddenly, the trees parted, revealing a deep ravine cutting through the valley floor. The sight made him stop in his tracks.

On the other side, partially hidden among the rocks and twisted roots, something gleamed faintly. The token.

His breath steadied as he looked for a way across. The walls of the ravine were steep, slick with moss and moisture. There was no clear way to climb down and back up without significant risk. He tested a rock with his foot, but it crumbled beneath his weight, tumbling into the depths below.

Transitions weren't new to him, but they were unpracticed, unstable. He had used them under Whyn's supervision, but this was different—this was on his own. He took a steadying breath, then reached out, weaving the ethers around him. A sphere of blue light flickered to life, humming softly at his feet.

The world twisted, space folding in on itself for the briefest moment. Then, he was on the other side. The ground beneath his feet solidified, but nausea slammed into him, a wave of vertigo that sent him staggering. He dropped to a knee, swallowing back the sick feeling roiling in his gut.

A rustling in the bushes made him stop. He turned sharply, scanning the dense foliage, magic curling at his fingertips as he gathered a fresh batch of ethers. The undergrowth shifted again, and then it emerged. A creature unlike anything he had ever seen. It moved with an unnatural grace, its elongated body rippling with lean muscle. Its deep-set eyes locked onto him, its maw stretching in a grotesque, unnatural grin.

Darien's breath steadied, his instincts screaming for him to act. He tensed, his magic surging to the surface, fire coiling at his fingertips. Then he remembered—Whyn's words. *You must not harm anything in the valley.*

His fingers twitched as he forced himself to think, to strategize. The creature was between him and the token. He couldn't retreat. But he also couldn't fight the way he wanted to.

The beast prowled forward, its movements measured, testing him. Darien raised his hand and gathered the ethers—not into fire, but into force. He shifted the air, forming a barrier just as the creature lunged. It slammed into the invisible wall, snarling as it skidded back. The impact sent tremors through Darien's arms, but the barrier held.

He couldn't keep this up forever. His mind worked through the possibilities. If he couldn't attack, he had to move.

Summoning the wind, he twisted the ethers into a concentrated burst, pushing himself sideways just as the creature swiped at him. He landed lightly, pivoting to keep his eyes on it. The beast circled, growling low.

Darien exhaled sharply, then did something he had never tried before. He reached out—not to strike, but to *push*. He focused on the energy surrounding the creature, weaving the air around it, pressing downward. The beast growled, shifting its weight uncomfortably as if the very air had thickened around it. It caused the creature just a moments hesitation, but that was all he needed.

Darien spun, drawing on the ethers once more, sending a concentrated pulse of force toward the ground beneath him. The energy propelled him past the creature, its swipe missing by mere inches, slowed by the air that still clung to it like unseen chains. He hit the ground running, closing the gap to the token.

The ravine yawned just past the beast, who was once again between him and his destination. The animal still struggled against the magic slowing it down, confused as to why it was unable to pursue its prey. The ravine beyond was too wide to jump under normal circumstances. He reached deep, pulling at the threads of time itself, *accelerating* his own movements—his breath, his pulse, the rhythm of his body syncing into something faster, sharper. The world seemed sluggish around him, the creature turning, reacting too late.

He launched himself forward, ending the spell he used on the creature and instead using the ether driven wind to push him into the air. He soared across the space and laughed as he felt the freedom of weightlessness. It was joyous and freeing. Halfway across, his body screamed in protest—his vision blurred, the telltale buzzing of overexertion flaring at the edges of his consciousness. He forced himself to scale back the magic, but in that moment, he knew—*he wasn't going to make it.*

Panic scratched at his throat, but he shoved it down. He had prepared for this. Trusting in the practice Whyn had drilled into him, he took a breath and called for a transition. The ethers roared in response, a sphere of blue light flickering into existence just as gravity began to claim him.

The world twisted violently, nausea slamming into his gut as space folded. Then, he was falling again— onto solid ground. He collapsed onto the grass, gasping, his limbs weak, his stomach churning. The token was still clutched in his trembling hand.

A shadow moved nearby. Whyn stood over him, watching with a knowing look. "You were successful."

Darien groaned, rolling onto his back, fighting the sickness clawing at his insides. "Yeah."

Whyn caught the token as Darien tossed it toward him without looking. "How do you feel?"

"Like I was just kicked through a storm."

Whyn gave a small nod, examining the pendant. "Transitions affect everyone differently. Some adapt. Others... struggle. I take it, based on your hasty entrance, that you encountered something in the valley."

Darien exhaled, forcing his body to calm. "Yeah. What was that thing?"

Whyn studied him for a moment before nodding approvingly. "A Leucrocuta. You've read about them, haven't you?"

Darien pushed himself up onto his elbows, still shaking off the last of his nausea. "Yeah... They're supposed to be tricksters, right? Luring their prey in with false calls. They pretend to be injured. I read about them weeks ago, but I never thought I'd actually see one."

"They're more than tricksters," Whyn said, slipping the token into his robes. "They're one of the larger predators in Olympus, save for... well that doesn't matter. They are dangerous, and very territorial. You did well."

Darien pushed himself up onto his elbows, shaking off the last of his nausea. Usually he would have asked

Whyn about the creature he mentioned. But with his head swimming he chose to let the matter pass.

"Are there more of them?" He asked, breath still ragged.

"Many," Whyn said simply. "You'll need to be ready the next time."

Whyn smirked faintly, motioning for him to follow. "Come. The sun is setting, let's get you cleaned up."

# Chapter 17: The Master Revealed

The days stretched on as Darien continued his training. The once difficult manipulation of the ethers now came naturally to him, and his repertoire of magical abilities expanded with each passing lesson. Fire, wind, speed, force—he had begun to master them all. But today, Whyn introduced something new.

"There is power in knowing," Whyn said as they sat in the shaded clearing outside his dwelling. "Seeing beyond where your eyes can reach, understanding what is happening beyond the walls around you."

Darien frowned, tilting his head slightly. "You mean seeing things from a distance?"

"Not quite," Whyn corrected. "Farsight is more than simply seeing," Whyn explained. "The ethers are connected, forming pathways between all things. Your ability to sense them around you is only a small window into just how vast and omnipresent they are. Every place, every object leaves an imprint in the ethers, and those with the skill can follow those threads, tracing the resonance back to its source. The farther the distance, the greater the energy required to hold the connection.".

Darien let the name settle in his mind. It felt right.

"As with transitions, distance is the challenge," Whyn continued. "The farther you wish to see, the more energy it requires. People are especially difficult. They move, they change, and the ethers struggle to hold onto them. Places, on the other hand, remain still. They are easier to reach."

Darien considered this. "Then the energy required to bring people across worlds—"

Whyn nodded before Darien could finish. "Yes. The transitions that bring people from Earth to Olympus require immense power. It is no simple act."

Darien leaned forward, his mind racing. "How does it work? How do you gather that much energy?"

Whyn's expression did not change, but something about his presence shifted—like a door shutting before Darien could glimpse inside. "That is a lesson for another time," he said. "Focus on what is in front of you."

Darien knew better than to press the issue. Instead, he exhaled, centering himself. "So how do I start?"

"Guide the ethers," Whyn instructed. "Control them. Then let your mind stretch beyond what is here. Choose a location, something distant but not unreachable. Let your mind travel through the ethers. You'll feel the urge to retreat into yourself, but do not give into it. Try to see Farkland Reach."

Darien closed his eyes, reaching out with the magic he had spent weeks honing. He gathered the ethers, weaving them into something finer, more delicate than he had before. He did not push them outward as he did with transitions, nor did he force them into tangible force. Instead, he let them *flow*, extending outward like invisible threads through the air.

Farkland Reach. The city he had fought for. Its towering walls, its narrow streets, the way its people moved like rivers through stone channels. He focused on it, felt the weight of its presence in his memory.

The world behind his eyes shifted, blurred at first, but something took shape. A cityscape, moving shapes—indistinct, like ink dissolving in water. He could see it, but it was not fully clear. The buildings were there, the streets winding in patterns he recognized, but the people remained indistinct. Shadows without faces, shifting figures that never fully resolved. Everything moved as though in slow motion due to the time scaling that occurred in the valley.

His concentration wavered, and the vision faded. The ethers snapped back, returning to the valley. Darien let out a slow breath, his heartbeat steady but exhilarated.

Whyn was watching him closely. "You did well."

Darien wiped his brow. "It's like looking through fog."

"That will change with practice," Whyn assured him. "Your connection to the ethers must strengthen. Clarity comes with time. Do it again."

Darien closed his eyes and turned his focus to the city, but his mind kept struggling to focus. His thoughts had instantly turned to those he had been missing these past few weeks. Evatra, Chorrun, and Rist, the closest friends he had made since coming to Olympus. Recently he was finding his mind wandering back to them, and back to his friends at The Academy. He guessed that by now they would be nearing the end of their last year. Graduating without him. His heart stung at the thought of Kara.

Guilt wracked him when he thought of her. They had talked of lives together, of a future beyond The Academy. Darien had let go of that so quickly upon accepting his fate here in Olympus. But now that he was learning transitions and farsight, the idea of communicating or even traveling back home again was beginning to open itself back up. How would he explain to them everything that happened?

"Darien," Whyn's voice jolted him back to the present moment. "Your mind is wandering. Focus."

Darien apologized and returned to the task at hand, returning Farkland Reach into blurry resolution behind his eyelids.

Over the following day, Darien continued to practice farsight with locations he had seen around Olympus. He learned that even if the area didn't have a name, he would be able to revisit through the ethers every detail of that location. He visited the place where he and Evatra had fought against Cyprin's raiders. The clearing where his first camp with the

Marauders had been. The village of Taitron. The still war-torn battle fields just outside Farkland Reach. The details were blurry but were coming more and more into focus with each iteration and bought of practice.

Despite his efforts, his mind kept returning to Rist, Evatra, and his friends who he had left behind at The Academy. Finally, after days of practice using the farsight, his curiosity was too much.

*I don't want to overdo it, though.*

He settled his mind on checking in with Rist and Evatra. He wanted to see his friends, but worried that the effort of reaching all the way through the ethers back to Earth would be an impossible task. He gathered together his memories of Evatra. His thoughts wound through the ethers in winding, twisting ways before finally settling in on Evatra, standing in a room with Totra-Dal. The two were looking at maps of an area Darien didn't quite recognize. Their motions were so slow that Darien couldn't tell what was happening.

He shifted his spell to rewind the images, manipulating space and time. The effort was great, but not more than he could handle. For several long minutes he sat rewinding time, allowing the images to stack and build on each other. When he felt he had enough build up, he reversed the spell, but faster.

Their voices came into clearer focus, though they were still slower and thus deeper than his memory of them.

"—save for those in the cycles obviously, happened-at least according to these records. If Darien's been taken anywhere that's not inside the mountain itself, he might have gone through here… but, see, this passage here—according to the scouts over the last century or so it's collapsed. So that means your best option is to enter here."

Totra-Dal pointed to several places on the map in slow, methodical motions. Everything appearing like it was playing at half speed. Darien sped up the images a little to bring everything into clearer focus. His heart jumped, and he felt a small burst of adrenaline as Evatra's voice filled his ears.

"So if we enter here," she said, pointing to another area on the map, "it looks like we'll be able to follow this around to his opening."

"Ah yes, that is precisely what I was thinking. This appears to be some kind of large open cavern. Maybe a meeting hall of some kind from ages long past. I think if you—"

The images froze again, coming to a near standstill and the sound of their speech dragged as he caught up in time with the present moment. Seeing how long time stretched for them while it passed by him instantly was disconcerting.

*She's going to go try to find me.*

Darien was touched, but he knew that it was a fool's errand. If Evatra went, she would likely find nothing but empty ruins. Depending on exactly where she went though, and how far Cyprin had expanded his forces or recovered, she could find much much worse.

He turned his attention to Rist, finding the ethereal nature of the dark robed figure. It took longer, the distance between them was significantly greater. Darien consumed the ethers at a prodigious rate, but he kept control. Finally, the dark robes of Rist, demure figure of Airlyn, and towering form of Breyman took shape in front of him. There were others there, but he couldn't tell who, or even what they were. Darien pushed his mind to rewind the events again, going for even longer than he had with Evatra. He then wound the images forward again, allowing their actions and words to come to almost real time.

"—against ussss, then our position issss more fragile than we believed."

"We have heard… whisperssss." Another voice said from beyond his view.

Darien struggled to understand the voices with their hissing tones.

Airlyn scoffed. "Whispers? A man tried to gut us, and you call it whispers?"

The unseen voice continued, unshaken. "Rumorsss of a cult—followers of Ccccyprin—growing in the shadows. Not just here in Peronia, but in other citiessss as well. We have no proof, no namessss, only murmurs among traderssss and scattered reports of dissssappearances."

Airlyn's glare was sharp as a blade. "And yet you said nothing? You chose silence over action?"

Another voice answered. "We did not wish to ssssspread fear without ccccertainty. Minotatha thrives on order. A panic could be assss dangerous assss an unseen enemy."

Airlyn stepped forward, hands clenched at her sides. "Well, now you have certainty. The assassin's blood is proof enough."

A heavy pause followed. Then, one of the council elders spoke, his voice firm. "If the cult existssss within our ccccity, then the bow must remain locked away. We cannot rissssk placing it in further danger."

Darien's spell ended as it caught up with the lagging time outside the valley. He sat there in confused thought as he considered everything that he had seen from both views outside the valley. His friends were in trouble. Evatra was about to throw herself into danger to save him. An ultimately fruitless endeavor, and one that would put her in more danger.

Rist, on the other hand… their discussion of assassins, cults, and Cyprin gave him even greater pause. They were in trouble, wherever they were. If he could get out of the valley he could go to Evatra, reveal that he was okay and then they could, maybe even together, find Rist and the others and help them. His allies needed him.

Darien paced through the valley, his thoughts racing. The images from his farsight weighed heavily on him—Evatra and Totra-Dal planning an expedition to find him, Rist and the others embroiled in a crisis that could shake Olympus. His allies needed him. They were in danger, and he was stuck here. He couldn't ignore it. He had to leave.

His feet carried him toward Whyn's dwelling before he realized he had even made the decision. He pushed open the door with more force than he intended, his pulse hammering in his ears. Whyn sat cross-legged in the center of the room, hands resting on his knees, eyes half-lidded in meditation. He didn't acknowledge Darien's entrance, but Darien knew he was aware of him.

"I need to leave," Darien said, his voice tense. "I saw them. Evatra's trying to find me. Rist and the others are dealing with some kind of cult connected to Cyprin. They're all in danger."

Whyn remained still. "And what made you look beyond the valley?"

Darien's frustration bubbled over. "Because I had to know! I can't just sit here while my friends are risking their lives. I can help them!"

Whyn sighed and opened his eyes, meeting Darien's frantic gaze with unnerving calm. "It is unfortunate."

Darien blinked. "What?"

"That you let your emotions override your caution," Whyn said evenly. "That you disregarded my instructions. You were not ready to reach beyond this place."

Darien clenched his fists. "I wasn't ready? You knew I'd want to check on them, eventually! Did you think I wouldn't care? Did you think I could just sit here, training, while people I care about are in danger?"

Whyn exhaled slowly. "And what will you do if you leave now? Charge into the unknown, half-trained, against forces you don't fully understand?"

Darien stepped forward. "I was brought here for a reason. You told me that. The cycles demand that I play my role. How am I supposed to do that if I'm locked away in this valley?"

Whyn studied him for a long moment. "Think your way through it, Darien. What happens when you leave?"

"I help them."

"You find them, perhaps. But what happens when you do?"

Darien faltered, his mind racing. "I... I fight. I stop whatever's happening."

"You *try*," Whyn corrected. "Without the training you need, without the mastery you must achieve. Leaving now means you may not be able to return. You are not ready."

Darien's breath came faster, his frustration mounting. "So I just abandon them?"

Whyn's voice remained infuriatingly level. "You trust them. They have fought before, they will fight again. You are part of this cycle, Darien, but not in the way you wish to be right now. Your training is not complete."

Darien ran a hand through his hair, his anger simmering into something closer to helplessness. "Why didn't you tell me?"

Whyn's eyes softened slightly. "Because your focus must be here. Your training, your understanding of magic, must come first. If you are to face what lies ahead, you must be more than you are now."

Darien let out a sharp breath, his shoulders sagging slightly. His heart still pounded, the desire to leave still burned, but logic settled over him. He hated it, but Whyn was right. He wasn't ready. Not yet.

He exhaled slowly. "Fine."

Whyn nodded, as if he had expected this outcome. "Then let's return to your training. There is still much to learn."

The valley air crackled with energy as Darien moved, his body a blur as he weaved between conjured obstacles. His movements were sharp, refined, his speed enhanced by the ethers coursing through him. Whyn watched from the sidelines, arms folded, his expression unreadable.

Darien leapt over a swirling torrent of wind, twisting midair and landing with a burst of force that sent dust scattering around him. A wall of flame erupted in front of him—his own creation—only to be immediately doused by a controlled stream of water he summoned with a flick of his wrist. The balance of power was instinctual now, an extension of himself rather than something he consciously controlled.

"Again," Whyn commanded.

Darien exhaled sharply and pulled the ethers once more, threading them into his muscles. He surged forward, his form shifting with unnatural speed, dodging invisible attacks and countering with bursts of wind and fire.

Whyn extended a hand, sending a pulse of force toward Darien. Instead of dodging, Darien planted his feet and pushed back. The collision sent a shockwave through the clearing, rattling the trees.

Whyn smirked. "Better."

Darien didn't wait for further praise. He lunged, a streak of fire trailing his fist as he closed the distance. Whyn sidestepped with ease, countering with a sweep of his hand. The ground beneath Darien's feet shifted, upending him, but he twisted mid-fall, catching himself with a cushion of air and rolling back to his feet.

"That was new," Darien noted, brushing the dirt from his sleeves.

Whyn only shrugged. "You'll need to expect the unexpected. When you fight other spellcasters, your abilities alone won't be enough."

A flicker of understanding passed through Darien. "So that's what this is about."

Whyn gave a slight nod. "Your magic is formidable, but you must learn how to counter the unexpected. A duel between spellcasters isn't won with strength alone—it's won by control, by understanding how to anticipate and counter abilities as they manifest. Each fighter can see the ethers shifting before a spell is cast, reading the magic as it takes shape. Battles are not just about force, but about adaptation. You never know what magic an opponent will use, so you must always be prepared, maintaining layered protections against elemental forces—shields woven into the very air around you, deflecting fire, nullifying wind, resisting force. Without them, a duel ends in an instant. But even with them, the battle comes down to creativity and instinct—how fast you can think, how well you can manipulate the ethers in ways your opponent won't predict."

Darien wiped sweat from his brow, breathing hard. "So the elements—some cancel each other out?"

Whyn nodded. "Fire and water will neutralize each other. Earth will disrupt lightning. Wind and force clash in strange ways, but their balance is precarious. Knowing this isn't enough—you must anticipate and layer your protections accordingly."

Darien frowned, rolling his shoulders. "What about those who can use multiple types?"

Whyn's gaze sharpened. "They are the most dangerous. A spellcaster with multiple disciplines can counter many at once, shielding their allies while disrupting opponents. Few can reach that level."

Darien's pulse quickened. "Could I?"

Whyn smirked. "Perhaps. But power means nothing without control."

They stood in silence for a moment before Darien spoke again. "But if the protections are so strong, how do these fights even end?"

Whyn's expression turned calculating. "More often than not, they end with steel. Spells will clash, shields will hold, and when neither side can overpower the other's defenses, it comes down to speed, agility, and a well-placed blade. A warrior who can augment their body with magic—enhanced strength, reflexes, speed—is often deadlier than one who relies on magic alone."

Darien considered this, clenching his fists. He had focused so much on magic, but now he saw the full picture.

Darien's pulse quickened. "Then let's go again."

Whyn chuckled. "Eager now, are we?" But he relented, lifting his hand. The air around them shifted, charged with potential. "Very well. No holding back."

They clashed again, their movements fluid, their magic colliding in bursts of power. Darien's control had never been sharper. He twisted the ethers, lashing out with speed, but Whyn matched him effortlessly. Their sparring continued until the sky began to turn golden, the day slipping toward dusk.

Later, after their training had ended, Darien sat alone in Whyn's study. His muscles ached, his energy drained as the magic of the valley which supplanted his need for sleep restored him, but his mind refused to rest. His fingers drummed absently on the desk, the thrill of the day's battle still lingering in his veins. He had pushed himself harder than ever before, had matched Whyn's speed and force in ways he hadn't thought possible only weeks ago.

Yet, something unsettled him.

His eyes flicked to the bookshelf, to the tome he had skimmed before. The history of Olympus, leading into the civil war. His breath slowed as he reached for it again, flipping carefully through its worn pages. At first, the words flowed as expected, chronicling the rising tensions, the conflicts that had torn the world apart. But then—abrupt silence.

Darien frowned. He turned a few more pages, his fingers trailing over the parchment. Whole sections were missing. The pages weren't just aged or frayed; they had been torn out deliberately, their jagged remains clear against the binding. His frustration grew as he tried to follow the narrative, but each time he thought he was close to an answer, the story stopped, leaving only fragmented sentences and broken thoughts.

He ran his fingers over the empty spaces, his pulse quickening. Someone had removed these passages. Someone had decided that whatever knowledge had been written here was too dangerous—or too revealing—to remain.

Why? And more importantly—who?

Darien sat back, exhaling slowly. He could feel the heat rising in his chest, a slow-burning anger coiling beneath his skin. He had spent months by now training, pushing himself further than ever before, learning things that were never taught at the Academy. And yet, despite all his progress, despite his relentless pursuit of understanding, he was still being kept in the dark.

The question gnawed at him through the remainder of the evening, lingering even as he forced himself through another round of training, his body moving on instinct while his mind churned. He thought of confronting Whyn immediately, of demanding answers. But something held him back. The time just didn't feel right yet.

Instead, he trained harder, pushing himself in ways he hadn't before. Refining his control over the ethers, he wove his defenses more quickly, strengthening his reflexes until countering Whyn's attacks became second nature. He focused on layering protections, shifting them mid-fight, anticipating the strikes before they even landed. He needed to be faster, sharper—because sooner or later, whatever truth was being kept from him would be something he had to be prepared for.

A few days later, after a particularly intense training session where Darien had nearly bested Whyn during a sword duel, he made his way toward where he know he would find his master. The sun moved across the sky, nearing it's peak. Darien approached carefully, his voice steady, measured looking up and the glowing orb.

*I wonder how the sun works here...*

Darien sat at the edge of Whyn's perception, watching as Whyn manipulated the ethers in strange ways that Darien couldn't quite pinpoint the nature of.

"Master," Darien began, trying to show respect and deference before moving in to probe some of the deeper and more controversial topics. "I have a question."

Whyn glanced up, studying him before nodding. "Go on."

Darien hesitated for a moment before speaking. "I wasn't looking to break any rules, but I needed to know more. Every time I dig into the history of this world, I find pieces missing, stories half-told. I thought maybe I'd finally get some clarity, but instead, I find that someone—*someone*—decided I shouldn't see what came next." Darien held up the book, gripping it tightly. "They didn't just omit details in the writing, they physically tore out the pages. Why? What was there that was so dangerous?"

Whyn's expression barely shifted, but Darien could see something in his eyes—calculation, caution. "Some knowledge isn't meant for everyone," Whyn said carefully, his tone measured. "There are things in Olympus' past that are better left untouched."

Darien scoffed. "That's not an answer... Master. Someone went through the trouble of tearing these pages out. Why? What was written here that someone didn't want me to see?"

Whyn sighed, setting his hands on his knees. "History is written by those who survive it. And sometimes, they choose what is remembered."

Darien's jaw tightened. "And who decided *this* shouldn't be remembered? You? Whytaren? Or was it Cyprin himself?"

Whyn's gaze hardened. "Enough, Darien. You're letting your emotions drive you. Focus on what's ahead, not the past."

Darien shook his head. "No. Not this time. You've taught me to question everything, to understand the forces at play. But when it comes to this—when it comes to Cyprin and whatever led to the war—you just expect me to accept ignorance? I deserve to know the truth, and I can't help but shake the feeling that you're involved in this somehow. Did you remove the pages? If so, why? Why don't you trust me to know what's in this book? Haven't I proven enough to you?"

A long silence stretched between them. The meadow felt quieter, as if the valley itself was holding its breath.

Whyn rubbed his face, exhaling. "You don't understand what you're asking."

Darien stepped closer, voice steady. "Then explain it to me. I wasn't looking for trouble," he admitted, voice steady but edged with frustration. "I was trying to understand. Every lesson, every battle, every word you've told me has been about preparing me. But how am I supposed to be ready when I don't even know what I'm stepping into? I read this book because I need answers, not because I want to question you. But they were taken away from me before I even had a chance." He exhaled sharply, shaking his head. "Why are these pages missing?"

Whyn sighed and rubbed his face with his hands, breathing deeply.

"You know, having this information can put you in much more danger than you are already in." Whyn said flatly.

Darien stood his ground. "I know. And I don't care."

Whyn sighed, examining the resolve of Darien's face.

"I suppose there's no waiting then. There is some of this I must tell you now, sooner than I had planned. Some I will still keep to myself."

Whyn held out his hand as Darien began to protest, "Not out of a desire to keep you ignorant, but out of a desire to hedge against the fact that we might fail. If some of the information I have were to get into the wider world, and more importantly to Cyprin, all would be lost."

Whyn stood and paced in slow measured steps.

"Had I not misjudged the timing of the cycles, this would not be so difficult." Whyn stopped and looked out across the meadow as if contemplating something, then looked back to Darien.

"The first of the answers you seek is one you're entitled to start with and one that will open more questions for you than answers. I can reveal my part in the cycle to you but before I do, I want your word of honor that no matter what, unless you are given permission by me, you will never reveal my presence to anyone. Doing so will put this world and your own in unimaginable danger."

Darien stared back at Whyn, perplexed by what answer he could possibly give that could be dangerous. Darien had grown up studying under Whyn, he knew more about him than almost anyone else at The Academy, even some of the teachers. They had spent countless hours training, sparring, and studying together. What answer could he give that would be dangerous?

*Then again, who knows what else he's hiding from me.*

"Darien, your word?"

"I promise." Darien answered flatly.

"You also need to know that once I answer these questions, there is no other path for you to take but the one that I offer. Once I begin to give you deeper answers, you can never go back. This knowledge, you will use to either save the worlds or cause them to be subject to the dark ones rule. The stakes are the highest imaginable."

Darien sat stunned into silence. What was Whyn talking about? Was it about his role as one of the Eldric? As a magician? Thinking quickly, he decided.

"Despite all the times you've held back information from me, kept me in the dark, I still trust you for some reason. It's not like I can go anywhere anyway and if there's more to learn, I don't want to go forward without knowing everything. You've taught me up to this point. If anyone is going to teach me more, it should probably be you."

An odd expression crossed Whyn's face. It contained shock, fear, and a hint of, was it pride? Excitement? Darien couldn't tell.

"You honor me with that more than you know, Darien. Let me tell you a shortened version of my story. It dates back longer than you are likely to believe, before the rise of Cyprin and the beginning of the cycles."

Darien nodded, indicating that Whyn should continue. A flash of memory of sitting with Chorrun in his hut when the story of the cycles was first told to him shot through Darien's mind. He smiled inwardly at the similarities and turned his full attention to the man sitting across from him, who was looking stone faced and somber. Something in the man's face and demeanor seemed to shift, but Darien couldn't quite say what. He chocked it up to being another trick of the light as the sun's beams filtered through the dappled canopy above, and focused his attention on the words Whyn began to speak.

"I was raised in a small subsistence community. We were farmers, blacksmiths, craftsman of all kinds. We made what we needed to survive and traded with those around us what we could now make ourselves. It was a hard beginning to life, but one filled with purpose and achievement. There is nothing so rewarding as seeing the crop you have tended all season become food on your family's table, or the shoe you fit on the hoof of your steed coming from your own forge. Using your own hands to shape the world around you is one of the greatest joys one can experience."

Whyn began weaving with blades of grass again, his fingers moving with idle mastery against the sharp green strands as he continued.

"When I was in my teenage years, however, I was identified as having certain... abilities... and was sent away to craft and hone those skills. I was in a class of maybe fifty or so students, many of whom could not keep up with the work. I, however, persisted and continued to absorb what knowledge I could. Eventually, there were only fourteen of us left, each with their own specialized skillset and each with their own partner who would complement their abilities. There were two of us, however, myself and one other, who held no single specialty, instead we were able to control our abilities and great amounts of power. Similar to your abilities, Darien."

Darien's mind began to race, wondering at the implications of Whyn having been raised as a spellcaster. As he listened, he saw the same shift in Whyn's appearance, but this time the man's very skin began to change. It began to fade in color as he spoke, gently transitioning away from the pink skin and becoming almost colorless in the late afternoon shade of the tree overhead.

"We were sent all over, doing various tasks, learning new skills, and doing the work of our own school for the people and those around us, not unlike our own version of The Academy. You see Darien, I was one of the best magicians there had ever been. From my class rose fourteen of the greatest friends and allies I had ever known. Rumors began to spread about our abilities. We became some of the greatest assistants to the lands of Olympus that history had ever known. The world called for us and we answered. Healing, protecting, teaching."

Darien sat, dumbfounded at the story he was being told. The implications of Whyn's history beginning to take shape in front of him, just as the physical shape of the man resolved into something familiar.

"You know the names of many of my colleagues. Talk of their abilities spread from our world to the sister worlds like your own. Names like Zeus, Hera, Ares, Athena, and Poseidon, all great spellcasters and even great people in their own right. They were the last class of spellcasters to come before the rise of the dark one and accomplished so many great things."

Whyn's voice broke for a moment as he was overcome by some internal emotion. Darien's eyes widened as he watched the grey eyes he had known for so long turn to solid black, the hair grow long and white, and the skin resolve itself from the pink skin of a human like himself, to a white, then almost black, and then finally into the soft grey skin of a troll.

"It was us who fought the hardest during both instances of our civil war. We had called him friend and ally before he was twisted by his desire for power and revenge against those he felt had betrayed him. The twisted, black hearted demon who now resides at the top of Olympus, where we studied and trained ourselves is only a shadow the man I once knew and trusted with my life. One of the hardest things I have ever had to do in my life Darien, was to imprison the man who I had called brother after his corruption. You see Darien, I was the one who cast the spell which began the cycles. I am Whytaren, the last spell caster to walk free in the lands of Olympus for three thousand years."

# Chapter 18: The Imprisoned Hope

The road northeast was a long one, and Evatra was grateful for the company. Though she had initially hesitated to bring others along, reasoning that the fewer people involved in this journey, the easier it would be to move unnoticed, she had ultimately relented. A handful of marauders had decided to follow her, loyal to her leadership even after everything that had happened. And then there was Cycnus.

He was a towering figure, his presence an imposing yet strangely comforting one. Evatra had been wary at first, unsure what to make of him. The wraiths had once been their enemies, and even though Darien's intervention had changed the course of things, old instincts died hard. Yet, over the days they traveled together, she found herself growing used to him. His movements were careful, his words sparse but deliberate.

They traveled by day, winding through mountain passes and deep forests, stopping to rest when the terrain allowed. The crunch of boots against gravel, the rustling of wind through the trees, and the occasional distant cry of unseen creatures filled the long stretches of silence. The scent of damp earth and pine clung to the air, mingling with the lingering smoke of their small fires. At night, the sky stretched endlessly overhead, stars burning fiercely in the clear air, offering their silent watch over the travelers.

The nights were spent in quiet conversation around campfires, exchanging stories as they prepared for whatever lay ahead. The marauders who had chosen to come along were grizzled and experienced, but they, too, found themselves listening when Cycnus spoke. His voice, though low, carried weight, like a distant echo of something lost long ago.

One evening, as the fire crackled and the rich scent of charred meat filled the air, Evatra finally broached the subject that had been circling her mind. "You were a wraith once. Before all this."

"I was," Cycnus admitted, his eye reflecting the flickering light. "Darien was the first who came to us not as an enemy, but as something new. He brought the truth with him—proof that the cycles had changed. That there was an opportunity. Some of us saw it. I saw it." He exhaled slowly, his eye dark with memory. "But it was not so simple. I was not always a wraith."

Evatra's brow furrowed. "What do you mean?"

Cycnus shifted, staring into the fire. "Before the darkness, before the curse that twisted me, I was born to a spellcaster—one of the last before the cycles began anew. My father was powerful, but his ambitions led him to Cyprin. He pledged himself, believing in the promises of the dark one. And in return, he offered me."

Evatra stiffened. "He gave you up?"

Cycnus gave a slow nod. "I was young, but not without ability. I had already begun training, learning how to wield magic. Cyprin saw potential, but not as a student—he saw as fuel. He bound me, drained me of my life, my essence, siphoning my power to strengthen his own. My father was there. He watched and said nothing. I cried out for him but—" his voice caught before he continued. "The pain felt endless, and in the end, I was left with nothing but rage. That was all I knew. Cyprin cast us out, imprisoned us in those caves. Our inability to be exposed to light kept us trapped until some poor soul would venture near, and then one of us would be free. Free to try to seek revenge on those who still held the life and freedom that had been so wrongly stolen from us."

The fire crackled, sending embers spiraling into the night. A wolf howled somewhere in the distance, its voice carried by the wind, adding to the oppressive quiet that followed Cycnus' words. The air smelled of woodsmoke, tinged with something sharper, the lingering memory of old hurts that seemed to settle around them.

Evatra let the silence stretch between them before she finally spoke. "And now?"

"Now, I fight to reclaim what was stolen," Cycnus said, his voice quiet but firm. "I do not know if I will ever be whole again, but I can choose what comes next. I can choose who I stand with."

Evatra absorbed his words, but another thought pressed forward. She leaned slightly toward him, her expression unreadable. "What about the battle at Farkland Reach? You fought there too."

Cycnus nodded, his gaze drifting past the fire as if staring into something unseen. "I did. It was the first time I fought as a free man in centuries."

Evatra studied him. "What part did you play?"

He let out a slow breath. "I did what I knew best—I reached into the power I had once been bound to, using it against those who had cursed me. When Darien entered the caves, I felt the shift in the world. We all did. I saw an opportunity."

Her eyes narrowed. "An opportunity for what?"

His jaw tightened slightly before he spoke. "To give him strength. To lend him what I had left."

Evatra narrowed her eyes. "And his injury?"

He looked away then, the weight of something unspoken settling between them. "I did not know it would happen."

The words were simple, but the regret in his tone was unmistakable.

Evatra let out a slow breath, rubbing her arms as the cool night air settled over the camp. "He wouldn't blame you. Not really. But I think you should tell him yourself one day."

Cycnus nodded, but said nothing more. The fire crackled between them, and the night stretched on.

The journey into the mountains was slow, the terrain growing more treacherous with each passing day. Winding paths yielded to uneven ground, jagged rocks, and thick underbrush. The scent of damp earth filled the air, mingling with the crispness of the mountain breeze. Evatra rode in silence, eyes scanning the landscape, noting every change in the environment.

One afternoon, she and one of the marauders, a younger troll named Callen, rode ahead of the group to scout the path forward. The quiet between them stretched, broken only by the occasional clink of armor and the dull sound of hooves against soil. Callen eventually spoke, voice low.

"Feels like a scouting mission, doesn't it?"

Evatra nodded absently, swinging off her horse as they reached a ridge overlooking a shallow valley. Something in the dirt caught her attention. She crouched, running her fingers over the impressions left behind.

The ground told a story. She could see the faint ridges where boots had pressed into the dirt, heavier prints where wagons had rolled through, and the scuffs of hooves—many of them.

                                                                         

"Recent," she murmured. "A large group moved through here within the last few days. Horses, carts, and armed men. Not just scouts."

Callen dismounted, crouching beside her. "Think it's Cyprin's forces?"

Evatra exhaled through her nose, her fingers tracing a partial bootprint that had been obscured by wind and shifting soil. "It's possible. The depth of these prints means they were carrying supplies. Either they're reinforcing something, or they were preparing for something bigger."

She picked up a bit of disturbed soil, rubbing it between her fingers. The dampness told her that rain had come through recently, but not enough to erase the markings. "They weren't in a rush, but they weren't lingering either. Whatever they were doing, it wasn't just a pass-through."

Callen shifted uneasily. "So if Cyprin's forces have been operating here, you think Darien's in those mountains?"

Evatra didn't answer immediately. She straightened, looking toward the jagged peaks ahead. The thought had been lingering in the back of her mind since they had found the first sign of movement. Was he really here? Could he have been taken underground?

"It's a real possibility," she admitted finally. "But we won't know for sure until we get inside."

They rode back to the main group, relaying their findings. The atmosphere grew heavier, the weight of what they were walking into settling on all of them.

As they prepared to search for the cave entrance, one of the marauders, Jorek, approached Evatra. His movements were cautious, his usual bravado muted. He rubbed a hand over the stubble on his chin before speaking.

"Evatra," he started hesitantly. "I know we signed on for this, but... going into those caves, that's different. The ruins of Zanarchin, Olympus itself—this isn't just some raid or skirmish. It's not quite what we were thinking it would be."

She studied him, understanding his unease. The prospect of adventure had been enticing, but standing at the threshold of something ancient, something unknown, was another matter.

"You're afraid," she said simply.

Jorek shifted, looking uncomfortable. "I'd be stupid not to be. We all would. This is different from anything we've ever done, Evatra. Raids, skirmishes, even battles—those made sense. But this? This is walking into something we don't understand. We'll help you find the entrance, but once we do... I think it's best if we make camp and wait for you to come out again."

Evatra's jaw tightened, irritation prickling at the edges of her thoughts. She understood. She really did. But understanding didn't make it any less frustrating.

"So that's it? You're turning back?" She tried to keep her voice neutral, but she wasn't sure she succeeded.

Jorek hesitated. "We came this far because we believe in you. But this..." He gestured toward the looming mountain ahead. "This isn't what we expected. We thought we'd be fighting battles, not stepping into something ancient and cursed. I have a bad feeling about this."

Evatra looked at him for a long moment. His words stirred something in her—an echo of her own doubts. But she couldn't allow hesitation. Not now. "If that's what you want, so be it. But understand this—once we go in, there's no turning back. If you're not coming, then you should leave. Staying put here isn't safe either. If Cyprin's forces are nearby, they'll find you."

Jorek looked down, guilt flickering across his face. "I just—" He trailed off, shaking his head. "We're not cowards. But we don't belong in those tunnels."

Evatra exhaled sharply, running a hand through her hair. A mix of emotions pulled at her—anger at being left, guilt for feeling that way, understanding for their fear, and an unshakable sense of inevitability. She softened her stance slightly. "I know. And I don't blame you for it. But if you're not going to see this through, you need to leave before it's too late."

Jorek nodded, though he still looked uncertain. "We'll make for Farkland Reach once you and Cycnus head inside."

She let the tension settle before offering a brief nod. "Thank you for coming this far."

The tension between them eased slightly, though something unsaid still lingered in the air. Jorek stepped away to inform the others, and Evatra turned her gaze back to the looming mountains. If Darien was truly here, she would find him. And if Cyprin's forces stood in her way, she would face them head-on.

As they entered the foothills of Olympus, the path toward the mountains grew more treacherous. Ahead: Towering peaks loomed ahead, their jagged edges disappearing into a near-permanent crown of mist. The air was thinner here, crisper, carrying the scent of cold stone and distant rain. Loose rock crunched beneath their boots, and the distant cries of mountain birds echoed eerily through the stillness.

Evatra pulled her cloak tighter around herself, her gaze fixed on the imposing landscape. The mountain ahead wasn't just any mountain—it was Olympus, the place where the cycles had turned for millennia. Where wars had been fought and legends forged. The idea of walking beneath it, through tunnels carved by hands long dead, left a weight in her chest she couldn't quite shake.

Finding the entrance itself was far from easy. The map Totra-Dal had provided gave a rough idea of where it should be, but as they scoured the rocky ridges and crevices, there was nothing resembling a clear entrance. Cycnus ran his hands over the rock face, his single eye narrowing as he studied the worn carvings that had nearly faded with time.

"This is old," he murmured. "Older than anything we've seen so far. If the entrance is here, time has buried it."

Evatra traced her fingers over what looked like the faint curve of an ancient symbol, almost indistinguishable from the surrounding rock. The markings, though faded, matched those on the map.

"It's here," she said, more certain than she had been all day. "We just have to dig."

Cycnus wasted no time, dropping to his knees and pulling loose dirt and debris away from the base of the stone. Evatra joined him, fingers quickly covered in dust as they clawed through centuries of earth and time. The others, sensing their urgency, stepped forward to help.

The work was slow and grueling. Layers of sediment had settled over the entrance, stones piled atop one another, some wedged so tightly it took Cycnus' full strength to pry them free. The further they dug, the more they uncovered—a weathered step leading downward, the remains of what had once been a grand archway now buried beneath dirt and time.

Then, finally, an opening. A hollow darkness yawning before them, exhaling stale air that smelled of ancient stone and something else—something deeper.

Evatra sat back on her heels, wiping sweat from her brow, her breath steady but her chest tight with anticipation. "This isn't being used," she said, glancing at Cycnus. "If Cyprin's forces were operating out of here, they'd have cleared it. Either they don't know about it, or they haven't reached it yet."

Cycnus peered into the darkness. "Collapsed, maybe. Or forgotten. But if we found it, they will eventually."

Evatra nodded, pushing herself up to her feet. She moved toward her horse, reaching into the saddlebags to gather what she would need. The tunnels stretched for miles beneath Olympus, and she couldn't risk being unprepared. She packed carefully—a full waterskin, dried provisions, flint, torches, and extra wrappings for warmth. Every metal object, from her dagger to her belt buckles, was wrapped in cloth to keep them from clinking together. Stealth might be the only advantage they had.

Her horse nickered softly as she adjusted the straps, brushing a hand down its mane. "You can't follow me into this one," she murmured. "But you've done well."

Jorek shifted on his feet and she turned to face him, clearly uneasy. "Evatra, you don't have to do this. We can find another way."

She exhaled sharply, shaking her head. "We've already been over this. Either I find Darien, or I don't. But once Cycnus and I enter, there's no turning back. You all need to move on. Unless you've decided to come with us after all?"

The tension between them thickened. Jorek looked like he wanted to argue, but he knew better. He finally nodded, glancing at the others before mounting his horse. "We'll head back. Stay safe."

Evatra didn't respond. She watched as they turned their horses, retreating down the winding path, disappearing into the haze. Only once they were gone did she let out a slow breath. She turned to Cycnus. "Ready?"

He nodded once. "Let's go."

Together, they stepped forward, leaving the fading light behind as they descended into the tunnels beneath Olympus.

The air in the tunnels was thick, damp with the scent of earth and the faint metallic tang of something old, something forgotten. Evatra moved carefully, each step measured, her breath slow and controlled. The flickering torchlight barely penetrated the darkness ahead, casting shifting shadows along the carved walls. Ancient reliefs and inscriptions had been worn down by time, their meanings lost to history.

Cycnus moved beside her, his massive form somehow ghostly in the dim light. He seemed unfazed by the oppressive weight of the underground. Evatra envied that.

Ahead of them, movement. Two figures stood near the next corridor, armored and armed—dark army soldiers, just like the ones from the battle of

Farkland Reach. Evatra's stomach coiled with tension.

She turned her head slightly, whispering, "Cycnus, can you still possess them? Like before?"

A moment of silence, then Cycnus' voice, low and resigned. "No. I am bound to this body now. My kind... we grew weary of our existence. Of wandering without form. We anchored ourselves to the bodies we took. If this one dies, I die. There is no returning."

Evatra absorbed the revelation. The stakes had changed. Cycnus was no longer an entity that could slip between hosts—he was as vulnerable as the rest of them.

She exhaled, steadying herself. "Then we do this the old-fashioned way."

She signaled to Cycnus. They moved like shadows, closing the distance with silent precision. The soldiers were speaking in hushed voices, unaware of their presence. One of them adjusted his grip on his spear, shifting his weight slightly. The momentary distraction was all they needed.

Evatra struck first, her blade sliding cleanly into the gap between the soldier's armor. His eyes widened in shock, but she was already pulling back, letting his body slump soundlessly to the ground.

Cycnus moved at the same moment, his powerful arms wrapping around the second soldier's throat, cutting off any chance of alarm. The struggle lasted only seconds before the soldier went limp.

Evatra exhaled. "That was too easy."

Cycnus nudged one of the bodies with his boot. "This is a forward guard. There are more ahead."

They dragged the bodies down a side passage, tucking them into the shadows where they wouldn't be easily spotted. The weight of what lay ahead settled over them. They had to move quickly.

The tunnels grew wider as they pressed forward, and soon, they found themselves in what must have once been a chamber of importance. The walls were lined with alcoves, crumbling shelves filled with relics coated in dust. Evatra ran her fingers over a broken stone tablet, the inscriptions too worn to decipher. A forgotten place of knowledge, now abandoned.

Beyond the chamber, a stone staircase wound upward, carved into the very bones of the mountain. Evatra motioned for Cycnus to follow as she climbed carefully, her fingers trailing along the wall for balance. The higher they ascended, the more the stale air thinned, the scent of damp earth giving way to something else—smoke, faint and distant.

At the top, they found themselves on an overlook carved into the rock. Below them, an open cavern stretched wide, its ceiling arched like the ribcage of some ancient beast. In the center, a group of figures stood gathered near a raised stone platform. The flickering glow of torches cast long, shifting shadows.

Tahmer stood at the head of them, his stance rigid, his voice carrying through the cavern. "We are behind schedule. Our master's patience grows thin. If the excavation does not yield what we seek soon, consequences will be severe."

One of the armored figures, his dark cloak half covering his battered armor, cleared his throat. "Tahmer, with all due respect, the deeper we go, the worse it becomes. We lost three men in the last collapse. If we continue at this pace without proper reinforcement, we risk sealing ourselves inside."

Tahmer turned his head slightly, his expression shadowed by the torchlight. "Then send more men to clear the passage. The ruins below hold what we need. A few casualties will not stop us."

The subordinate hesitated. "If we push too hard, we may cause another collapse. We need time."

Tahmer stepped forward, closing the space between them. His voice dropped, laced with something far colder than frustration. "Time?" He let the word settle before continuing. "The only thing you need to concern yourself with is following orders. The mountain will not stop us. Fear will not stop us. *You* will not stop us. If we must tear through the very foundation of Olympus itself, we will do it."

Another soldier shifted uneasily. "But we don't even know if what we're looking for is still intact. The records are millennia old by now, there's no guarantee that—"

"You think I don't know that?" Tahmer snapped. "You think I haven't considered every possibility? That HE hasn't? Our master has seen the signs. The ruins are here. And if we don't find them, if we don't retrieve what was lost to get him the answers he requires, we will answer for that failure in ways you cannot comprehend."

Silence gripped the chamber. The soldiers exchanged uneasy glances, but no one dared to contradict him further.

Evatra, watching from the ledge above, exhaled softly. Whatever they were searching for, it wasn't just old ruins. It was something dangerous. Something that, if recovered, could shift the balance of power in ways she didn't like.

She turned to Cycnus, whispering, "We need to move. Now."

They stepped back from the overlook, keeping low as they moved toward a more defensible position further along the rocky ledge. The cavern below stretched far, the torchlight flickering against the jagged walls, sending long, distorted shadows dancing across the stone. They were outnumbered—badly. If they were spotted now, there would be no chance of escape. Caution was the only path forward.

A sudden, wet sucking sound filled the cavern, unnatural and thick. Evatra froze, pressing herself against the stone. The tension in the air shifted, an anticipation that even she could feel. Down below, Tahmer lifted his head, an eager gleam in his eye. "Finally," he murmured, stepping forward. "A report from Minotatha."

Evatra strained to hear, her pulse quickening as a dark figure emerged from a side tunnel. The soldier wore the same dark armor as the others, but there was something different about him—his movements were precise, almost mechanical, and his presence demanded attention.

Then, the real shock. From the tunnel behind him, Rist stepped forward, his dark robes flowing as he moved into the firelight. Evatra's breath caught. Following close behind him were Airlyn, Breyman, and—her heart clenched—a Peronian warrior carrying an ornate, powerful-looking bow across his back.

Tahmer's lips curled into a smirk. "Well, well. I must admit, Boronoth, I expected you to fail. Or perhaps, in your vengeance, kill them outright. But you succeeded. And for that, your devotion to Cyprin will be rewarded. But where is the fourth?"

Evatra watched as Boronoth, presumably the Peronian warrior, stood stiffly. Even from this distance, she could see the tension in his shoulders.

"He wassss not with them. They ssssaid he was to meet them at the sssssouthern shores due to his injury during the battle at Farkland Reach."

Tahmer took a few slow steps toward them, hands behind his back, his tone somewhat annoyed but eyes looking over the three present members of this cycles heroes. "The southern shores? Well, that is plainly a lie. The human was sent off into some other place during our transition when I came here. It is no matter. We will have the truth from them soon enough. Nevertheless, Boronoth, you have brought me quite the prize. Our master will be pleased."

Evatra's grip tightened on the hilt of her weapon. Whatever was happening here, they were running out of time to act and Darien wasn't even here.

# Chapter 19: The Answered Questions

Darien could only stare. His mind reeled, grasping at memories, searching for clues buried in the past, moments he had overlooked. Every lesson, every cryptic remark, every glance that had seemed filled with some hidden meaning—had all of it been leading to this? His teacher, the man who had shaped his life, had been lying to him. Not with words, but by omission.

It had been his magic that brought Darien here. His actions had torn Darien from his home, his friends, and thrown him into this world of war and prophecy. Had he chosen Darien for this? Had he planned it all along? Was he just a pawn in some grand scheme?

His thoughts spun wildly. He had spent his life trusting this man, believing his lessons were meant to prepare him for something, but not this. He had never questioned why Whyn had pushed him so hard, why the lessons always seemed just outside his grasp, just beyond what others were learning. Why me? If he was telling the truth, then how much more had he been hiding?

His hands clenched into fists, his breath coming in short, ragged bursts. "You lied to me."

Whyn—Whytaren—sighed, rubbing his temples as if the weight of the moment pressed down on him just as much. "I never wanted to deceive you, Darien. I—"

"You LIED!" Darien's voice cracked, raw with betrayal. He surged to his feet, pacing in frantic circles. "Everything—everything you ever told me was a lie! You—" he gestured wildly, his mind unable to settle on just one accusation. "You brought me here! This was your doing!"

Whytaren lifted his hands, placating. "Yes, but not in the way you think. I did not choose you, Darien. I did not pull you from your world on a whim—"

"Then how?!" Darien spun on him, his breath coming fast. His heart pounded in his chest like it was trying to escape. "How are you even here? How are you alive?! You were supposed to be—"

He faltered, his mind racing. If he had hidden his identity, then what else had he done? Had Whyn manipulated the cycles? Had he cheated death? Had he been playing this game for longer than Darien could even fathom?

Whytaren's expression shifted, but his voice remained calm. "This is not the moment for all the answers, Darien."

"Not the moment?" Darien laughed bitterly. "When is the moment? After you've dragged me even deeper into whatever plan you have? After you've kept me in the dark for years longer? I trusted you, and you—" He exhaled sharply, his voice dropping. "You weren't even who you said you were."

Whytaren looked at him with something close to sadness. "I am still your teacher, Darien. That hasn't changed."

"Yes, it has!" Darien snapped. "Everything has!"

The weight of unspoken words stretched between them. Darien could feel it now—Whyn was still holding something back. He wasn't answering. He wasn't denying anything either, but that only made it worse.

Had he ever cared about Darien as a student? As a person? Or was he just shaping him into something else?

Darien's vision blurred with anger, his breathing ragged. "I have nothing left! No home, no friends, no choices! And now I find out that you were behind it all? That you could have told me—could have trusted me—but you didn't?"

Whytaren finally exhaled, his gaze steady. "You are not ready to understand."

Darien scoffed. "And I suppose you get to decide that too?" He shook his head, stepping back. "You're just like them. Just like the people who rip pages from books, who take knowledge away and decide who gets to know the truth."

A flicker of something crossed Whytaren's face, and then he spoke, his voice quiet but firm. "That was me too, Darien. The books, the missing pages. I kept things from you, from many, many people, because I had to."

Darien turned away, his mind a maelstrom. He felt the ground beneath him shift—not physically, but something deeper. His world had already changed when he was pulled into Olympus. Now, it had shattered entirely.

Whytaren watched him carefully, his expression unreadable. Then, after a long silence, he spoke. "You have two choices, Darien. You can keep being angry, let it consume you, and walk away. Or you can calm down and get the answers you claim to want. But I will not fight you. And I will not argue with you. The choice is yours."

Darien's jaw tightened. "You say I have a choice. But if I walk away, I doom all of Olympus and the other worlds to a fate worse than death. I have no choice."

The last four words were spat into existence with contempt and disgust.

"That is not untrue." Whytaren said, the calmness in his voice irritating Darien even more.

The fire in his chest told him to storm off, to put as much distance between himself and this deception as possible. But the other part of him, the part that had spent years learning from this man, forced him to pause.

His breathing slowed. He turned back, his anger still there, but more controlled. "Fine. Explain it to me. But no more half-truths. No more secrets."

Whytaren nodded, his gaze steady. "Then sit and listen."

Darien sank onto a nearby rock, his breathing still uneven but slowing. His mind still reeled, but the raw edge of his anger had dulled, replaced by a simmering frustration. He had screamed, raged, accused—but none of that had brought him the answers he needed. His chest rose and fell as he tried to collect himself. This wasn't over. Not by a long shot.

Whytaren studied him for a moment, then continued. "You want to know how you got here? How I brought you here." His voice was even, his tone controlled, as if carefully measuring each word. "The cycles are meant to be voluntary. An instructor from the Academy had already volunteered this time. But when the transition was to be made, I intervened. I saw something in you, something that had never been in any cycle before. I made a choice."

Darien's jaw tightened. "You *chose* me over them? Over someone who volunteered?"

"Yes," Whytaren admitted. "I watched over you for years, studied your growth, your potential. The fire within you—it was unlike anything I had ever seen. I knew you were different. That you could change everything."

Darien clenched his fists. "So you redirected the transition to bring me instead."

Whytaren nodded. "Yes. And the timing was imperfect because I thought I had more time. I had grown too invested in watching over you, too distracted by my place at the Academy. The cycles are precise, but I made a mistake. I brought you here before you were ready."

Darien exhaled sharply. "And you never told me. Why?"

Whytaren's expression darkened slightly. "Because knowing would have made you a target before you were ready. There are forces at play that you do not yet understand. If you had known everything from the beginning, it would not have helped you—it would have put you in greater danger. Even now, there are truths you are not ready for."

Darien scoffed. "So you get to decide that too? Just like you decided to rip me out of my life?"

Whyn sat stoically calm. His long fingers pressed together and his now black eyes peering at Darien, waiting for him to calm again.

Darien exhaled sharply, the weight of it settling in. "And the cycles themselves? How does Cyprin even get imprisoned?"

For the first time, Whytaren hesitated. His lips pressed together, as if considering whether to answer at all. "That is another thing I cannot reveal. Not yet. But I will tell you this—before you face Cyprin, you will know the truth of everything you ask. Even the knowledge of my survival is dangerous. Until you learn to shield your mind, even a stray thought in the presence of the wrong person could betray us both and prevent us from finally ending the cycles."

Darien's pulse quickened. "End the cycles? What does that even mean? What would have happened if the original volunteer had gone instead of me?"

Whytaren exhaled, his gaze steady but measured. "The cycles would have continued. The pattern would have repeated. But Cyprin has been preparing. The last few cycles, he has conserved his strength, studied every failure, honed his strategies. He is no longer simply enduring—he is planning to break free in a way that cannot be undone. I saw this, and I sought a way to stop him."

"But how do the cycles end?" Darien asked, feeling frustrated and the complexity of the answers.

"The cycles continue because of the spell. The spell works to bring all four members of The Eldric to Olympus to collect the weapons–"

"Yeah," Darien interrupted, "Why do we have to do that, anyway? That seems pointless. Sending us all over Olympus to get these weapons, only to use them to challenge Cyprin and then reimprison him. It seems like if you just put them all in one place, it would happen a lot faster."

Whytaren's irritation at the interruption did not go unnoticed. But given the situation, Darien didn't much care.

Whyn folded his hands together remaining calm, "The weapons are there to create the journey. The original four I brought together to cast the spell, the ones who held the weapons, including the sword you now carry, knew each other so well, they were so attuned with their neighbors as allies, friends, and comrades, that they were willing and able to do anything for each other, to give anything for the other. The weapons are scattered to create the journey. The journey bonds The Eldric together, as nothing like traveling together does, so that when they do come to face Cyprin together and complete the ritual, they know that they can rely on each other."

Darien nodded. He knew the value of teamwork from his time at The Academy. Had he not trusted Kara, Philip, and even Trey in every fight, he would have used precious time worrying if they would do what was necessary.

"Okay, fine. But how do the cycles end? You say you think I can do that, but when he's beaten he'll just come back again, won't he?"

Whytaren shook his head, "Not necessarily. The Cycles provide a method of imprisoning Cyprin. Of cutting him off from the flow of magic, just as he did to the world. It was a clever bit of magic, if I say so myself, and one that likely frustrates him to no end given his lust for power. But it does not truly defeat him. To be beaten he must be faced on the field of battle. He must be slain as the mortal man that he truly is. Either by magic or by steel, his heart must stop beating."

Darien narrowed his eyes. "And you thought training another spellcaster would do it. Someone to do your job for you."

Whytaren's eyes narrowed, the first hint of true anger covering a dangerous rage beneath the calm demeanor that Darien had seen since coming to the valley crossing his mentor's now grey face.

"Do not forget who you are speaking to. I am not simply the sword master you thought me to be. It is I who fought against and *killed* my dearest friends so long ago. I fought in wars you cannot even yet imagine. You knew the people of Farkland Reach for days, weeks. I was fighting the friends I had known and built bonds with for decades. Do not presume to know what I have sacrificed, or that you can comprehend the sorrow that entails."

Darien sat stunned at the swiftness and intensity of the words.

"I'm sorry."

Whytaren nodded his acceptance of the apology and allowed his tone to soften again.

"That being said, you are not entirely incorrect. I was looking for someone to do what I cannot. There are aspects of the spell I wrought that limit me. I cannot face Cyprin, the stakes are simply too high. So I spent the last ten cycles searching for someone who I thought could. Someone who could challenge him not just with magic, but with the ability to see beyond what others could, an innate, inborn ability. Watching you at the Academy, I believed it might be you."

Darien thought for many long minutes. Absorbing the information he had gathered thus far. So many moving pieces, so many things falling into place that he had wondered for the days, weeks, and months since coming to Olympus.

"Why didn't you teach me to shield my mind? If knowing of you, of this place," Darien gestured to the landscape around them, "was so dangerous. Why was that not the first thing I learned?"

Whytaren's face remained unreadable. "There are things you still do not understand, things that must be revealed in time. You ask why I didn't teach you to shield your mind sooner—because everything must come in its time. The skills you have now? They are the basics. And while you have mastered them faster than I anticipated, through sheer natural talent, you can only learn so much in a given time. Even I, who I saw modestly was one of the greatest of my generation, spent five years training before I was taught how to use a transition. You have used them, and to great effect, I might add, in only six months of training. It is impressive work, one that would have made you the leader of your class, just as Cyprin and

I were three thousand years ago. But it does not mean you are ready to take on additional work more quickly."

Darien accepted this, seeing the wisdom in Whyn's pacing of instruction, even if he didn't like it. Taking a deep breath, he asked the last question that was on his mind, at least for the moment.

"And why can't you face Cyprin yourself?"

Whytaren took a slow breath. "That is something I cannot tell you yet. Not because I don't want to, but because knowing it now would put you in danger. Cyprin has had three thousand years to plot. Even in his imprisonment, he has done nothing but think, plan, and adapt. I know his mind, he will have made plans within plans, that he is no doubt executing even now. He has no access to magic when locked away, but his mind remains sharp."

Darien exhaled sharply, shaking his head. "I understand why you kept some of this from me, but that doesn't make it any easier to trust you. You're not even who I thought you were. You kept secrets, not just about this war, but about yourself. How do I trust someone when I don't even know what they really are?"

Whytaren's expression softened slightly, though his tone remained measured. "That doubt is fair. I have kept my secrets for a long time. A plan that takes centuries to create and execute in secret is not so easily shared without hesitation. You were not meant to be pulled into this yet, and for that, I regret the burden placed upon you before you were ready."

They sat there in silence for several more minutes, the weight of the conversation pressing down on them both. The wind rustled through the valley, cool against Darien's skin, but his mind still burned with the remnants of his anger. It was easier to stay mad, to hold onto the frustration, but he was tired. Tired of questions without answers, tired of fighting against something he could not yet define.

Whytaren shifted slightly. "Food often settles the mind, even when the body does not crave it. You should eat."

Darien blinked, surprised by the abrupt shift, but then something in him twisted. It had been weeks since he had last eaten a proper meal. The thought of food sent a pang of longing through him—not just for sustenance, but for the comfort of shared meals, of laughter, of simpler times. Memories of the Academy surfaced: late nights at the dining hall, stolen bits of bread during study sessions, meals shared with friends who now felt so distant.

He exhaled and nodded wordlessly.

Whytaren stood, leading him back to their dwelling. The fire crackled softly as Whytaren set to work, moving with practiced efficiency as he prepared a simple meal—a stew of root vegetables, its earthy aroma filling the space. Darien sat cross-legged near the fire, watching the flickering flames dance across the walls, his thoughts still tangled but quieter now.

They ate in silence. The food was warm, filling, but more than that—it was grounding. A moment of normalcy in the midst of chaos. Darien let himself focus on that, even as the weight of everything still pressed against him. There would be more questions, more battles to fight. But for now, he just ate and enjoyed the quiet company.

# Chapter 20: The Hero Returns

The training continued, each day bleeding into the next in a blur of exertion and magic. Darien threw himself into his lessons, but he kept his silence. He executed tasks, followed Whytaren's instructions to the letter, but offered no words in return. It was his quiet protest, his way of maintaining control in a world that had been ripped from him. If Whytaren noticed, he gave no indication. He merely provided careful, measured instruction, never pushing, never pressing for conversation.

The silence between them was thick but not strained. It was something that settled between master and student like an unspoken agreement. Darien was angry, and Whytaren allowed him that.

Yet with each passing day, the lessons grew harder. Darien expanded his abilities in ways he hadn't thought possible. He refined his control over the ethers, weaving them into new forms, testing limits that had once seemed untouchable. Fire that once burst outward in raw, explosive force now curled around his fingertips, contained and shaped into delicate patterns. Water did not just flow; it danced, suspended in the air at his command before freezing into razor-sharp shards. He learned to manipulate wind into solid forms, creating temporary platforms beneath his feet, allowing him to leap impossibly high or glide for short distances.

One day, he combined what he had learned, sending forth an arc of lightning only to guide it along a current of water, allowing it to bend and twist toward its target instead of traveling in a straight line. Another time, he used fire and wind together, creating a vortex of heat so intense that even stone blackened beneath its touch.

Still, he did not speak.

Whytaren did not comment on the silence. He simply continued, introducing the next phase of training when the time was right.

It was time to learn to shield his mind.

"The mind is the last true battlefield, Darien," Whytaren said one morning, breaking the long-held silence. "If you cannot protect it, then all of your power, all of your skill, will mean nothing."

Darien only nodded. He had known this lesson was coming. Whytaren had warned him about it before. He had also warned him that he was not yet ready to face the full truths of the war he had been pulled into. If his mind remained unguarded, he was vulnerable.

"The ethers flow through us, around us. They are the conduit through which magic is performed, but they are also the medium through which thoughts can be touched," Whytaren continued. "Your task is to create a barrier, not with brute force, but with precision. Too strong, and you will cut yourself off from the ethers entirely. Too weak, and you will leave yourself open to invasion. Balance is everything."

Darien listened, absorbing the information, then closed his eyes. He could feel the ethers as he always had, wrapping around him, shifting with his intent. But this time, he had to do something different. He had to hold them at bay while keeping just enough access to maintain his connection to magic.

He visualized a wall—not one of stone or steel, but something fluid, something reactive. He focused on the way the ethers reacted when they met resistance, using that energy to push back without severing the connection completely. The process was delicate, demanding. More than once, his barrier collapsed entirely, leaving his mind exposed, his magic unresponsive. But each time, he rebuilt it, fine-tuning the edges, adjusting the structure until it held.

Then Whytaren struck.

It was not a physical attack, but an intrusion—something foreign pressing against his mind, tendrils of magic searching for an opening. Darien gritted his teeth, shifting the point of access, diverting the connection, making it harder for Whytaren to gain a foothold. But after only a few seconds, Whytaren was through, pushing magically controlled ether through his mind and probing into every part of his being. The sensation was incredibly uncomfortable.

"Good," Whytaren murmured. "But not good enough. Again."

The days blurred together as Darien trained relentlessly. He found new ways to integrate his magic with his swordplay, refining techniques that allowed him to shift seamlessly between raw power and refined precision. He used wind not just for speed but to guide his blade mid-strike, redirecting his momentum at the last second to throw off an opponent's defense. He combined force magic with fire, slamming his sword down and releasing an eruption of heat that sent shockwaves through the air. His footwork became sharper, aided by currents of wind beneath his heels, allowing him to move with an almost unnatural grace.

But the mental training was even more grueling. Every night, while others might have rested, he spent hours either reading ancient texts or reinforcing his mind against Whytaren's relentless attacks. His teacher had made it clear—his defenses had to be constant, unwavering. It became a part of him, a reflex, until he could maintain a shield even as he slept. And yet, no matter how far he progressed, he still couldn't fully keep Whytaren out.

Then, one morning after a month of silent struggle, Darien stood in the training clearing, his sword humming with power. The morning air was crisp, cool against his skin, but already charged with the tension that crackled between them. Whytaren stood opposite him, his stance measured, his own blade resting easily in his grip. The training space had become familiar, yet it felt different today—heavier.

They circled each other, and then, without warning, Whytaren struck. His blade cut through the air like lightning, and Darien barely had time to deflect, sparks erupting as steel met steel. The force of the impact sent a sharp tremor up his arm, but he did not falter. Whytaren pressed forward, attacking with a flurry of quick, precise movements, each one aiming to break Darien's guard. Darien countered, using wind to subtly shift his momentum, twisting his body at the last second to avoid the worst of each blow.

Then the real battle began. Whytaren's mind surged toward Darien's, seeking an opening even as their blades clashed. Darien gritted his teeth, reinforcing his mental defenses, shifting the access point to the ethers away from Whytaren's probing tendrils. But Whytaren was relentless. He feinted high with his sword, forcing Darien to raise his guard, then attacked his mind in that instant, pressing his etheric will forward in a sudden, forceful strike.

Darien staggered back, gasping, but recovered quickly. His warning system flared, his body sending signals of strain, but he ignored them. He had to push through.

He adapted. Instead of only defending, he began using his mind as a weapon. He visualized a spear of thought and thrust it forward, targeting Whytaren's own access point. The older spellcaster's eyes widened slightly as he adjusted, shifting his own defenses to block Darien's intrusion. But Darien had expected that.

Their swords blurred as they fought at inhuman speeds, the world around them slowing in contrast. Leaves and dust swirled in the air, suspended in the wake of their movements. Darien took control of the wind, using it to pull himself into a spin mid-strike, bringing his sword down with punishing force. Whytaren blocked, but just barely, skidding backward from the impact.

Darien didn't let up. He fused his force magic into his blade, sending a concentrated pulse of energy through it at the moment of impact. The resulting shockwave cracked the ground beneath them, forcing Whytaren back further.

And then Darien saw his opening.

With a roar, he locked blades with Whytaren, forcing their swords together with immense force. At that same moment, he launched his etheric attack—an aggressive, unrelenting probe, not meant just to block, but to invade.

Whytaren's defenses snapped, caught off guard by the sheer ferocity of the attack. For the first time, Darien's mind broke through, pushing into the depths of his teacher's thoughts.

And what he found froze him.

Pride. Overwhelming pride. Not just admiration for his progress, but something deeper—an unshakable, quiet love. Every lesson, every sacrifice, every carefully measured instruction... it had all been for him. For Darien. Not as a student, not as a piece on some grand board, but as someone Whytaren truly, deeply cared for.

Darien's breath hitched. His sword lowered slightly, and the connection severed. He felt it still—the warmth, the pride, the undeniable truth of what he had just seen.

He staggered back, his body trembling, but not from exhaustion. For the first time in weeks, he spoke, his voice quieter than he expected.

"Thank you," he said, his throat tight. "For everything."

Whytaren met his gaze, his expression unreadable for a moment. Then, he gave a single, slow nod. No words were needed.

The days of training had taken their toll, leaving Darien in a state of exhaustion that made him miss the spectre of sleep. The quiet of the valley pressed down on him, his mind drifting between the rhythm of past battles and the weight of future ones. Every strike of his blade, every surge of the ethers, had been honed with purpose. The weight of it all gnawed at him, persistent and inescapable. Every muscle burned, every fiber of his being demanded rest, but his mind refused to be still. His breath was steady, but his thoughts raced beyond the valley, beyond the silent nights and the endless cycle of preparation.

Evatra. Rist. Breyman. Airlyn.

It had been days in the wider world—perhaps more. The thought gnawed at him, refusing to be ignored. He closed his eyes and reached out with the ethers, the energy surging around him, bending to his will. The connection formed almost immediately, as if the urgency of his emotions made it sharper, clearer.

It was not sight as he had once understood it. He was not merely looking—he was moving, his consciousness untethered, flowing through the ethers like a river seeking its course. The valley fell away beneath him, the physical world dissolving into an endless weave of unseen currents, pulsing energy that twisted and churned in a rhythm older than time itself. He willed himself forward, following the pull of his thoughts, reaching beyond space, beyond distance.

Shadows of places flickered past him—faint, distant echoes of where he had been, where he could be. The Academy, its great halls shimmering like a half-forgotten dream. The battlefields of Farkland Reach, stained with the memory of war. He did not stop. He could not stop.

He was weightless, bodiless, his awareness stretching farther and farther, until suddenly—clarity.

A sharp inhalation, a feeling like snapping into place.

Evatra stood on the rocky overlook, her stance tense as she peered down at the open room of stone below her. The ledge she stood upon was narrow, barely more than a jagged outcrop jutting from the top walkway of the space. Her eyes were locked on the figures below.

The space below was wide and dark, an ancient maw in the rock, framed by half-worn carvings that spoke of a civilization long past. Fires burned along the perimeter, their glow flickering against the jagged walls still in the changed time scale of the valley. Shadows stretched long across the stone floor, almost shifting as figures moved beneath them at a pace almost imperceptible to him.

Then he saw them.

Rist, Breyman, and Airlyn, being led forward. Their hands were bound, their bodies stiff with the weight of their situation. Torchlight caught on the metal restraints, making them gleam in the dim cavern. Their faces were grim, set in expressions of determination, though Airlyn's eyes darted around, calculating, searching for something unseen.

Before them, Tahmer loomed, his dark presence commanding the space around him. His posture was relaxed, almost casual, but there was no mistaking the power that radiated from him. The air itself felt heavier near him, charged with something unnatural. He watched his prisoners with the quiet amusement of a predator who already knew how the hunt would end.

Darien's heart pounded. The moment stood frozen in perfect, agonizing detail. Despite not being there, he felt the cold bite of the mountain air. The damp stone of the tunnels and the distant scent of burning torch oil filled his nostrils. He felt the tension in Evatra's shoulders, the weight of the situation pressing down on her like a crushing force. And beyond that—Tahmer's presence, dark and immovable, like a black hole at the center of it all.

He didn't need to rewind time. The image was stark enough on its own—a vision burned into his mind like a scar.

His mind was made up. He had to go. Now.

His eyes snapped open, breath coming faster. He pushed himself to his feet, muscles protesting the sudden movement, but he didn't care. If he didn't act now, all hope of the cycles could be lost. His friends—his family—needed him.

He turned sharply, finding Whytaren watching him from the entrance of the dwelling. There was no surprise in his dark eyes, only quiet understanding.

"I have to leave," Darien stated. "I have to go now."

Whytaren's expression didn't change. "If you leave, you risk everything we've built. If your injury flares at the wrong moment, it will be over. Cyprin will have won."

Darien's jaw tightened. "Then they still have the other three. If what you said is true, if the weapons don't matter but the bond between the Eldric does, then by your own logic, I must go. If I fail, they have to be there to carry on the cycles. You may have lost your friends all that time ago, but mine are still alive."

Whytaren's eyes flickered, and Darien saw the words land like a blow. The silence between them stretched, heavy with meaning.

"I can't let them die," Darien continued. "You wouldn't have given up on your friends either. You know there's no other way."

Whytaren's shoulders rose and fell in a slow breath. For the first time in their long discussions, in their arguments and lessons, he hesitated.

"You are not ready," he said finally.

"I'll never be ready if I sit here while my friends are slaughtered."

Whytaren exhaled sharply, then, with a slow nod, turned toward the small chest at the back of the dwelling.

Darien watched as Whytaren pulled out supplies—rations, a reinforced cloak, and equipment he had set aside long before Darien even knew he would need them. But it was the armor that caught Darien's eye.

It was the finest he had ever seen—ornate, beautiful, yet lethal in its precision. The metal, though ancient, gleamed as if newly forged, intricate engravings of celestial patterns and golden sunbursts dancing along the surface. Every piece was fitted together seamlessly, designed not just for protection but for elegance, for power. The craftsmanship was beyond anything modern smiths could replicate.

Whytaren lifted the chest plate, running his fingers over the delicate engravings. "This was the armor of Apollo, twin brother to Artemis," he said, his voice softer than usual. "In the final battle, she betrayed him, slew him in the name of Cyprin. His body was lost, but his armor remained, hidden away. Its enchantments faded long ago, but its legacy remains."

Darien reached out hesitantly, letting his fingers brush against the smooth metal. He could feel the weight of history in it, the ghosts of battles fought long before his time. "It's incredible."

Whytaren nodded. "It will serve you well. The enchantments may be gone, but they can be restored—if you find the right means, if you learn how." It was clear that Whytaren meant that he would have to return for that particular lesson. But the fact that he had the pieces stored away meant that he had always known this moment would come, whether he wanted it to or not.

Next, Whytaren went to his private quarters, where Darien had laid him after he had lost consciousness in his effort to prevent Darien's death at the loss of control of magic all that time ago. It felt like another life given how far his abilities had come since then. He returned with the sword. The jeweled handle, gleamed in the flicker of sunlight.

"What are you doing? Shouldn't that stay here?"

Whytaren shook his head. "No."

The word was said simply. No expression, no inflection, no emotion. But by it he communicated everything. This sword was meant to be used to take down Cyprin. It was not just a relic, not just an amulet or token, it was a weapon, forged for a purpose and it was time for it to return to it's makers design for the object. It was a weapon of war that had kept Cyprin imprisoned for millennia, and it was time to use it to defeat his agents in what would likely be the first battle between spellcasters, himself and Tahmer, in three thousand years.

Finally, Whytaren reached into the folds of his robe and pulled out a small metal token, its surface etched with ancient symbols. He held it out to Darien. "This will allow you to return to the valley. But only for seven days. After that, the magic that allows you to re-enter will fade. The valley protects itself from transitions beyond its boundaries. The only reason you were able to enter before was because I brought you here."

Darien took the token, his fingers curling around the cool metal. "Seven days."

Whytaren nodded. "Make them count."

# Chapter 21: The Friends Reunited

Darien stepped beyond the valley, feeling the air shift around him as if the world itself recognized his departure. A sensation he had long forgotten washed over him—fatigue, the kind that only true sleep could cure. His limbs felt heavier, the energy that had once sustained him no longer humming beneath his skin. The stillness of the valley had been deceiving; out here, the weight of reality pressed against him, unrelenting.

How long had it been? Weeks? Months? He turned, glancing back at the valley's entrance. The protective enchantments shimmered faintly, an invisible veil ensuring that only those permitted could enter. It felt strange to be on the other side of it now, like stepping beyond an unspoken boundary that had tethered him to something greater than himself. He tried to piece the timeline together. It had to have been nearly a year inside the valley. Here in Olympus, only a handful of weeks had passed. The realization sent a cold shiver down his spine. He would spend no more than a week here in the wider world of Olympus but Whytaren...

Whytaren would return to an isolated existence. He would experience those months alone. For all his measured wisdom, for all the secrets he had withheld, he had been a presence—one Darien had come to rely on, even when he didn't want to. The thought of him remaining in solitude, waiting, made Darien's chest tighten. Months for Whyn, spent in quiet isolation, the only company being his own thoughts. Darien felt a pang of guilt, but he couldn't let that hold him back. He had made his decision. His friends needed him.

Before leaving, Darien had used farsight to return to Totra-Dal's room, mentally tracing his way back to the maps scattered across the wooden table. The vision took shape slowly, the act of rewinding time through the ethers more difficult the further back in time he went. He clenched his teeth against the pressure in his mind, the sensation like swimming upstream against a raging current. Every second backward felt like pulling against the weight of the world.

The world blurred, shifted, and then solidified.

He saw Evatra, standing over the maps, her finger trailing along marked routes, discussing their next move. Though Darien had never been in that exact location, he had a direction, a destination. The energy it had taken to hold the vision left him breathless, his limbs weak, but it was enough. He could get close—close enough.

He had also donned the armor—the armor of Apollo.

The chestplate gleamed in the dim light of Whytaren's dwelling, the intricate engravings of celestial patterns and golden sunbursts catching the flicker of the fire. The metal seemed almost alive, reflecting light in ways that made the etchings appear to shift and glow. Ornate, but functional. Regal, yet forged for battle.

He reached for the first piece, the weight of history pressing against his palms. As he lifted it to his chest, he felt the old magic within it—long dormant, waiting. The plates were heavier than he expected, yet perfectly balanced, made to fit a warrior of Apollo's stature. He adjusted the fit, feeling the rigid metal press against him. Too stiff. Too foreign.

Whytaren had guided him through the process, silent as ever, watching. "Use the ethers," he had said at last. "Make it your own."

Darien took a slow breath, reaching inward. Obediently, the ethers flowed into the metal, wrapping around it like invisible hands. The armor shifted, the plates aligning, molding to his body—not a separate entity, but an extension of himself. The sensation was unlike anything he had felt before.

It was a merging, as if the armor itself was recognizing him, acknowledging the new wearer. The chestplate settled against him, no longer foreign but familiar. The vambraces wrapped smoothly around his forearms, each segment adjusting with fluid motion as he flexed his hands.

He looked down, watching the engravings glow faintly in response to his touch. This had once belonged to Apollo. A warrior. A spellcaster of old who had fought against Cyprin.

He flexed his fingers, feeling the movement in the bracers, the subtle give in the armor where he needed mobility. The weight settled, not just on his body, but in his mind. This was real. He was going back, stepping into a war he barely understood, wearing the remnants of a legend. The thought was humbling.

Now, as he stood outside the valley, clad in armor that bore the echoes of a forgotten past, Darien let out a slow breath. The weight of the armor, the journey ahead, the seven days he had to return—it all pressed in on him.

He was on his own and now he had to determine his next actions. He knew what he was planning but had worked hard to keep his mind shielded so that Whytaren wouldn't be able to figure out his plans. He knew he wouldn't have approved of what he was planning.

Darien had seen the battle ahead—Tahmer, the Peronian Boronoth, and several soldiers from the remnants of Cyprin's dark army had filled that cavern. There were likely more in the various tunnels that stretched off from that central chamber. He needed help, and he had an idea of how to get it.

One of the nights after his heated argument with Whytaren, in an act of quiet rebellion, Darien had pulled one of the forbidden texts from the shelves of Whytaren's dwelling. His fingers had hovered over the bindings, skimming across the dust-coated tomes, their covers etched with symbols that pulsed faintly with latent magic. He chose one at random—or perhaps, he told himself, the ethers had chosen for him.

The book felt heavier than it should have, as if knowledge itself weighed upon its spine. As he cracked it open, the pages crackled with age, and an unnatural chill swept up his arms. His eyes darted over the ancient script, his heart pounding as the words unfolded before him.

Transitions. Not just through space, but through worlds.

His breath hitched as he read further. There was a way. A way to reach across immeasurable distances, a technique few had mastered—one that could allow him to go anywhere, provided he understood the principles. A cascade transition. A technique both magnificent and terrifying. A manipulation of the ethers so volatile that even the most experienced spellcasters dared not attempt it lightly. Darien swallowed hard as the implications of the text sank in. He had caused a cascade transition before—unintentionally. And had Whytaren not been there to stabilize it, it would have torn him apart.

He remembered the sensation vividly—the raw energy surging, spiraling out of his control. The way the flames had nearly consumed him, his essence pulled in every direction at once, caught between forces far greater than himself. The power had nearly killed him, but now, here he was considering doing it on purpose.

But the book also held answers. If he could learn to guide the cascade—to use the merging of the ethers to fuel his movement rather than let it consume him—he could reach anywhere. He could reach them.

The text described the process in meticulous detail—a technique that allowed the ethers to merge violently, creating a surge of energy that, if harnessed correctly, could funnel the caster to a precise location anywhere in existence. But the warning beneath it was clear: Only those with true mastery of both transitions and farsight could attempt such a feat. Without a solid anchor, without pre-existing knowledge of the destination, the caster could be lost—forever.

Darien exhaled, his mind spinning. A combination of farsight and transitions. It wasn't impossible, but it was risky, especially the inclusion of language translation. He didn't know how it worked, but he knew how to do it. He had been stretching the limits of both for months now. But this? This was dangerous. Reckless. But did he really have any other choice, given that Whytaren refused to leave the valley?

He knew of only two people in the universe he could trust right now. And if he was going to make this work, he had to do it quickly.

He took a slow breath, steadying himself as he reached out. The ethers stirred, responding to his will. Not in a slow, controlled way as before—but violently, a river breaking through a dam, rushing forward too fast to contain. His heart pounded as the energy built, an unstoppable force surging toward the moment of release.

He had never felt anything like it. This was power untethered. He wasn't just summoning the ethers, he was commanding them, forcing them into motion with his intent alone. It was overwhelming—raw destruction colliding with creation, two forces warring to maintain their balance. He had to guide it, had to shape it into something usable before it consumed him entirely.

The magic tore through space, threading between the unseen fibers of reality, searching, stretching outward in search of familiarity. His mind strained, his focus bending under the weight of what he was trying to do. The transition had to be precise. If he let go too soon, he would be lost. If he pushed too hard, the ethers would collapse upon themselves, and he would be swallowed whole.

The sensation was indescribable—his body pulled in every direction at once, weightless and yet impossibly heavy. He felt the fabric of the universe twist around him, bending, reshaping, merging. It was both too much and not enough. His mind reached further, stretching beyond the known, past distances that should have been impossible.

Then, at last, he felt it. A familiar thread, a resonance buried deep in his memory. A place he had lived, studied, grown. A place tied to him in ways even he hadn't and still didn't fully understand.

His body lurched as the transition snapped into place. The force of it threw him forward, yanking him through the collapsing ethers. It was like being pulled through an ocean current of energy, his body stretched impossibly thin, his consciousness slipping between the fabric of space itself. He was neither whole nor broken, existing in the in-between, his awareness flickering between what had been and what was becoming.

Light streaked past him in violent flashes, colors he had no name for blending into a swirling vortex. The air was thick with pressure, as though he were plummeting through an endless sky with no ground to stop his fall. Sound warped, distant echoes of voices long past bleeding into the present. His own heartbeat pounded like a war drum, reverberating through his skull, anchoring him to himself. He had to hold on. He had to keep the image of his destination fixed in his mind or risk being lost in the ether's ever-consuming tide.

And then, as suddenly as it began, the energy released him.

He slammed onto solid ground, his knees hitting cold, familiar stone. The ethers pulled away like a receding wave, leaving him gasping, his vision swimming from the disorienting shift. Silence rang in his ears, and for a long moment, he knelt there, his fingers splayed against the stone floor, his breath ragged.

The transition had worked.

Darien forced himself to lift his head. A pale, sterile sheen from the artificial glow of LED lights washed over the spartan dormitory room. The walls, bare and unadorned, had once been comforting in their simplicity, but now they felt oppressive, suffocating. The familiar hum of the ventilation system droned softly in the background, blending with the faint mechanical whir of automated temperature controls. The air was dry, processed, lacking the organic richness of the valley's untouched wilderness.

The room was exactly as he had left it—a narrow bed with stiff, gray sheets tucked military-tight, a simple desk covered in neatly stacked notes and textbooks, a wardrobe filled with clothing of a style he no longer wore. The Academy had always been practical, structured. He had lived in this space for years, yet standing here now, clad in Apollo's armor, he felt as if he were an intruder in his own past.

Everything about the space seemed smaller than he remembered, as if he had outgrown it—not in size, but in presence. The very air felt different, the cold efficiency of this world clashing with the sheer weight of history resting on his shoulders. He wasn't a student anymore. He was a warrior, carrying the remnants of an age that had long since passed.

Darien exhaled slowly, his fingers tightening at his sides. Then, nausea hit him like a crashing wave. His stomach twisted violently, his head spun, and the floor beneath him tilted as though the transition had left part of him behind. He barely kept himself from retching, his body rebelling against the sheer force of what had just happened.

His vision blurred, his breath came in short, ragged gasps. He clenched his fists, digging his nails into his palms, grounding himself through sheer force of will. His body wanted to give in, to collapse, but he refused. Not here. Not now.

Several long moments passed as the worst of it began to fade. The pressure behind his eyes eased, the weight in his stomach settling into a dull ache instead of a raging storm. He forced himself to focus, to push through the remnants of vertigo.

He had made it back. But the world he had known felt distant, like a dream he had long since awoken from.

"What the hell?!"

The voice snapped Darien out of his haze. He knew that voice.

He turned sharply, his movements still sluggish from the transition, and found himself staring at Philip. His wide bodied, bull-like friend, who he had fought with an uncountable times in the arena of The

Academy, stood frozen near the doorway, wide-eyed, his expression shifting rapidly between confusion and disbelief. Darien watched as Philip's gaze traveled over him, taking in the ornate armor, the sword at his hip, the sheer impossibility of his presence.

"Philip?" Darien's voice came out hoarse.

"Darien?" Philip took a hesitant step forward. "Is that... is that really you?"

Darien exhaled sharply, lifting his hands to the clasps of his helmet. With a faint hiss of shifting metal, he removed it, letting the cool air touch his skin. His dark hair fell messily over his forehead, his face etched with exhaustion, but there was no mistaking him now.

Philip let out something between a laugh and a breathless curse. "You look like a goddamn warlord. What is this? Where have you been?"

Darien shook his head, suddenly overwhelmed. "It's... a long story."

Philip gave him a once-over again, still disbelieving. His mouth opened, closed, then opened again before the words finally burst out. "What the hell is going on?! Where have you been?! You just—vanished! Do you know what people have been saying? Do you have any idea what you've put us through? I thought—hell, we all thought you were dead! And then, Whyn disappeared too! The same day! No explanation, nothing! You just blinked out of existence!"

Darien barely had time to process before Philip took another step closer, his eyes scanning him up and down, trying to reconcile the image before him. "And what—" Philip gestured wildly to the armor, the sword, the sheer impossible presence of him. "What is this? You look like you walked out of some ancient war. You—"

Philip let out something between a laugh and a breathless curse, rubbing his face with both hands. "You have got to start explaining this, man. Now." Darien struggled with what words to use to communicate the urgency. He was quiet for several beats, which Philip clearly didn't appreciate.

"Listen, I promise I'll tell you everything. But I only want to do it once. It's a lot to take in. First—where is everyone? Where's Kara? Where's Trey?"

Philip looked like he wanted to argue, but answered Darien's questions, anyway. "Trey went home," Philip said, the words tumbling out, his frustration barely masked beneath the relief. "His uncle died—he had to leave for the funeral. Kara…" He let out a slow breath, his gaze flickering toward the window. "She's probably on the roof. She spends all her time up there now. Since you disappeared… she's not doing okay."

Darien's stomach clenched. Kara. His friend. She had been more than that for longer than he could remember. Guilt at his relationship with Evatra pulled at him. He was going to have to explain that too. But that was later. He barely managed to swallow past the lump in his throat. "I need you to go get her, and don't tell anyone else what's going on."

Philip opened his mouth as if to argue, then shut it. He let out an exasperated sigh and scrubbed a hand over his face. "Fine. But you owe us both one hell of a story."

Darien nodded, watching as Philip turned and hurried out of the room. Before he fully left he remembered.

"Have her grab her gear for the Arena. All of it."

Philip turned back to look at Darien, a look of deep confusion on his face, but he went without asking any more questions.

Darien exhaled, glancing around, really looking at the space now. His things were gone. The room wasn't his anymore. Philip was staying here alone now. But even stripped of his belongings, there was still something familiar, a faint echo of the life he had once had. Yet, for the first time, he realized it wasn't home.

Darien sat on the edge of the bed, his fingers absently tracing the seam of his armored vambrace. The room was silent except for the faint hum of the ventilation system, the steady rhythm a stark contrast to the storm raging inside him. He had waited for what felt like hours, but the clock on the desk revealed it had only been five minutes.

His mind raced, his body tense—but then, a strange sensation stirred in his abdomen. It was sharp, hollow, foreign.

He was hungry.

He blinked, startled by the realization. He let out a short, breathless laugh. He had forgotten what hunger felt like.

Between the valley's magic sustaining him and the endless training sessions, the need for food had become a distant memory. Now, though, with the weight of everything crashing down on him, his stomach twisted in protest, demanding nourishment in a way he hadn't experienced in what felt like a lifetime.

The sheer absurdity of it all sent another chuckle through him. Here he was, a walking legend in ancient armor, fresh from an impossible journey across space and time, sitting in his old dorm, waiting for his friends—and the first thing his body decides to do is remind him that he needs a sandwich.

He shook his head, still grinning faintly, when the door burst open.

Philip stepped in first, looking exasperated, and behind him, Kara stormed in, her expression set in familiar frustration. She carried a small bag of gear that clinked as the equipment moved against itself.

"Whatever it is you have to show me," she said, voice sharp with warning, "it better be damn good. I am tired of people trying to make me feel better—"

She stopped mid-sentence, her bag dropping to the floor. The words died in her throat as her gaze locked onto him.

Darien had expected some kind of reaction, but not this kind of silence. Kara just stood there, her blonde hair swaying slightly from her sudden stop, her blue eyes wide as she took him in. The armor. The sword. The sheer impossibility of him standing before her.

She moved then, slowly, as if approaching a wild animal, one wrong move away from bolting. Her fingers twitched at her sides, then lifted, reaching for him—softly, sweetly, like she was about to cup his face, reassure herself that he was real.

Then she smacked him. Hard.

The slap rang through the room, his head snapping to the side, the metal of his armor doing absolutely nothing to lessen the sting. If anything, it just made it worse. His ears were ringing.

Philip winced.

Kara shook out her hand, muttering something under her breath about how his stupid face was still as annoying as ever, then reeled back to hit him again.

The second slap never landed. The moment her palm collided with the chestplate, pain shot up her arm, and she yelped in frustration and pain, shaking out her fingers furiously.

"What the hell, Darien?!" she shouted, cradling her injured hand.

He just sat there, blinking, taking it. This was fair.

Kara, however, was not finished. She tried punching him next—bad idea. Her fist connected with the solid metal of his shoulder guard, and the sharp impact had her stumbling back, hissing through her teeth.

Philip barely had time to react before Kara turned to him, eyes ablaze. "Let me go," she demanded.

Philip hesitated. "Kara—"

"Give me your axe."

Darien's eyes widened. "Wait—"

"I am going to take his head off!"

Philip let out a nervous laugh, gripping her shoulders as she squirmed and kicked in his grasp. "I *like* my axe, thank you very much. And I think we all like Darien's head right where it is."

Darien sighed, rubbing his jaw. "Kara—"

"No! You disappeared! No warning, no explanation, no nothing! And now you just show up looking like you walked out of a prophecy?! Are you kidding me?!"

She bucked again, nearly breaking free before Philip tightened his hold. "*Would you stop?!*"

"Not until I hit him at least one more time!"

Philip groaned. "Darien, do *something!*"

Darien held up his hands in surrender. "Kara, I swear I will explain everything, but you breaking your hand on my armor is not going to help!"

She glared at him, breathing heavily, strands of hair falling over her face. Then she pointed at him, finger shaking.

"You better start talking fast, Darien Glade, or I swear I will find a way to stab you."

# Chapter 22: The Journey Retold

Darien exhaled, rubbing his face as Kara's glare bored into him. Philip looked just as bewildered, though his stance was far less aggressive. The tension in the room was thick, but they didn't have time for this.

"We can't stay here," Darien said firmly, his voice cutting through the lingering chaos of Kara's outburst.

Philip frowned. "What do you mean? Stay where? What the hell is going on?"

Darien shook his head. "I need your help, but you need to know something first. This isn't a game. This isn't the arena. It's real danger. People will die. We might die. But you're my closest friends, and I need you. If you're willing, I want you to come with me. I'm asking you to trust me."

Kara crossed her arms, still seething, her blue eyes burning into him. "Trust you? After you vanished without a word? After you show up looking like some kind of—some kind of warrior god?!"

"I know," Darien said, trying to rein in his frustration. "I know how this looks. But you need to listen to me. Something weird is going to happen. You're going to see something blue, and when you do, you need to touch it. One right after the other—quickly. Philip, get your gear together."

Philip exchanged a glance with Kara, both looking more skeptical by the second. "What? Why? What does that even mean?"

Kara let out a harsh breath. "And what exactly are you dragging us into this time?"

Philip and Kara both started talking at once, questions tumbling over each other. Darien clenched his fists, his patience wearing thin.

"LOOK AT ME!" he roared. His voice rang sharp through the dorm room, and both of them froze.

He gestured at himself, the heavy armor gleaming under the artificial lights, the sword at his side radiating an ancient presence. "Do you really think I'm making this up? Do you think I'd come back looking like this if it wasn't serious?"

Darien kept his face earnest, as he took a step towards them, trying to let some calm return to his tone.

"Obviously, something bigger is happening," he continued, his voice steady, commanding. "I'm asking for your help, and it's important. Do you really think I would disappear for no reason? Do you think I would keep you in the dark if I didn't have to? I need you both.

But if you're coming, you need to decide now. Are you in or not?"

Silence.

Philip let out a slow breath, nodding reluctantly. Kara, arms still crossed, ground her teeth before finally muttering, "Fine."

Darien nodded as he saw Philip began to get his arena equipment and armor shoved into a bag as well. Darien exhaled sharply.

"Okay. Now just do what I say. No questions. I'll explain everything, but not now. First, we get out of here. Do you have your gear?"

Kara nodded, Philip finished stuffing the last bit in his bag, and slung his axe over his back.

Darien closed his eyes, reaching out. The ethers responded instantly, swirling to his command, bending to his will as he prepared the transition. Kara and Philip didn't see it the way he did—they just saw him suddenly go silent, standing there with his eyes shut, his fingers curling slightly like he was grasping something invisible.

"What is he doing?" Kara muttered.

Philip frowned. "I have no idea."

Darien's eye twitched. "Shut up and touch it when it shows up."

They both flinched at the sudden order but exchanged another glance and complied.

Then it appeared. A sphere of blue light, flickering into existence between them, followed by a slight sucking sound that steadily grew louder. Darien strained with the effort it was taking on him. Two long distance transitions was a lot. The buzz that told him he was doing too much began. He couldn't stop. He tried to ignore it, but it got louder, threatening to consume him.

Philip reacted first, reaching out. The moment his fingers brushed the energy, it pulled at him, drawing him into the cascading flow. Kara hesitated for the briefest second before cursing and lunging forward, her hand following his. Darien let himself go into the magic. Buzzing still growing louder and louder in his mind. The transition engulfed them, the dorm room vanishing in a flash of blue.

A heartbeat later, they were somewhere else.

The entrance to the tunnels, exactly where Darien had stood minutes ago before leaving. He had studied this place in excruciating detail before departing, ensuring that when he returned, it would be here. The magic shimmered faintly around the entrance, flickering like heat off stone. The air was thick, heavier than the crisp sterility of the Academy.

The moment the transition ended, Darien collapsed to one knee, the buzzing in his skull growing unbearable. The sensation was worse than before—his wraith-inflicted injury pressing in, the aftershock of two transitions in such rapid succession wracking his body with exhaustion. His stomach clenched, nausea twisting through him, but there was nothing left in him to give.

He dry-heaved, gripping the cold dirt beneath his fingers, his body shuddering from the strain.

Philip and Kara were motionless, sprawled beside him, unconscious from the abrupt shift. Darien squeezed his eyes shut, focusing on breathing, on pushing back the overwhelming need to collapse then and there.

Minutes passed. The nausea ebbed. The buzzing dulled to a distant, persistent hum, a reminder that he was still pushing the limits of what his body could handle. It was frustrating, but it was his existence. His price for his prior victory. Slowly, deliberately, he forced himself upright.

By the time Philip and Kara stirred, Darien had a fire going. A small camp had been set up—rudimentary, but enough. The soft crackling of burning wood filled the air, a welcome contrast to the silence of the half buried tunnel entrance behind them Darien could see where someone, or a group of someone's, had dug their way into the blackness inside. The smell of something cooking—a simple stew made from foraged roots and dried meat—wafted toward them, the aroma grounding Darien as much as the warmth of the flames.

Darien knelt in the dirt, using the tip of his finger to carve rough lines into the earth. The firelight flickered across the uneven terrain as he worked, sketching out the layout of the tunnels as best he could remember from his farsight. Philip and Kara sat across from him, their faces shadowed with lingering uncertainty, but they were listening. That was enough.

"Alright," Darien said, drawing a large circular shape in the center. "This is the main cavern where they're being held. Rist, Breyman, Airlyn, and Evatra. From what I saw, Tahmer is there too, which means we need to be careful. He's powerful, and he's not alone."

Philip rubbed his hands together, glancing between the crude map and Darien. "And you're sure about this? You're sure they're still alive?"

Darien nodded. "I haven't seen anything to suggest otherwise. If they were dead, Tahmer wouldn't be standing over them like a prize. They're valuable to him. He wants them for something."

Kara exhaled sharply. "So what's the plan? We just run in there and hope for the best?"

Darien shook his head. "No. We move carefully. These tunnels go deep, and we'll use them to our advantage. If we can take out guards quietly before reaching the main chamber, we do it. If things go south, we'll need to be ready for a direct fight."

Philip frowned. "And by 'take out,' you mean—"

Darien looked up at them, meeting their eyes. "I mean kill them."

The words hung in the air, heavy and unflinching. Kara's fingers twitched, gripping the edge of her knee. Philip's throat bobbed as he swallowed.

Darien sighed, running a hand through his hair. "Look… I know this isn't what you signed up for. And if you want to back out, do it now. But this is war. I won't lie to you—people will die. If we're not willing to do what needs to be done, then we're already dead."

Philip shifted uncomfortably. "I don't know if I can—"

"I didn't know either," Darien admitted. "Not until Farkland Reach. Not until I was standing there with a sword in my hand, with people charging at me trying to kill me. I was lucky—I had the others, I had the wraith inside me, I had strength I didn't even understand. But even then, it was brutal. It was terrifying."

He let the words sink in before continuing. "You two are even greener than I was. I won't pretend to be able to prepare you for what it's like, because nothing I say will make that first moment easier. The first time you take a life, the first time you watch someone die—it doesn't leave you. But we don't have a choice. If we don't do this, they die, and Cyprin could win. And he won't stop here."

Kara inhaled slowly. "And if we freeze up?"

"Then you adapt," Darien said. "And you survive. Because if you don't, we all die."

Philip exhaled sharply, running a hand down his face. "Hell of a pep talk."

Darien smirked faintly. "I do my best. It's good to see you guys."

Philip chuckled lightly, shaking his head. "Yeah, you too, man. Even if you look like some ancient war hero out of a storybook."

Kara, however, didn't laugh. She was still staring at him, her expression unreadable. The firelight flickered in her blue eyes, shadows shifting across her face as she studied him. Then, without warning, she moved.

She closed the distance between them in a few quick strides, her hands reaching for his face. At first, Darien thought she was going to hit him again, but her touch was gentle—hesitant, even. Her fingers brushed over his cheek, tracing the edge of his jaw as if she were trying to memorize the contours of his face, make sure he was real.

Her breathing was uneven, as if she was fighting something inside herself, something too big to contain any longer. "You were gone," she whispered, voice raw. "And you didn't even say goodbye."

Darien's throat tightened. "I didn't have a choice."

"You never do, do you?" Her voice wavered, anger flickering behind her eyes, but so did something else— something softer, more vulnerable.

Before he could respond, she kissed him.

It wasn't tentative or unsure—it was raw, filled with the weight of everything left unspoken. The anger, the relief, the fear, the longing. For a brief moment, the war, the danger, the uncertainty of their future melted away, leaving only this. Only them.

When she finally pulled away, she didn't step back. She stayed close, her forehead nearly touching his, her breath warm against his skin. "You don't get to disappear on me again," she whispered. "Not without a fight."

Darien swallowed hard, emotions warring inside him. The guilt, the longing, the reality of what he had left behind and what he had gained. He couldn't promise her that. He couldn't lie.

"A lot has happened," he said instead, his voice quiet. "More than I can even explain right now."

She studied him, her gaze searching, but she must have seen the truth in his eyes, because she nodded, stepping back, wrapping her arms around herself as if steadying herself from everything that had just happened.

Philip cleared his throat loudly. "Alright. So that happened."

Kara let out a breath that was almost a laugh, shaking her head as if trying to clear it. Darien still felt the ghost of her lips on his, but there wasn't time to dwell on it. Not now.

Philip and Kara turned toward their belongings, gathering what little armor they had from the Academy. It was standard, practical—meant for sparring, not war. The plates were scuffed from years of drills, the leather worn from countless hours of training. It was standard, practical, but nothing close to what Darien had now. He stood, watching as they adjusted the straps, tightening buckles with determined but inexperienced hands.

Darien stood watching as they adjusted the straps, their fingers moving with the precision of routine but not the confidence of real battle. Philip struggled with a buckle, muttering a curse under his breath before yanking it into place. Kara tightened her chest piece, her knuckles white as she fastened the last strap.

"I'm gonna do something now." Darien told them as he examined their armor. "That isn't going to be enough for what's coming."

Darien extended his palm toward them, and the ethers responded instantly. The air around their armor shimmered, the dull metal hardening, reinforcing itself under his will. The enchantments flowed through him, strengthening the protective layers, sealing weak points, molding it to their forms like a second skin.

Philip looked down at his chest plate, tapping a fist against it. "Whoa. That's... different."

Kara flexed her fingers, rolling her shoulders as the armor adjusted to her movements. "Feels... better."

"It'll hold," Darien assured them. "Better than what you had before."

He inhaled sharply, forcing himself back to reality. "We've already taken too long. Every second we sit here talking, the window to get to them gets smaller."

Philip and Kara both snapped back to focus, the weight of what they were about to do settling on them fully.

"We go now," Darien said, rising to his feet. His fingers tightened around his sword hilt, the firelight glinting off Apollo's armor as he lowered the helmet on his head and led them towards the tunnels.

# Chapter 23: The Agents Fall

The tunnels stretched before them, the air thick with the scent of damp earth and something fouler—blood, decay. Darien's grip tightened on the hilt of his sword as he stepped carefully over the twisted remains of a soldier. The corpses were fresh, their wounds still glistening. Evatra had fought here.

Philip let out a slow breath, but his eyes darted across the bodies, his hands tightening into fists. "This... this isn't normal," he whispered. "What *are* they?"

Kara hesitated before kneeling beside one of the bodies, her face pale. "Gods... What *is* this thing?" she muttered, forcing herself to look at the wound. "And who—who did this?"

Darien exhaled slowly, eyes fixed ahead. "They used to be like the others," he murmured, just loud enough for Philip and Kara to hear. "Once, they were races of Olympus—goblin and troll, most likely. But Cyprin's magic twisted them, warped them into something else. Shadows of what they were meant to be."

Philip swallowed hard. "So, they were people?"

"In a way," Darien said, voice flat. "But not anymore."

Philip hesitated, then asked, "Are these the things you fought at Farkland Reach?"

Darien gave a single nod. "Yeah. And bigger ones, too."

Silence stretched between them. Philip and Kara exchanged uneasy glances. They had never seen Darien like this—never heard him speak with such weight, such certainty. The boy they had trained with, laughed with, had become someone far beyond anything they had known.

Darien's breath came slow and steady, his fingers flexing around the hilt of his sword. The cavern ahead pulsed with the flickering glow of torchlight, shadows shifting and twisting against the stone like living things. The air grew colder, thick with the weight of something unseen, something waiting.

They moved in silence, pressing against the jagged rock walls, every step measured, every movement deliberate. The scent of damp earth and sweat mixed with the faint, unmistakable tang of blood. The tension in the air coiled tighter, a wire drawn taut, ready to snap. They crept closer, hearts pounding in their chests. The flickering torchlight cast shifting shadows across the cavern walls, stretching their fear into something tangible. Every instinct screamed at them to stop, to turn back, but they moved forward, drawn by the weight of what they might find.

They reached the same ledge where Darien had used his farsight to glimpse Evatra before. The cavern stretched below them, a dim glow flickering from scattered torches, barely illuminating the jagged stone. Darien peered over the ledge, his breath steady but his grip tightening on the hilt of his sword.

Below, the captives were spread across the chamber. Evatra and Cycnus were bound, their bodies battered, heads slumped forward in exhaustion. To their right Breyman and Airlyn hung in similar restraints, their bruised forms barely moving. And across from them, chained tightly against the cavern wall, was Rist—shackled with thick iron that seemed to shimmer with unnatural energy.

Tahmer stood before them, his expression unreadable as he leaned in close to Evatra. He spoke in a low voice, but even from this distance, Darien could see the tension in Evatra's bound form, the effort she made not to react. Then Tahmer moved, and Darien caught a glimpse of the bloodied knife in his grip.

Kara's breath caught in her throat, her gaze flicking rapidly between the figures in the chamber. Philip swallowed hard, the weight of the unknown pressing into his gut like a stone.

Darien pulled them back into the shadows. "We don't have long," he whispered. "Philip, you take left. Kara, right. Stay low. We need to know how many soldiers are in there."

Philip nodded, slipping away like a shadow. Kara followed, her bow at the ready. Darien remained still, watching, counting. Twelve soldiers. Maybe more hidden. They needed to be smart.

Minutes passed, and Philip and Kara returned. Philip's face was grim. "They're watching the main exits. No way out if we don't clear them first. Only way out would be back. But I don't think they'll squeeze through that exit in the shape they're in."

Darien nodded. "We go in quiet. Pick them off when we can. But if we get spotted, we move fast and hit hard."

"And Tahmer?" Kara asked.

Darien's eyes locked onto the man who had haunted his steps since that battle in Farkland Reach. "He's mine."

A sharp whistle cut through the air as Philip launched the first strike, hurling a knife into the throat of a nearby soldier. The man staggered back, choking on blood before collapsing, his weapon clattering to the ground. A beat of silence—then chaos erupted.

The cavern exploded with movement. Kara loosed an arrow, catching a beastly figure in the chest. It let out a strangled cry before slumping against the wall. Another lunged toward her, but she was already in motion, rolling away and nocking another arrow. Philip roared as he drove his axe into a soldier's shoulder, the impact sending the man crashing to the ground.

Darien held his sword steady, every movement sharpened by instinct and years of training. He and Philip moved in perfect sync, as if no time had passed since their last fight together. Philip would swing high, forcing an enemy back, and Darien would finish the opening with a precise thrust. A beast lunged for Philip's flank, but Darien was already there, his sword slicing through its shoulder before it could reach his friend.

Philip grinned despite the chaos. "Just like old times."

Darien smirked. "Try to keep up."

They pressed forward together, bodies weaving through the chaos, covering each other's blind spots without thinking. Philip caught a soldier's axe on the haft of his own, twisting it aside as Darien spun low, cutting the enemy down in a single motion. A monstrous form with jagged armor roared as it came for them, but Darien and Philip acted as one—Philip slammed his boot into its chest, sending it stumbling back, and Darien finished the job with a precise strike through its exposed throat.

More creatures surged forward out of the hallways— twisted forms that had once been men, now barely recognizable, but Darien and Philip stood their ground, fighting side by side, just like they always had.

Across the room, Tahmer cursed. His eyes locked onto Kara, who had taken down three guards already. With a snarl, he grabbed a blade and made his move toward her.

Darien felt it before he saw it—the shift in the air, the sharp pull of instinct screaming for him to act. He surged forward, faster than ever before, the ethers whispering at the edges of his consciousness.

Steel rang as his blade met Tahmer's, stopping him just inches from Kara's exposed flank.

Kara didn't hesitate. She darted away, drawing two daggers as she moved. Without waiting for orders, she turned and sprinted toward Philip, joining him in the fray.

Darien squared his stance, meeting Tahmer's sneer with cold resolve. The battle around them faded into the background.

"You should have stayed dead," Darien growled.

Tahmer grinned, eyes flashing with dark amusement. "And you should have run while you had the chance."

Their blades met in a vicious clash, steel grinding against steel, the impact sending vibrations up Darien's arm. He pushed forward, forcing Tahmer back a step, but the man twisted, redirecting the force and lashing out in a counterstrike. Darien barely caught it, pivoting as their movements blurred into a deadly dance of precision and instinct.

Tahmer's footwork was sharp, controlled—too controlled. Darien's eyes narrowed. *He's using magic.*

A chill ran down his spine, but a flicker of confidence sparked in his chest. He had been right. Tahmer wasn't just a brute with a sword; he was something more, something dangerous. And for the first time, Darien understood the weight of what he was up against.

*He is a spellcaster.*

But he held back. He wouldn't reveal the full extent of his magic—not yet. He had already shown a glimpse when he moved to protect Kara, but he needed to keep Tahmer unaware of just how deep his abilities ran. Let him think this was still a fight of blades, of strength and skill alone that he could manipulate. That illusion was an advantage Darien wasn't ready to give up.

Tahmer struck again, faster this time, his blade singing through the air in an arc too swift to be natural. Darien ducked under it, countering with a strike aimed at Tahmer's ribs. The man twisted out of reach, but Darien was already moving, pressing the attack. Sparks flew as their swords met again, each strike heavier, more desperate.

From the corner of his eye, Darien saw Kara and Philip still holding their ground, cutting down Cyprin's soldiers with brutal efficiency. He was proud at how they were doing, but this—this was his fight.

Tahmer sneered. "I expected more."

Darien didn't answer. He lunged instead, faster than ever before, willing the ethers to respond in his movement alone. Tahmer's smirk faltered as Darien's speed surged, his blade slicing just past Tahmer's guard.

Tahmer bared his teeth, realization dawning in his eyes.

"So," Tahmer murmured, stepping back, blade held loosely in his grip. "You've been hiding something, too."

His voice was probing, his stance shifting, as if analyzing Darien anew.

Tahmer's eyes gleamed with something unreadable, a predator recognizing another. "Where did you learn it? The ethers are hidden from the world and you—" He tilted his head, studying Darien. "You didn't have it before. Not in Farkland Reach. So tell me, how does a swordsman gain power like yours in just a few weeks?"

Darien didn't answer. He kept his grip firm, his breathing steady, his mind shutting itself like a fortress. His boots shifted slightly against the cavern floor as he began to move, pacing to the side, forcing Tahmer to do the same. They circled each other, steel glinting under flickering torchlight, both waiting for the other to make the first move.

Then, a flash of motion—Tahmer struck. Darien caught the blow on his blade, steel screeching against steel, and twisted, forcing Tahmer to retreat a step. But the man only grinned.

Darien tightened his grip on his sword. He kept his expression blank, unwilling to give Tahmer anything. "You assume a lot."

Tahmer chuckled. "Do I?"

A sudden shift. Darien felt the press of magic against his mind, subtle but invasive. The pressure tried to worm its way inside, clawing at his thoughts. But Darien was ready. He shut it down with ease, severing the tendrils before they could take hold. A pulse of satisfaction ran through him as he saw Tahmer's smirk falter.

"That's not going to work on me," Darien said, voice calm, almost amused.

Tahmer's expression twisted into something between frustration and intrigue. "So, you *do* understand what you're up against."

Darien rolled his shoulders, keeping his stance measured. "I understand more than you think."

The cavern around them buzzed with battle—clashing steel, cries of pain, the steady rhythm of Philip and Kara carving their way toward the captives. But in this space between him and Tahmer, time stretched, coiled tight with tension.

Then Tahmer's grip tightened on his sword, and the stillness shattered.

They moved, their blades clashing in rapid succession, each strike faster, sharper. The ethers swirled around them, bending to their will, and in an instant, the battle changed. The world outside their fight slowed, as if trapped in a dream. Every movement from the soldiers, every distant shout, became sluggish, stretched by the sheer speed at which Darien and Tahmer moved.

Darien surged forward, his sword a blur of silver light, and as Tahmer barely managed to parry, Darien willed the wind to gather beneath his feet. He stepped onto the currents, using them like a bridge, twisting through the air as if gravity itself were an afterthought. He vaulted above Tahmer, landing behind him in a single fluid motion, forcing the spellcaster to spin, barely keeping pace. Sparks flew as the edges of their weapons screeched together. Tahmer retaliated, flicking his free hand upward— ether tendrils lashed out toward Darien, dark and writhing. Darien twisted mid-air, calling upon the winds again. They wrapped around him, lifting him out of reach as the dark tendrils lashed upward, missing him by inches. Then, as he descended, he wove the currents into a push, rocketing forward like an arrow, his blade flashing as he struck at Tahmer's exposed side. He landed and countered, using the ether to propel himself forward, striking in a flash of steel and light.

Tahmer stumbled back, his breath uneven. He was keeping up, but only barely. The confidence in his eyes flickered, replaced with something closer to frustration. Darien pressed the attack, weaving between sword strikes with near-weightless movements, the wind carrying him effortlessly from strike to strike. Tahmer's blade met only air where Darien had been a heartbeat before, his movements guided by an intuition that bordered on preternatural. Each time Tahmer adjusted, Darien was already gone, using the ether to stay one step ahead, his mastery undeniable.

"You're stronger than before," Tahmer growled between labored breaths. "This isn't just training. Someone taught you. Who?"

Darien sidestepped a swipe meant to take his head, his smirk unwavering. "Wouldn't you like to know?"

Tahmer scowled and lunged, but Darien was already moving, stepping aside and bringing his blade in a tight arc toward Tahmer's exposed side. At the last moment, Tahmer released a burst of ether, shoving Darien back just enough to avoid the killing blow.

Their battle stretched on, a dance of magic and steel, until finally, time snapped back into place. The rest of the cavern sharpened around them, the sounds of battle resuming in full clarity. A faint buzzing filled Darien's ears. The injury that he was worried would overcome him beginning to show itself. He was thankful for the reprieve, but the pain in his side was becoming impossible to ignore. His body was beginning to wear down, and the fight wasn't over.

His eyes flicked to Kara and Philip—both still standing, still fighting, but their movements had slowed. Their stamina was waning. He exhaled sharply and willed a thin thread of ether toward them, infusing their limbs with renewed strength. Instantly, he saw the shift—Philip's swings regained their former speed, Kara's movements sharpened with fresh energy. It was subtle, but it was enough.

Tahmer chuckled, wiping a trail of blood from the corner of his mouth. "Interesting," he mused, pacing in a slow, deliberate circle. "You truly have mastered it. The ethers bend to you with ease."

Darien kept his stance, adjusting to the dull ache spreading through his side. "You're running out of time, Tahmer."

"Am I?" Tahmer's tone was casual, almost amused. "Or are you beginning to realize the truth?"

Darien didn't respond, waiting for the inevitable trap. Tahmer continued, pacing slowly as he spoke, his blade still at the ready. "Cyprin is not the dark lord, they claim. He was simply a spellcaster who defied the order of things and was betrayed by his own. The histories you cling to, that you have no doubt studied to gain such mastery over these abilities—they're lies. Twisted fables passed down to justify an endless war. The spellcasters of old clung to their traditions, refused to grow beyond themselves. The world was tearing itself apart under their stagnation, but Cyprin saw a better way. He and his allies—fourteen spellcasters in total—tried to change things from within. They sought to unify, to guide, to protect. But when the others saw the truth, they turned on him. Half refused to accept that the world needed change, and the other half feared the consequences of power being wielded differently."

Darien scoffed, shaking his head. "You expect me to believe that?"

"You think dark magic is corruption? You think Cyprin's forces are chaos? No, Darien. They're the last hope. His only option following three millennia of imprisonment. It is the last gasp of a dying world that refuses to let go." Tahmer's voice was measured, steady. "Why do you think you're here? Why do you think you were given this power? You are meant to end this. Join us and assist us in ending these cycles forever!"

Darien felt the weight of the words settling in, an unsettling sense that there was truth buried in the tale. His grip tightened. "You're twisting history to suit your own means," he snapped.

Tahmer smirked. "Then look for yourself. See the truth."

Darien hesitated. He didn't want to. He didn't want to find that Tahmer wasn't lying. But doubt crept in, gnawing at the edges of his certainty. Carefully, cautiously, he reached out—his mind brushing against Tahmer's like the barest whisper of wind against a locked door. He didn't push, didn't pry, just skimmed the surface, searching for cracks, for deception.

He found none.

His heart pounded as he pulled back quickly, bracing himself for a hidden attack. But none came.

Tahmer tilted his head. "No tricks, Darien. No lies. You can see I tell no lies."

Darien's expression hardened. "You could be using the very dark magic you claim is necessary to shield and twist your own thoughts. Just because you believe it doesn't make any of it true."

Tahmer shook his head. "I do not lie Darien."

Then a sudden rage filled Darien. Where it came from, he wasn't sure. But he felt it, as sure as he felt the ethers twisting around and through him, as sure as he breathed.

Darien felt his control snap. The edges of his vision burned red as his blade flashed forward. Tahmer barely dodged, rolling away with an agile grace that only fueled Darien's fury. But the troll wasn't retreating—his hands surged with dark ether, fingers curling into claws as he twisted, hurling a bolt of blackened energy toward Kara and Philip.

Darien barely had time to cry out before it struck. Kara twisted mid-air, the blast grazing past her with a scorching heat—but Philip wasn't so lucky. The attack hit him square in the chest, sending him flying across the chamber. His body crashed against the jagged stone wall, landing in a twisted heap of limbs and shattered armor.

Darien's world went silent. The buzzing in his ears swelled, but he ignored it, his vision filled only with Tahmer. The troll was still moving, his blade coming up in a desperate attempt to block, but Darien was beyond caring. His rage consumed him, surging through his limbs like fire, and he struck with all the fury that had been building since the battle began.

Their blades met again, but this time, Tahmer was too slow. Darien forced him back with relentless blows, each strike heavier, faster, pushing him toward the edge of the cavern. Sparks flew, and for the first time, there was fear in Tahmer's eyes.

"You have no idea what you're doing!" Tahmer spat, trying to regain control. "You're throwing away everything! You could be—"

Darien didn't let him finish. He pressed forward, steel flashing, his mind empty of anything but the next movement, the next strike. A feint, a twist of his wrist, and his sword cut deep across Tahmer's torso. The troll gasped, falling to his knees, his weapon clattering to the stone floor.

Breathing hard, Darien reached down and wrapped his fingers around the hilt of Tahmer's own sword. It felt heavy, final, in his grasp. He lifted it, staring down at the defeated spellcaster.

Tahmer looked up at him, bloodied and gasping. "You don't understand... you never did."

Darien's grip tightened. "No more resurrections."

He brought the blade down in a clean, merciless arc that severed neck from torso. The cavern was filled with the sound of steel meeting flesh, and then—silence.

The buzzing in Darien's ears roared to a crescendo, swallowing him whole as darkness overtook him, and he collapsed to the solid stone floor, lost in the pain of convulsion.

# Chapter 24: The Students Return

Pain was the first thing Darien noticed. A dull, heavy ache that sat deep in his bones, spreading through his body like a slow tide. His fingers twitched against rough fabric, the weight of a blanket pressing down on his chest. The air smelled different—earthy, tinged with unfamiliar herbs. He wasn't where he had fallen.

His thoughts were slow, clouded, his body sluggish as he drifted between awareness and darkness. Then came the sound—soft breathing, a faint shuffle of movement. The pressure of exhaustion clawed at him, urging him to stay under, but instinct pushed back. Something had happened. He needed to remember.

Flashes of battle surged through his mind. The cavern. The fight. The blood. Philip—

His breath hitched, his muscles tensing involuntarily. The effort sent a spike of pain through his ribs. A quiet gasp reached his ears, and a warm hand touched his arm. "Darien?"

His eyelids felt impossibly heavy as he forced them open. Blurred shapes swam in his vision before sharpening into something familiar. Kara. Her face was drawn, dark circles ringing her tired eyes. She hadn't left his side.

"You're awake," she breathed, relief and exhaustion warring in her voice.

"How long?" His own voice felt foreign, hoarse and dry.

"Five days."

His stomach twisted. Too long.

The room around him came into focus. It was small, simple, but alive with scent and texture—walls of carved stone, cool and damp beneath his fingertips, their rough surfaces lined with faint etchings, histories long forgotten. A cot beneath him, its mattress thin but firm, smelled of dried lavender and faint traces of medicinal oils. A dimly lit lantern flickered on the far wall, its flame casting shadows that danced against the stone like ghosts of the past. He didn't recognize it. He wasn't in the valley anymore.

His heart pounded as he forced himself upright, his body screaming in protest. "Where's my stuff?"

Kara hesitated, then gestured to a worn satchel resting in the corner. Darien was moving before she could stop him, his balance wavering as he staggered forward. He fell to his knees beside the bag, fingers clawing through its contents with growing urgency.

His hands brushed past familiar items—his blade, still stained with battle; his torn cloak, stiff with dried blood. His fingers trembled as they fumbled deeper, growing more frantic with every second. The bag felt too empty, the weight of what he searched for absent. His breath hitched as he pulled out a few more scattered belongings—bandages, a waterskin, a dull whetstone—but not the one thing he needed.

His chest tightened. Had he left it behind? Had it been lost in the caves, buried beneath rubble and corpses? The thought sent a fresh wave of panic through him. He shoved aside another layer of cloth, his vision tunneling as desperation clawed at his ribs.

Relief hit him so hard his shoulders sagged, the weight in his chest loosening just enough for him to breathe. He curled his fingers around it, pressing the cool metal into his palm, reassuring himself that it was real. He hadn't lost it.

The emotion of the events crashed over him, so strong it nearly buckled him. He clutched it tightly a crutch, the cool metal anchoring him to reality. He was still too weak, but this... this he had.

Kara knelt beside him, watching him carefully. "Darien, you need to rest—"

"I need food," he corrected, his grip on the token unrelenting. He reached for the ethers, drawing energy into himself.

A warmth spread from his fingertips, slow at first, then rippling outward in waves. He barely had time to react before the raw scrapes along his forearms smoothed over, the bruises paling before vanishing entirely. The soreness that had settled deep into his muscles eased, replaced by a strange lightness, like he had just awoken from a deep, dreamless sleep.

Kara's sharp intake of breath cut through the quiet. "Darien..."

He looked up at her, his own breath catching. Her wide-eyed expression mirrored the disbelief pooling in his chest. He flexed his fingers, watching the last traces of his injuries fade from the energy the ethers provided his body. But even as his skin stitched together and his body restored itself, a deep hunger gnawed at him. The ethers could mend, they could sustain, but they couldn't replace. His body still craved food, a sharp reminder that he was not beyond mortal needs.

He swallowed hard, the dryness in his throat making the thought of food all the more pressing. "Philip..." he rasped, his voice barely above a whisper. "Is he—?"

Kara's expression tightened, but she didn't hesitate. "He's alive. But it's close. The healers say it could go either way."

A pit formed in Darien's stomach, but before he could respond, Kara reached beside her and lifted a small wooden bowl. "Drink this," she said, pressing it into his hands. "The healers gave it to me. Said it would help."

He peered down into the murky liquid, the scent of bitter herbs filling his nose. He grimaced but lifted it to his lips. The taste was sharp, almost sour, and it clung to his tongue like thick residue. He coughed but forced himself to swallow.

"It's foul," he muttered.

Kara huffed out a tired laugh. "Yeah, well, it's medicine. It's not supposed to taste good."

Darien set the bowl aside and pushed himself up, legs shaky beneath him. He ignored Kara's protests as he steadied himself. "I need to see Philip."

She hesitated, crossing her arms. "Darien, you just woke up. You're still weak. You need to rest."

Darien clenched his jaw. "I don't have time for that. Philip doesn't have time for that. Besides, I'm stronger than you think."

Kara exhaled sharply, frustration flashing in her eyes. "And what do you think you're going to do? Just walk in there and magically fix everything?"

"I have to try," he said, voice tight. "I won't just sit here doing nothing. You can't stop me, anyway."

She stared at him, lips pressed into a thin line. For a moment, he thought she would keep arguing, but then she exhaled and looked away. "Fine. But if you collapse on the way there, I'm not dragging you back."

Darien nodded, steadying himself. "I won't."

The walk was short but felt endless. His body no longer ached from battle, but a deeper weariness weighed on him, not of injury, but of something more consuming. The corridor outside his room was narrow, walls lined with shelves of dried herbs bundled in twine, their sharp, earthy scent mixing with the acrid tang of burning incense. The floor was uneven beneath his bare feet, a mixture of smooth-worn stone and woven reed mats that muffled his footsteps.

The room Philip lay in was dimly lit, warm and humid from the smoldering coals in a brazier nearby. The scent of herbal poultices clung to the air, thick and slightly cloying, mingling with the faint metallic tang of blood. Hanging charms, carved from polished bone and twisted vine, dangled from the ceiling, swaying gently as if responding to an unseen breath of wind. Low chants echoed from a nearby room, distant murmurs of the healers at work, their voices blending with the flickering light and the rhythmic crackling of the embers.

Philip lay still, wrapped in bandages, his breathing shallow but steady. The pallor of his skin sent a fresh wave of dread through Darien's chest. Darien hesitated, then pressed a trembling hand to Philip's chest. He reached for the ethers, letting them flow through him, willing them to mend what was broken. A soft glow pulsed beneath his fingers, faint tendrils of energy weaving through Philip's body. The shallow cuts along his arms sealed, bruises lightened, and the tension in his muscles eased.

Kara gasped behind him. "It's working..."

For a fleeting moment, hope surged through Darien. But then, as the magic spread deeper, something pushed back. The energy couldn't reach beyond the surface, couldn't touch whatever dark wound still festered beneath. The ethers flowed, but they did not mend.

Darien's breath hitched as he withdrew his hand. Philip looked like he had before, wounds healed and body mended—only something still lingered. Something in Tahmer's magical attack on his friend had done more than he knew how to mend. The magic had done all it could. The rest was up to him.

*This is my fault.*

Darien sank to his knees beside the cot, the wood creaking under his weight. His friend's breath came slow and shallow, his skin too pale beneath the dim glow of the lanterns. Tears welled in his eyes as he looked at his friend's broken body, struggling to fight for survival. He had brought Philip here. His friend had hesitated, but he had pushed.

*This is MY fault.*

Darien sat frozen, his breath shallow, his chest tightening under the crushing weight of guilt. His hands trembled where they rested on his thighs, fingers curling into his palms as if trying to grasp something solid, something real. But there was nothing. Only the sickening knowledge that Philip lay there because of him.

His vision blurred, the dim glow of the lanterns smearing into soft halos of gold. The sounds of the room faded, swallowed by the pounding in his skull. Why hadn't he been faster? Stronger? Why hadn't he stopped this before it had begun? His shoulders hunched forward, his head falling as a raw exhale left his lips. No amount of magic could change what had already happened.

A hand touched his shoulder, light but grounding. Kara. He knew it was her without looking, but he didn't move, didn't acknowledge it. The warmth of her touch barely cut through the cold pressing into his bones. The price of victory had been too high. His fingers curled into a fist. He never should have let them come.

Kara stood behind him, silent. There was nothing left to say. He stayed there for what felt like hours before the weight of time pressed in. He had just over a day to reach the valley, and there was still too much to do.

With one final glance at Philip, Darien forced himself to stand. He turned to Kara, voice tight. "I need to talk to the others."

She studied him, hesitating before crossing her arms. "You should be resting. You're barely standing as it is."

Darien shook his head. "I don't have time for that. And I don't need to. You saw me heal."

Kara's eyes narrowed, her arms crossing tightly over her chest. "You're not all healed," she shot back, her voice quieter now but no less firm. "Not everything is just bruises and wounds, Darien. Some things don't fade so easily."

He stood there, looking at her adopting an impassive conversation that allowed her to say her piece, but didn't allow for anything but acceptance of his goal.

Kara let out a slow breath, frustration flickering across her face. "Fine. But don't expect them to be in any better shape than you. They went through hell."

He nodded and made his way toward the next chamber. The space was dim, filled with the quiet murmur of conversation between Breyman and Rist. Airlyn sat apart, arms folded tightly across her chest, her eyes snapping to Darien as he entered.

Darien stepped into the chamber where the rest of the Eldric were recovering, relief washing over him like a tide. He hadn't allowed himself to think about what he would find—if they would all still be here, still breathing. But they were. And for a brief moment, nothing else mattered. The air was thick with the scent of herbs and burning oils, the remnants of whatever healing methods had been used to keep them alive. Breyman sat propped against a wall, his arms folded over his chest, watching the room in wary silence. Rist stood near him, unharmed but contemplative, his presence as unreadable as ever. Airlyn sat at the edge of her cot, rolling her shoulder with a wince, but the sharpness in her gaze had lost none of its edge.

They all turned to him as he entered, but for a heartbeat, no one spoke. Then, Rist pushed off the wall, his sharp eyes scanning Darien before the faintest hint of a smile ghosted across his face.

"So," Rist spoke first, his voice calm but carrying something rare—something close to relief in the now unfamiliar icy tone of the dark robed figure. "You're alive."

Darien let out a breath he hadn't realized he was holding. "And so are you."

Darien stepped further in, clasping Rist's forearm in a firm grip, the closest thing to an embrace he could allow himself. "It's good to see you."

Airlyn scoffed, though there was no real venom behind it. "We were the ones chained to walls, remember? While you were off doing gods-know-what."

Darien's expression darkened. "What did he do to you? What did he want?"

Breyman exhaled, shaking his head. "You. He wanted you. He thought we were keeping something from him, that we had answers we just refused to give. We told him the truth—we had no idea where you were."

Rist nodded. "He thought we were hiding you, or lying. But we had nothing to tell. He didn't take that well."

Darien studied them, his gaze sweeping over their worn expressions, the stiffness in the way they carried themselves. The bruises, the half-healed wounds. He could help.

He took a step forward, hesitating before speaking. "Let me heal you. I have the ability now—if you'll allow it."

Breyman's brow furrowed, studying him for a long moment. "So you do have power."

"Yes," Darien said simply with a short nod of his head.

Airlyn's expression darkened. "Where? How?"

"I'll answer what I can," Darien responded, gesturing to her bandages and bruises on her exposed skin. "But let me repair some of the damage first."

Breyman let out a slow breath, stretching his arm with a grimace before nodding. "I would be grateful."

Airlyn rolled her eyes but said nothing. She shifted on the cot, testing her injuries, but the tightness in her shoulders betrayed her pain. "I don't need your sorcery," she muttered. "I'm fine."

Rist snorted, shaking his head. "That's ridiculous. If he can heal, refusing is choosing pain for the sake of whatever pride clouds your judgement."

Airlyn shot him a glare. "Oh, so now you're the authority on what's wise? I seem to recall you sitting in chains the whole time without a scratch while the rest of us were getting beaten."

Rist smirked, folding his arms. "And yet, here I am, still standing, while you sit there refusing perfectly good offer from an ally. Interesting."

Airlyn huffed, looking between them before finally letting out an exasperated sigh. "Fine. But if this makes things worse, I swear—"

Darien smirked, stepping closer. "Trust me. You'll be fine."

As he placed his hands over her wounds, a soft glow pulsed beneath his fingertips, warmth radiating outward. Airlyn sucked in a sharp breath, the pain easing as bruises faded, cuts sealed themselves. The tightness in her shoulders eased, and she flexed her fingers experimentally, as if expecting something to still be broken.

She looked up at him, something unreadable in her expression. "Huh," she muttered. "That's... unsettling."

Breyman, watching closely, chuckled. "Not going to complain, are you?"

Airlyn shook her head, rolling her shoulder again. "No. Not right now."

Darien turned to Rist, but the dark-robed figure raised a hand. "I don't need it."

Airlyn scoffed, giving him a look. "Hypocrite."

Rist merely shrugged. "I'm not made the same way you are. Your wounds need healing. Mine never existed in the first place."

Darien hesitated but nodded. He had no idea how much truth lay in Rist's words, but he wasn't going to press it now.

The group sat together in silence, Breyman and Airlyn examining their newly healed wounds. Breyman with amazement, and Airlyn with some mix of annoyance and curiosity. Eventually, the silence was breached by Airlyn's cutting tone.

"So, you lived. How did you find us? How'd you get away from Tahmer? And where, by the goddess Laira have you been?"

Airlyn asked the questions in an accusatory way, which made Darien feel a shot of annoyance. He pushed back his urgent desire to tell her exactly what he thought of her attitude and stuck to the important details.

"I have been in a place where I studied magic. That's how I found you. I cannot tell you where. I cannot tell you with whom."

Airlyn began to protest, but he raised a hand to stop her.

"I know. That's not the answer you're looking for. You want to know. You want details, but I cannot give them to you. If I do, it places everything, Olympus, us, the cycles, *everything* at risk. Yes, I learned magic. Yes,

I've gotten pretty good at it. But as you can tell, I'm not healed. I can't do everything, and I still have a lot to learn. Which is why I have to go back." The three sat in silence, looking at him for several long heartbeats.

Breyman leaned forward, elbows resting on his knees, his expression a mixture of curiosity and frustration. "So you disappear, and suddenly you come back wielding magic? That's not exactly something that just happens, Darien. How did you learn? Who taught you?"

Darien exhaled through his nose, crossing his arms. "I told you, I can't say. It's not just about me. The knowledge I have—it's dangerous. If I say too much, I put more than just us at risk."

Airlyn scoffed, shaking her head. "That's convenient."

Rist, still leaning against the wall, watching the conversation unfold, finally spoke. "You know we'll follow you, Darien, whether we understand or not. But you have to give us something. You're asking us to fight alongside you while you carry secrets that could change everything. How do we trust what we don't understand?"

Darien's jaw clenched. "I don't expect blind trust. I know it's frustrating, but I swear to you, everything I've done has been to keep you safe. If I could tell you, I would. But I won't risk it."

Breyman sighed, rubbing a hand over his face. "Then at least tell us what's next. What happens now?"

Darien hesitated. "I have to go back. There are things I need to learn, things that I need to prepare for. We don't have much time."

Airlyn shot up from her seat, fists clenched at her sides. "What can you tell us, then?" she cried. "I didn't come to Olympus to lay down my life, to give up everything, leave my family in tears as I entered the transitions, to be kept in the dark!"

Her voice echoed through the chamber, thick with frustration, grief, and something unspoken—fear. The silence that followed was deafening, as Darien looked at her, confusion creeping into his mind.

He frowned, his gaze shifting between them. "What do you mean, 'lay down your life'? Why would you say it like that?"

Breyman inhaled sharply, glancing at Rist, who remained impassive. Airlyn clenched her jaw, but she refused to meet Darien's eyes. Something cold coiled in his stomach.

"What aren't you telling me?" Darien pressed, his voice low, demanding.

Airlyn let out a shaky breath, shaking her head. "How do you not know? Darien, everyone who comes here knows. It's not a secret. We all chose this. We accepted it."

The weight of her words sent a chill through him. His pulse thundered in his ears. "Chose what? Accepted what? What exactly did I supposedly sign up for?"

A heavy silence stretched between them. Airlyn opened her mouth, closed it, then shook her head as if trying to reconcile something that didn't make sense. Breyman rubbed his temples, avoiding Darien's gaze. Even Rist, unreadable as ever, took a moment longer than usual before speaking, his voice quiet but deliberate.

"Darien," he said, voice even, "we die here. The Eldric never return."

Darien's breath left him in a sharp exhale, his mind reeling. Betrayal slashed through him like a blade. Whytaren. The one person he had trusted most. He knew. He had to have known. And yet, he never said a word.

His hands curled into fists at his sides. "So that's it? We were all just sent here to die? No one thought to tell me?"

Airlyn's frustration faltered, something softer flickering in her eyes. "We thought you knew. Everyone who comes does. It's always been this way."

The words crashed into Darien like a hammer, the weight of them sinking deep into his chest. He shook his head, disbelief twisting his features. "You're telling me that all this time, all of you knew? That this was—this was supposed to happen? And no one thought to tell me?"

Airlyn took a step back, her expression wavering. "Darien—"

"No!" His voice was sharp, filled with something raw. "He knew. He had to have known. He was the one who prepared me. He was the one who sent me here!"

Breyman rubbed a hand down his face, the exhaustion plain in his posture. "Darien, it's not like that. We thought you came knowing what this meant. The Eldric always know. They always accept it. That's why they come."

Darien let out a sharp breath, his fists clenched. "And I didn't. No one told me. You all just assumed I was walking to my death with a smile on my face? That I knew I was meant to be sacrificed?"

The silence that followed only deepened his fury. He had been lied to. Trapped in half-truths and omissions. Sent here like a lamb to slaughter without even the courtesy of knowing the knife was coming.

"Well, not anymore." Darien's voice was like steel, his stance shifting as the fire in his chest grew into an inferno. He looked at each of them, one by one, his resolve solidifying with every breath. "The cycles end with us. No more sacrifice. No more accepting this as fate."

Breyman's brows furrowed. "Darien, that's not something we can just decide."

"Maybe not. But I'm deciding, anyway." His voice was unshaken, his conviction unwavering. "I didn't come here to die. And neither did you. We're not giving our lives to a system that's already taken too much. The cycles will end. I will end them."

Silence filled the room, thick and heavy. For the first time since they had arrived in Olympus, hope flickered in the shadows. And this time, it wasn't blind faith—it was a promise.

The next twenty-four hours passed in a blur. Plans were made, strategies discussed, and Darien explained everything he could to the other members of The Four. He told them about the time difference in the valley, how weeks there were only days outside of it. That was how he had learned so much, how he had changed so quickly. He could see the understanding settle into their expressions, though it did little to fully ease their tension.

Eventually, he found himself walking through the village, Kara at his side, when a familiar voice rang through the air.

"Darien!"

Evatra ran to him, her steps unsteady but urgent. The relief in her voice was unmistakable, her expression a mixture of elation and exhaustion. She reached him and threw her arms around his shoulders, holding him close. "You came for me. I was looking for you, and somehow, you ended up rescuing me."

Darien hesitated for only a moment before returning the embrace. "I couldn't leave you there," he said softly, feeling the weight of everything that had happened between them.

Evatra pulled back just enough to look at him, her hands still resting on his arms. "I knew you'd find me," she said, the warmth in her voice undeniable but not overdone. There was something unspoken in the way she looked at him—gratitude, trust, maybe something more.

As they parted, Darien caught sight of Kara's expression. Her jaw was tight, her eyes flicking between them with suspicion.

Evatra turned to her, the confidence in her expression fading slightly. "Oh."

Kara's gaze flicked between them before she said simply, "Kara."

Evatra's shoulders tensed, and she took a small step back. Her fingers curled slightly at her sides, her earlier warmth retreating. Darien had told her about Kara—about their relationship—but in a way that had made it seem like it was over. Now, standing in front of her, she realized how wrong she had been.

Kara's gaze shifted between Darien and Evatra before she nodded slowly. "Yeah."

Darien felt a heat rising in his face. He cleared his throat and gestured between them. "Uh, yeah. Kara, this is Evatra. Evatra, Kara." He hesitated, rubbing the back of his neck. "You should... probably say hello."

Kara crossed her arms, watching as Evatra withdrew, the confidence in her expression dimming. There was something unspoken in the way she stepped back, as if bracing herself. The air between them had shifted, and though no words had been exchanged, it was enough to make Kara's mouth press into a thin line.

The tension in the air was thick, but Evatra only smiled, seemingly unfazed. "It's good to meet you. Darien's lucky to have you watching his back."

Kara gave a curt nod, but her expression remained unreadable. Darien, caught somewhere between embarrassment and confusion, had no idea what to do next. The silence stretched a beat too long before he exhaled and forced a smile. "Uh, we should keep moving. Still a lot to do."

Evatra took a step back, nodding, her expression carefully neutral. "Right. Of course."

Kara, arms still crossed, lingered a moment before turning to follow him. But the tension didn't break—it lingered, thick and unspoken, hanging between them like something unfinished.

Darien didn't push it. Not now. Whatever this was, whatever this had become, it wasn't something that could be resolved with a few words. Not yet. He could feel the weight of it pressing down, an unspoken promise that this conversation, this conflict, wasn't over, but it would have to wait.

As the final light of the following day faded over the village, Darien stood with the others, the weight of departure pressing against him. They all knew he was leaving. There was no grand speech, no unnecessary words—just the shared understanding that they each had their part to play.

He looked to the members of The Four, his gaze steady. They had spent a good portion of the last day discussing next steps. They had their plan, and Darien had his own part to play. "You know what to do."

They all nodded, though tension still lingered. Airlyn crossed her arms, her usual sharpness present but tempered by something softer. "I hope you know what you're doing, Darien."

For the first time, there was no bite in her words— only something that felt almost like friendship.

Breyman stepped forward next, his large frame casting a long shadow in the dim light. "Luck, Darien. You're going to need it."

Darien extended his hand. Breyman huffed a quiet laugh before reaching out, his massive fur-covered paw easily engulfing Darien's hand in comparison. Darien gripped it firmly, or tried to given the sheer difference in size.

"I'll make my own luck," Darien said, his voice sure, unshaken.

The silence that followed wasn't heavy, wasn't uncertain—it was filled with resolve. Darien had his path, and they had theirs. Each would work in their own way to begin the end of the cycles.

Darien turned then, his gaze shifting to Kara and Evatra, who stood together yet apart, neither wanting to force a conversation but both unwilling to walk away just yet. He felt the weight of their eyes on him, different but equally intense.

He looked at Kara first. "Look after Philip for me," he said, his voice steady. "I'll check in when I can."

Kara hesitated for only a moment before nodding. "I will."

Then, his eyes met Evatra's. He wanted to say something—needed to—but the words weren't there. Not now. Instead, he gave her a small nod, a silent acknowledgment of everything that had happened. She returned it, a quiet understanding passing between them.

The moment stretched, charged with unspoken things, until Kara shifted beside him, arms still crossed. Her expression was unreadable, but the tension in her posture said enough. Whatever had been left unsaid between the three of them would stay that way—for now.

Darien exhaled, rolling his shoulders back. "I need to go."

Neither of them spoke. They only watched as he turned, stepping forward into whatever came next, the question of where his heart lay lingering just

behind							him.
Darien reached out with the ethers towards the amulet that he brought forth from his pocket. The energy of the colliding sources of his power pushing into the cold solid metal. As he did, it began drawing on the ethers itself, even after he ended the magic that he put into it the ethers flowed and he saw a small pinprick of blue light appear just in front of him. The object grew and the telltale sucking sound, the noise like air being sucked through a straw filled the air. He turned once more, looking at each member of the party gathered behind him individually.

*We can do this. We have to.*

Without another word, he reached out and touched the transition and returned as he had promised he would to the Valley of Nyseion and the master who awaited him there, hopefully with answers to yet unasked questions.

# Pronunciation Guide

Aghemnon — AG-em-non

Altruis — AL-tru-is

Atreya — a-tr-AY-uh

Chorrun — COR-un

Cyprin — SIE-prin

Cycnus — SICK-nuhs

Darien — DARE-E-un

Evatra — eh-VAT-ra

Evedra — eh-VED-ra

Evindor — EV-in-dore

Hephaesion — heh-FAY-shun

Hiranor — HEER-in-ore

Jodin — JO-din

Kara — CAR-uh

Laytri — LAY-tree

Leucrocuta — loo-cro-KYOO-tah

Lotry — LO-tree

Lystra — LIST-ruh

Marenya — muh-REN-yuh

Nyseion — NYE-see-on

Peronia — Per-OH-nee-uh

Ristvahkbain — RIST-vahk-bane

Scillan — SILL-uhn

Tahmer — TA-mer

Taitron — TAY-truhn

Terrae — TARE-ay

Torin — TORE-in

Totra-Dal — TO-truh-doll

Veritrium — Ver-EE-tree-uhm

Whyn — Win

Whytaren — WHI-tar-ehn

Zanarchin — ZAN-ar-kin